Energize: From the Logs of Daniel Quinn

http://www.thomasrmanning.com

Cover Design: Ronnell Porter http://ronnelldporter.wix.com/design

ISBN: 978-0-9895068-1-6

I cannot begin to express how grateful I am to the wonderful friends and family I have in my life. Thank you all for the support and encouragement. A special thank you goes out to Jorge, Pat, Lauren, and most of all, my wife Cecelia.

Without all of you, this book would not have been possible.

*Dedicated to two beautiful boys who call me daddy.
Jameson and Parker, I love you.*

ONE

Two security guards and one captured mercenary stood shoulder to shoulder in a cramped shuttlecraft, which sounded like the beginning of a bad joke but unfortunately it wasn't. I'll let you guess which guy I was. I had shackles around my wrists if it helps any. The short range shuttles of the Earth Star Alliance measured about three and a half meters long and three meters high, basically a box. The crew compliment of a shuttle was a dozen men, but I never understood the math. If three of us couldn't move without bumping into the other, how could twelve people fit? Honestly, I didn't care much how it worked. I just wanted a distraction from my current situation. As a prisoner, all I could do was stand between the two guards and watch as we approached one of the ESA's flagships, the Echelon.

Anyone who laid eyes on her would be a fool not to appreciate the beautiful craftsmanship used in constructing the vessel. At 1000 meters long and 600 meters high, the Echelon traveled throughout space as one of the most massive starships in human history. She, along with her sister ships Destiny and Triumph were designed in homage to the naval battle cruisers and carriers that once sailed Earth's oceans. Lights shone through windows, signal beacons blinked from bow to stern, and the silver metallic plating of the hull itself was seamless.

Though this ship technically belonged to the ESA, an infection of mutiny had spread among the crew a few years ago. Now they operated by their own designs and commands, while hiding under the ESA flag. I only knew this because I was a crewman when it happened. The Echelon was my first adventure into outer space, but after the mutiny I left and was rewarded with nightmares, relentless nightmares that haunted me night after night. Even now as I stared at her I could see shadows and images running through my mind, threatening to unlock memories I had buried long ago; memories of betrayal, blood, and murder.

If I didn't think of a way out of this, I would most likely never see the stars again. The person in control of the Echelon didn't like me very much. I didn't really like them either so our relationship was mutually hateful.

One of the officers holding me captive leaned forward and brought his hand to the touch screen display on the shuttle's computer console.

"ESA Echelon, this is Tier One Lieutenant Colin Dowell and Ensign Harold Scott. Requesting permission to dock. Priority code 397."

The radio crackled with static for a moment, and then a voice spoke back to Dowell.

"Message received, docking procedures pending. Identify code 397 for database confirmation."

"Shuttle 4 is transporting Daniel Quinn," Dowell said, though as he finished a smirk formed on his face and he covered his mouth to muffle his laughter. He composed himself and continued. I rolled my eyes.

The operator on the Echelon would now be searching my name in the database. He would find it listed as 'Wanted Red Level 1: Daniel Quinn - Murder, Mutiny, and Evasion of ESA operatives'.

"Code 397 identification confirmed. You will escort the prisoner to the brig upon docking. Be cautious officers, his file lists him as very dangerous. Docking Request granted. Welcome home."

The comm signal dropped and the two officers busted out laughing. Scott hunched over and wrapped his arm around his stomach as his laughter filled the small space. I just stood there. Yes me, the dangerous murderer and mutineer.

"Seriously," Scott said directly to Dowell, completely ignoring my presence. "This guy is the one Captain King has been searching for?" He hooked his thumb in my direction. "I mean look at this guy."

What about 'the guy' was he referring to? My messy brown hair? My ragged grey pants and jacket, which were covered in more holes and tears than I could count? Scott stood right in front of me, our eyes almost level with each other. He scoffed at me and continued his rant.

"I thought we were after someone threatening, someone who could put up a fight, but this guy walked right into our trap. It's like he wanted to be caught!"

I rolled my eyes at that one. I most certainly had no intention of being caught, but I had been a little too careless when Dowel and Scott found me. Dowell had to place a firm hand on Scott's shoulder to calm him down.

"It doesn't matter who he is or what he's done. The Captain wants him. Once we're onboard the Echelon we will transfer him to maximum security and he won't bother anyone again."

I didn't like the sound of that. To be honest I would rather open the hatch and get sucked out into space than be onboard the Echelon, but not all was lost. They clearly underestimated me and while I wasn't terribly strong, the size and limitation of movement inside the shuttle gave me an idea. The timing had to be perfect. I would also need some help.

If you took a good look at me, you would see my stubble-ridden face, green eyes, and messy hair; in other words, nothing out of the ordinary. However, there was more to me than meets the eye, specifically my right eye. During my first escape from the very ship I was looking at, my right eye was forcibly taken from me. The memory of it was horrific and it's something I don't like to think about, but in its place a bionic eye was equipped in my orbital socket. Losing the eye and gaining the new one hurt like hell, more physical pain than I ever thought possible, but now this eye gave me an advantage in certain situations. There was just one catch. The circuitry and cybernetics used to integrate it into my orbital socket weren't entirely compatible with human tissue.

With an exaggerated blink of my eye, the device turned on and a wave of irritation and dizziness plagued my vision. I hunched over and grunted, closing my eyes hard and trying to adapt to the pain.

"Hey! What's wrong with you? Getting space sick or something?"

"Yeah," I muttered. "Something like that."

As the pain slowly dissipated I opened my bionic eye and watched a display screen appear before me. It showed various readings, such as my blood pressure and heart rate. It also showed me the height, distance, and even clothing material of the two security officers. Numerous options displayed in my vision.

The shuttle jerked slightly as the autopilot computer activated the docking procedures. I had very little time left. With focus and concentration I managed to switch the eye's display to theoretical analysis, a mode that allows me to theorize possible actions depending on my surroundings. I thought hard about what I had to accomplish.

The two guards took their positions on each side of me and moved me a couple of steps towards the exit door. I knew from ESA protocol that there would be two additional guards waiting on the ship to assist in my escort to the security wing. If that happened, it would be too late. I had to disengage the guards on the shuttle before those doors opened.

The outer hull of the small vessel merged together with the starship. When the impact jostled us, I made my move. I would only have a couple of minutes before the depressurization process completed.

I threw my shoulder into the guard in front of me, hitting him in the midsection and slamming his back into the wall. The impact snapped his head back and it too hit the wall, which knocked him unconscious. Simultaneously I threw back my leg, connecting right between the other guard's legs. I heard a grunt. With his hands over his manhood I spun around with my hands folded together and hit him hard across his jaw. He fell to the floor with his shipmate.

My bionic sight may be a pain in the eye sometimes, but it can be a life saver.

Two guards were down for the count, with two more on the other side of the doors. I used the few precious seconds I had to grab the guard's keys and unlock the shackles that held my hands at bay. I rubbed at my red and irritated wrists, then stood at the door as the depressurization completed and the two sets of doors opened. Before I even locked eyes with the guard on my left, I swung the shackles at him hard. His head jerked sideways and he fell to the ground with a deep gash in his forehead.

I quickly turned to the opposite guard before they could use a sedative or stun gun on me, but it was a woman, nearly a foot shorter than I was. She wore the security uniform, but her eyes were staring at me wide, her hands flattened against the bulkhead behind her. She expressed fear. Like an idiot I stood there a moment staring at her. I rarely ever thought of myself as a scary person, but it wasn't the first time someone looked at me like that, like I was going to hurt them.

Memories attempted to invade my consciousness again, but I quickly shook my head and tried to recall my position on the ship. I deactivated my bionic eye and looked to make sure the downed officer was still breathing, and then turned back to the woman.

"Excuse me," I muttered as I ran past her, further into the ship.

I know what you must be thinking. If I just turned back toward the shuttle I could launch it and escape. That's when the Echelon would pull me back with a tractor beam. Shuttles are useless without a departure or arrival clearance. Of course, they could also just blow me up. That would have been easy. My only choice was to move deeper into the ship.

The layout of all the decks was relatively similar. With the exception of specialty decks like the Terran Garden or Sports Complex, every deck had two long corridors running parallel to each other. These corridors ran all the way from the front of the ship to the rear with multiple access hallways connecting the two of them together.

My first order of business was to find out what deck I was on. I kept looking at hallway intersections and doorways, but I couldn't see anything that listed my location

That's when the klaxon alarm sounded.

Flux me, I thought as I continued down the corridor. People peeked outside their apartment doors, concerned with the commotion. No one attempted to stop me, but there were plenty of shouts behind me; guards screamed at me to stop while people told them which direction I ran in.

Finally I reached a stairwell that read 'Deck 17'. I stopped a moment to think. I needed to be sure of my destination or my chances of escape would be slim to none. The answer came to me a moment later as heavy footsteps closed in on me. If I could hear them over the alarm that meant they would be on me in seconds. I threw my shoulder into the door and it burst open. I skipped every other step as I ran for deck fourteen.

There was a noise above my position and I caught sight of a guard descending on me from the upper deck. His enormous figure and tight uniform told me there was no chance in hell I could take this guy in a fight, even if I played dirty, so I used the one advantage I had, the stairs themselves.

When the guard was right on top of me, his arms outstretched, I threw my hand forward, grabbed his collar and pulled on him hard. I leaned over the railing as he sailed past me, cursing and grunting down the steps. With a quick deep breath to allow my lungs to catch up with me, I continued up the stairs until a large sign next to the door read 'Deck 14'. I threw open the door and poked my head out to see if any guards waited, but for the moment the immediate area was clear. I assumed that a number of guards were being posted at every stairwell and elevator. It wouldn't take long for my position to be revealed, so I made sure my bearings were correct and continued down the hall.

At this point my legs carried me on autopilot while the klaxon alarm impaired my ability to think clearly. Was I supposed to turn left at this access hall or the next one? I ran right past a number of guards waiting by the main deck elevator doors, and they pursued me at once. I heard them announce my location and call for back-up.

Flux I was tired, but I pushed forward. I felt like if I stopped running for even a second, my legs would turn to jelly and I would be caught. I saw the target door fifty feet ahead, and with every ounce of energy I sprinted hard to it and nearly stopped when I saw guards run around the corner ahead of me.

Don't stop, keep moving. Reach the door. Come on!

I threw my hand out to grab the frame so I didn't accidentally pass the door up. When it opened I leapt inside, allowed the doors to close and smashed the control panel with my elbow. That would hopefully give me some time as the guards would have to open the bulkhead and activate the manual release.

The large, domed room I entered was the cartography station. Each of the four walls revealed sectors of the galaxy that the ESA had previously mapped. A large table was erected in the middle with a holographic display above it, showing stars, nebulas, and planets. A lone officer stood at the table and stared at me. The dressing of his uniform told me he was a part of the science department. I took notice that he didn't have a weapon, so I advanced on him. Quickly, he turned and tried to key in something on the computer screen. I ran up to him and pulled him away.

"No you don't!" I said to him. He was as tall as me, around six feet, but he was just skin and bones, not the body of a fighter. I tried to put my best intimidating face on.

"I need to know where I am, right now!" I said with a bit of exaggerated gruff in my voice.

"Y-y-you're in s-s-sector five, about t-t-ten kilometers from the border to sector f-f-four."

This man was scared, no doubt my acting skills were better than I thought, or maybe he just heard the klaxon alarm and the guards banging on the locked door behind me. With my free hand, I used the console to key in my location and send it out in a broad sweep of sector three and four. Sector three was my last position before the ESA captured me and I hoped that my transmission would be received. When I was satisfied I did it correctly, I took notice of the screen that the science officer was working on.

Various maps and constellations were displayed onscreen. Stars were circled by hand and connections were drawn from one planet to another. It looked like new star systems were being mapped. I keyed in a few commands and the map zoomed out.

"No! Please don't do that!" He said. He threw his arms around, distracting me. I didn't have time for this so I let him go and his body spun in a circle. When he faced me again I delivered a backhand to his face, knocking him out. I have to admit, I actually felt badly for doing it. He was no security officer, in fact I wouldn't have been surprised if he wet his uniform, but he still did what he could to try and stop me.

"Sorry," I said to his unconscious form. "If it makes you feel any better, the bruise you'll have will most likely save your life." I didn't want to imagine the reprimand he would receive if he was accused of allowing me access to the system.

The information on the screen was massive, too much to look at with the guards close to opening the door and seizing me. I grabbed a small, pebble sized device I had concealed on my person and placed it on the control screen that displayed the charts and maps being studied. I leaned down close to it until my lips were almost touching it.

"Authorization Quinn. Record and transfer data stream."

At my voice command the device began blinking, slowly at first then faster and faster as it uploaded all the data it could. I listened closely to the commotion outside the room.

"Get ready men! Doors will be open in one minute!"

Flux, this was going to be close. I started swaying, cracking my knuckles and smacking my hands against my legs as I watched the device absorb everything that it could. With just enough time left the device indicator light went dark. I picked it up and attached it back to the accessory around my neck. The doors opened and two dozen guards piled in, all with stun guns. Looking at their uniforms, I categorized them as Tier One Security Specialists. These men were the best of the best in the ESA. There was no more running. I put my hands up in surrender.

A slender, womanly figure entered the room and the guards parted to allow her access to me. She wore a command uniform of blue and grey. Her hair was cut short and she stared at me with daggers in her dark brown eyes, though her mouth was turned up in a wide grin. As soon as I saw her my heart sank and my stomach grew nauseous. I hadn't seen her in over five years. The memories I tried to suppress earlier smashed through the gate, flooding my mind with images and feelings I couldn't handle.

I was suddenly back in a familiar room, a small but manageable space for someone with my living habits. I wasn't exhausted anymore from all the running, nor was I scared of being caught. I was happy and excited. Something was happening on this night, something I had prepared for. My body moved through the room, my mouth stretched out in a wide smile. I remember going into my bedroom to change out of my uniform. That's when everything changed and the room seemed to darken into a moment that would leave a scar on my soul, the moment when I saw my bedroom covered in blood and a body lay dead in front of me.

The present returned as quickly as it had left. I was back in the cartography room. Only small remnants of the vision remained in my mind. Captain Sarah King, the woman standing in front of me, was still grinning. In the time that I relived my memories the guards had completely surrounded me. As I looked into her eyes my thoughts grew reckless and angry, pouring out the intense hatred I had for her.

Kill her!

The words echoed in my mind as loud as the alarms did throughout the ship. A small part of me in the darkest corners of my mind wanted to end her life. She was certainly close enough. I would instantly be killed once I took her throat in my hands, but I should have just enough time to end her.

I lowered my shoulders and let out a sigh. I wouldn't kill her. I couldn't.

"Quinn," she said to me, the voice sending chills throughout my body, causing the hairs on the back of my neck to stand up. "I cannot tell you how nice it is to see you. It's been a long time."

What was I supposed to say? My entire thought process froze. I don't think it was fear. The hatred counteracted that. I tried to calm my thoughts, as impossible as that seemed.

Just keep talking to her, I thought as I grit my teeth together.

"Not long enough," I said.

King looked amused by my response, but otherwise unaffected. She stepped closer, the look of her, the smell of her was the same as I remembered years ago. The senses sent shockwaves through my body.

"We have been looking for you for a long time, Quinn. I see the years haven't been terribly kind to you, but you did manage to replace your eye! Let's hope you manage to hold onto that one" she said as she laughed softly, and then she deeply inhaled through her nose. "At least you keep yourself clean, despite your filthy persona."

"Well, the dirtier you are the itchier the body gets. Who likes that?" I could only throw sarcasm at her for so long.

"Listen, why don't you just do what we know you're going to do? Throw me in jail, or kill me here and now. Just do it quickly please."

King circled me, eyeing me up and down. "No inquiries about old friends? I know Lieutenant Hobbes has missed you terribly." She stuck out her bottom lip as she finished her sentence.

The name hit me like a punch to the gut. Jason Hobbes had been one of my closest friends for as long as I can remember. The last time I saw him was when I fled for my life to escape the Echelon the first time. Jason helped me escape. In my last memory of him I screamed and pounded on a shuttle door as I watched the guards seize him. I knew he would die after that, but was it possible he was still alive?

I lunged at King and wrapped my hands around her uniform. With a boiling rage I growled out at her.

"Where is he? What have you done with him?"

Every guard raised their weapon at my head, but King put her hand up to stop them from firing at me.

"He's doing well enough I suppose," she muttered. "I'm sure you'll have plenty of time to see him now that you're back where you belong."

I let go of her collar and backed away from her.

The amusement in her voice sickened me. I took a deep breath and tried to tell myself that she was toying with me, trying to break me mentally. Some small part of me wanted to surrender just for the chance to see Jason again. The two of us did everything we could to protect each other. We were like brothers.

As I stood there in disbelief, King's eyes traveled over my body and locked onto the ring that hung around my neck. She stepped closer. One of her guards recommended against it, but she raised her hand to silence him. With her opposite hand, she slid her fingers under the ring, palming it. I felt my heart racing, hammering against my chest.

"Drop . . . the ring . . . now," I growled out. She let go of it, her eyes widening. I palmed the ring and closed my hand tight around it. "I keep this on me to remember what I lost," I said to her, my voice growing colder by the minute. "I keep this to remember everything you took from me . . . *Commander!*"

Sarah King flinched when I called her by her previous designation. For a brief moment the tables seemed to turn. That didn't last long of course. She had the guards and the ship and quickly regained her composure.

"Speaking of taking things from others," she said, her voice cold and calculated. "You have something I want. Tell me where my artificial intelligence program is and you will be treated somewhat fairly."

I couldn't think of anything else to say to her, so I laughed. I wish I could say it was a pleasing, satisfied laugh. I think at that point I lost my mind. She pursed her lips and furrowed her brow.

"We'll see how amused you are when we break you Quinn," she said. "Then you will tell us everything."

At that exact moment, the ring I held onto trembled. My breath stopped as I felt it, but no one took notice of my expression. A short static noise echoed through the room, and then a high pitched man spoke over the intercom.

"Captain King, this is lookout," the voice said.

"I read you lookout, I'm currently indisposed, if you could please wait…"

"I'm sorry sir, but this can't wait. We are picking up a vessel on scanners, no known registration."

For the first time in hours, I felt a genuine smile creep up on me. My hands trembled with anticipation. There was actually a chance I could still get out of this.

"Check all transit, delivery, and cargo drops on our schedule and see if it matches any design in the ESA database. Do it quickly. We need to know if it's hostile or just passing through."

King watched me as she waited for her lookout to scan the vessel. She was smart. If this ship was the one I hoped for, the timing had to be quick and precise. We waited. She waited. The guard hadn't arrested me yet. I was shocked no one seemed to hear my heart slamming against my chest like a drum.

"Captain, lookout. We do not have any scheduled rendezvous nor is the ship listed in our database. It's approaching visual range."

Any second now.

"Hey *Commander*!" I said loudly. King almost jumped, but her expression of hate didn't falter. "I forgot to tell you, it's not just Quinn anymore, it's Captain Quinn." I finished the statement with a wide grin, teeth showing, and my eyebrows rose as I pointed right at the stone attached to the ring. The diamond that had once rested on the ring was replaced with a clear colored micro-drive, the same one I just used to steal a huge amount of ESA data.

"Next time try looking right under your nose, or in this case . . . mine."

"No! Grab him!"

Too late. In one single second, I watched as King and her guards leapt toward me. The stone emitted a scanning beam covering my entire body, which then shifted my entire being off of the Echelon. Imagine someone grabbing every single part of your body and pulling you at a velocity so intense, that you traveled from one side of a planet or ship to the other in seconds. That's exactly what happened to me. I was pulled, my mass and energy teleported from the cartography station to a small closet sized control room, the walls and floor a dirty shade of copper.

I was on the bridge of my ship. Technically I was lying on my back and my body felt like it had just fallen from the ceiling three meters above, but I wasn't going to complain at the moment. Instead I turned my head to the empty navigation station and yelled out.

"Al! Get us out of here now!"

The control console lit up and began computing coordinates. At the same time a voice came through the speaker system, a couple of the lights blinking as it spoke.

"You do not have to scream sir. Activating slingspace velocity now."

The engine growled and the deck plates trembled. I raced to the front window to see, only for a second, the ESA Echelon off my starboard bow. Less than five seconds later my ship turned and shot forward into a speed faster than light. I counted to ten, pinched myself, and dropped to the ground.

Somehow I once again escaped the jaws of the beast...and for now I was safe.

TWO

"I want to know how I ended up on that damn ship," I said to my computer console.

An hour had passed since my nearly fatal run in with the Echelon, but now I was cruising in the opposite direction at full slingspace velocity. I always thought the term sounded odd, but the act of traveling faster than light derived from old fashioned slingshots and catapults centuries ago. In addition to my main engine core which controlled my thrusters, my ship had a secondary core specifically built to charge enough power over time to launch the ship forward into slingspace.

Unfortunately this could cause problems. My ship is so old that it can't operate with both the thrusters and slingspace drive at full power at the same time. In order to escape the Echelon, we had to drop out of slingspace, power down its core, and then activate the thrusters. Once Al maneuvered her into a new position, we shut down the thrusters and primed the slingspace core. We repeated the process a few times to make sure the Echelon couldn't track us. If the two cores were ever activated at the same time the ship could shake apart.

Now that we had jumped a few times and masked the exhaust trail of my ship, I felt I could rest a little easier. The jumps had depleted my fuel tanks considerably and I had questions about everything that had occurred, but at least I was back on the bridge of my ship. I named her the Kestrel Belle.

The Kestrel class star cruiser, designed to mimic the shape of a falcon was created before the ESA and other agencies constructed newer, state of the art ships. She was small, quick, and easy to maneuver with only one crewman—me. Though I guess that wasn't really true. I had a lot of help from the advanced artificial intelligence that was installed into my ship's mainframe. He wasn't technically sentient, but I had a funny feeling if I told him that he would take offense.

"Captain," he said, his voice strangely human except for an occasional monotone vocal intonation. "I ran several diagnostics on the Starcade, specifically the job the ESA used to capture you. I found abnormalities in the source code."

I remembered the job post. The Starcade was an enormous, intergalactic bulletin board used by mercenaries, bounty hunters, and anyone else who operated outside the law. If someone needed a job done with no questions asked, they posted it to the Starcade and waited for a potential application process. Depending on the type of job it was, be it smuggling supplies, infiltration, or even assassination, mercs would bid for the opportunity to get the job. If the employer liked the resume and fee, then a deal was made and the job started.

Two days ago, I was hired for a simple escort. I would travel to an installation where I would be used as a hired protector of a high ranking government official. I had to admit, the details were scarce, but that wasn't anything new. Sometimes Starcade submissions were nothing more than one or two words like 'Target Pursuit' or 'Smuggle Operation'. I was confident I could accomplish an escort job, so I put in my fee. I was accepted immediately.

That's when the red flags should have been going off in my head. I didn't know of any job that hired a merc after one submission. Maybe this job was high priority and they couldn't afford to wait. That was possible, but there was one other reason I should have realized it was a set up.

My reputation as a mercenary was less than stellar. In a short few years submitting my name for jobs on the Starcade, I had been accepted less than a dozen times, and my completion rating wasn't exactly 100%. In fact, I'd be lying if I said it was over 50%. I was young, naive, and didn't know how deep and terrifying some of these jobs would be. It was no secret that I wasn't the most trustworthy bidder.

When I was hired two days ago, Al and I had discussed the oddity of the quick hire and instructional transmission. It stated that I had to wait on a space station in sector three for a shuttle to pick me up. Weapons and armor would be provided to me when I arrived at my destination. Did this all sound odd to me? Yes. Was it completely unheard of in the history of the Starcade? No. In the end, I decided that I needed the money, and took the job. You know how it ended, with my incarceration and transfer to the Echelon.

"So let me guess," I said to Al. "The source code was a native ESA signal."

"That is correct Captain. In fact, multiple ESA signals were in the Starcade, all different jobs and requirements."

Stars above, I thought. Sarah King was combing the damn galaxy for me, and it worked. I considered my options and tried to think of a location I could travel where I would be safe, well moderately safe, and at the same time could shop out for information. I could only think of one such place.

"Al, set a course for Galaxy One Alpha."

"Yes sir, altering course now. Stand by."

The ship modified its course and I felt my equilibrium shift causing a slight bout of dizziness. After a while it was something you got used to. I sat down on the cold, metal floor and angled my head under the computer console so I could remove the panel underneath it. A red glow emanated from inside illuminating a vast array of circuitry. In the center was a square shaped motherboard, one that many of the wires and chips were connected to.

I took the ring that still hung on the necklace and held it close to my eyes. The knotting was a shimmering silver color which led around and met on each side, tying together where the diamond sat, or used to. I carefully detached the micro-drive from the ring and connected it to the motherboard above me.

"Sir," Al said. I was so deep in thought that his voice boomed in my ears and caused me to jump. Thankfully I didn't drop the small device. "Why are you touching me?"

That comment made me laugh. When he was first installed on the ship, he was a lifeless, emotionless computer program that didn't understand simple human concepts. After years of traveling with me, lonely and depressed, I took to talking to Al like he was my best friend. He adapted to me as much as I did to him, growing his own unique personality. He requested I name him shortly after, so I called him Al because the abbreviation of 'A.I.' on his motherboard was written in a font where the capital 'I' looked like a lowercase 'l'. It wasn't the most original way to name him, but he didn't seem to mind.

"I'm reinstalling the micro-drive you lent me. I downloaded some information that may prove to be useful."

"Understood. I was content with the results of the successful teleportation I initiated. For a moment I was concerned you would not survive the process," he said to me. I nearly dropped the micro-drive.

"Are you telling me there was a chance I wouldn't have teleported off that ship?" I asked.

"Incorrect sir. You would have teleported, but the percentage of completing the process with your full mass was only 57%."

Well, it was nice to know my ass wasn't flying around somewhere in deep space at the moment. I took in a breath and let it out slowly, continuing to connect the drive to his mainframe. When I was finished, I closed the panel and waited in my chair. The rest was up to him.

"Accessing data . . . Classified. That is unacceptable. Bypassing . . . Coordinates, data logs, star charts, and personnel review . . . sir there is a formidable amount of information here. It is odd though that the data patterns are erratic."

"How so?" I asked. The records that he listed made it seem like the ESA was searching for something.

"There are a variety of records, however none of them are listed consistently or collectively. If I had to guess, I would say that this data has been intentionally scrambled to confuse anyone who illegally tries to access it."

Well gee, who would want to do that? I chuckled to myself.

"So what you're telling me is that you are looking at a pile of puzzle pieces. Can you put it all back together so it can be accessed?"

". . . Interesting use of terms Captain. Following your train of thought, I would say yes. With time I should be able to re-sequence the collections."

I could feel the tension in me evaporating. In a matter of hours Al would have complete access to the files I took from the Echelon. I could only imagine what kind of data was listed, and even more so, what it could do for me. Depending on what Al could find, maybe I could prove that I was an innocent man, falsely accused of murder and mutiny, or maybe it had valuable information that I could use. After my run in with King and discovering that Jason Hobbes was alive, maybe I could find and help him. Of course, none of this would come to pass if all it turned out to be was a blueprint for a kitchen refit.

"Alright," I said, trying not to sound too excited. "I'm going to try and rest. Let me know when you've finished."

The Kestrel Belle wasn't all that large. Beyond the bridge was a single corridor. The Captain's and crew quarters were on the left, and the mess hall was on the right. At the end of the corridor which was an overall length of about thirty meters, a set of stairs led down to the second floor which held the armory and main access to the cargo bay. There was a third floor as well that led to engineering.

A ship this size was meant to operate at full capacity with half a dozen people. Of course, having an advanced artificial intelligence program onboard allowed me to cheat the system. Although, even with AI on the ship I still felt the need for some type of human interaction. Even in space the crew quarters grew dust.

I punched in the code to my quarters and the door opened to a small, rectangular-shaped room. There was an old fashioned oak dresser attached to the left wall and a full sized bed in the middle. The right wall was bare, but with the touch of a camouflaged panel it would open a secret compartment which held my tactical gear and rifle. I had to give the designers credit, the secret compartment was awesome.

I pulled open the top drawer of the dresser, retrieved a small canister, and twisted the cap open to reveal a number of white pills. I took one and swallowed it, hoping it would do its job and keep unwanted images and memories from invading my mind while I slept. If I didn't take one of these, I wouldn't sleep, plain and simple.

The mattress groaned and squeaked as I sank into it. Maybe it wasn't happy to see me but I was more than happy to see it. Reaching back behind me, I hit the panel on the wall that controlled the lighting, lowering it several levels until I was satisfied. The hum of the engine, the rattling of the deck plates, and the vibration of the ship acted as a lullaby to me. Before I could think a single thought about my next step, my eyes were closed and I was asleep.

"Captain Quinn to the bridge!" A voice roared over the intercom, my arms and legs flew up and my heart jumped into hyperactive.

"Flux!" I cursed. My head felt like something was sloshing around inside and my eyelids didn't want to open.

"Al," I croaked out. "You realize since we're the only ones onboard that you don't have to follow regulation right?"

"I did not consider that sir. Shall I relay the information to you presently?"

"I just got to sleep, but what the hell? Go ahead."

"Actually you have been sleeping for forty-seven minutes."

Seriously? It didn't feel like it. I massaged my face with my hands, smacking my cheeks to try and coax myself awake.

"Captain," Al continued. "After successfully reorganizing and combining the collective databases, I now have a full analysis of the most common word in the collection. Empyreus."

"Should I know what that is?" I asked him.

"It is not surprising, actually. I searched every database I could link up to from our current position and found what you would call 'only a handful' of submissions of the word."

"Okay, I'm with you so far. So what is it?"

Al paused for a moment. I realized what I did shortly after and cursed myself for doing it.

"Captain . . . you are not with me. You are in your quarters."

Al was great, but sometimes he took things a bit too literally. I rolled my eyes and waited, hoping he would get the point and continue.

"In the few articles I managed to access, empyreus is a mythological energy source, vastly superior to anything known to any alien race associated to man. The power of empyreus is even greater than that of Earth's sun, producing at least twice as much energy, and unusually stable."

"What do you mean unusually stable?" I asked him.

"Consider the types of energy that humankind has used over their existence. Fossil fuels, fusion, plasma, and antimatter all have the potential to be toxic or largely unstable and can create chaotic devastation if not properly handled. Empyreus is neither toxic nor unstable."

Stars above, I thought. If this stuff was real, it would be the most sought after and valuable source of energy in the known galaxy.

"But it's only a myth?"

"Correct sir. While there are multiple reports on the energy itself, I cannot trace any of the information back to its point of origin. Without a source, or evidence of its existence, the power has been labeled as a myth and legend."

"So then why is Sarah King after it?" I shuddered as I said the name out loud.

"That is unknown sir, however from a large number of logs encrypted in the data I analyzed, it seems they were searching for something. Probes were sent out to various corners of the galaxy, programmed to only look for certain energy signatures."

"So they received a positive signature from a probe searching for this empyreus stuff?" If the Echelon had already found a positive signature from an energy source they thought to be empyreus, then this was most likely a waste.

"Technically, no. They began to receive data from all probes at regular intervals. All of the data was stored in the directory you collected in order to be examined and decoded. I would estimate at this current time that they would not find anything useful for a matter of months. However, I found something. While all probes have been sending back data, one in particular has been doing so erratically."

I tried to wrap my head around everything Al was telling me. If this empyreus really existed, it could change the playing field on so many levels, but for whom and for what? I could only imagine what Sarah King and her tainted crew on the Echelon had in mind, but to the right bidder this secret could be worth an enormous amount of money. If I could sell this information, I could live comfortably for a long time and potentially even right a few wrongs from my past.

The probe. Al said one of them was sending back data erratically. My head juggled the information around. Maybe it was damaged by a meteor or other space debris, or something as simple as a defective unit. We didn't exactly live in an age where our machines worked at 100% efficiency 100% of the time. Something told me this was different, that someone had found this probe and was doing their best to stop its transmission. Al came to the same conclusion when I told him my theory, which meant that we not only discovered empyreus, but also a possible range of coordinates where it might be located.

The question now was how to put the word out. The ESA already infiltrated the Starcade. Placing my own post of the information would be like telling them, 'Hey! I'm over here and I've got your data!' so that was out of the question. This time I was going to have to shop around the old fashioned way, face to face.

"Alright," I said, my mind a mixture of excitement and exhaustion. "Let me know when we reach Galaxy One."

"Acknowledged," Al said.

The room stayed silent after that. I laid there on my back for some time and closed my eyes only to find it impossible to keep them shut. My mind was racing too fast to sleep. I turned to my side, then my stomach, stretching out my arms and legs. Eventually I think I won the battle for sleep because when Al announced we were approaching Galaxy One Alpha, my eyes were crusted shut and my left leg hung off the bed with no feeling past the knee. I knew that would feel uncomfortable in a few minutes.

I stood up and walked out of my quarters towards the bridge. With every left step I took, hundreds of imaginary needles stabbed me in the leg. I grabbed the banister attached to the corridor and used it reach the door. I didn't even try to reach my command chair, but dropped into the tactical station chair behind it.

"Captain," Al said as I approached my chair. "Have you injured your leg?"

"Pins and needles," I groaned. "Don't say anything. Don't ask. Just pins and needles."

Al didn't make a sound after that. As the intense sensation subsided, I moved to my chair and leaned over to look at the display screen. The command, navigation, and tactical stations were all a similar layout. Each had a display screen that was about twenty inches from corner to corner. Surrounding it were smaller touch screens with multiple tiles of programs and controls. The command station actually had two of these stations on each side of my chair. Directly in front of me was a sphere, which I used to manually control the ship. Above that was the main viewing shield. In broader terms it was just a window transparent enough to see what was in front of me, but the material was constructed to be durable enough to handle debris and some weapon fire. The ship had dropped out of slingspace and was directly on route with the station.

As we passed into visual range I switched my right view to the live camera feed. Galaxy One Alpha was a space station, the central hub of human and alien activity in this corner of the galaxy. A large dome sat on top of a saucer-shaped platform big enough to fit multiple cities inside of it. Attached to the dome were multiple spheres, each one corresponding to a different operation such as manufacturing, science and research, and my current destination, the star port.

"Attention vessel," A low voice growled over the intercom. "This is Galaxy One Alpha Tower Command. We have you on our scanners and require identification."

"Daniel Quinn, Captain of the Kestrel Belle, registry FAL0812."

Every time I gave my name openly over communication channels my heart would beat faster and my sweat glands quickened their production. Sarah King never made the accusations against me public and in doing so couldn't outwardly put a price on my head. I thought I knew the reason why she did this; a combination of information I held that she needed and her own personal pride. She loved to play the game of cat and mouse and wanted the pleasure of hunting me alone so she could take out her vengeance on me. No one would rob her of that as far as she was concerned.

"Kestrel Belle," tower command said. "You are confirmed for docking. Proceed to platform nine."

THREE

The inside of the docking bay resembled the inside of a hollow metal planet, which itself was tucked inside a bigger metal planet. The station was designed this way so that the outer station's doors could open and let ships in and out. Once those were closed, the inner doors opened to the dock itself. If the doors were ever opened at the same time the entire dock area would decompress, sucking ships and people out into space. This hasn't happened yet as far as I knew, but I stayed aware of it when I visited the station.

Over a hundred platforms were connected to a handful of staging areas where shipments and cargo were checked over by control tower security. Once cleared past the staging area, you would then continue down a long walkway that led to the main elevator, which provided access to the main port terminal of Galaxia City.

Once the Belle was inside the dock, I let Al maneuver her to platform nine. The Belle slowly lowered onto the empty platform and trembled slightly as she met the floor. The landing gear groaned under the weight before finally locking into position. When my display read that we were on the ground, I cut power to the engines.

"Optimal landing Al," I said.

"Why would it not be sir?" He asked. I rolled my eyes.

The port was busy today. Every platform I could see outside the front shield had a ship on it, their crews all waiting in line to have their cargo inspected and cleared. Luckily for me I had no cargo so I could walk past that traffic jam. I took a deep breath going over my plan one more time in my head, then stood up.

"Al, keep the ship on conservative power. Remain online and attempt to access those coordinates from the faulty probe. I should be back within a couple of hours."

"Acknowledged Captain," Al said. I left the bridge and walked toward the rear of the ship, climbing down a set of stairs and stepping onto my cargo bay. This was the primary entrance and exit to the Belle. The bay was the largest room, resembling a mini warehouse with scaffolding on each wall and nets and ties for any cargo I might bring aboard. Next to the door was a lever, which I wrapped my hand around and pulled down. The door squealed and creaked as it lowered to the floor.

The temperature was cool and the sounds were plentiful as I stepped out onto the platform. Humans and aliens alike were arguing with each other or aiming their aggression towards security for holding up their delivery. I eased my way past them and walked toward the elevator.

"Good evening," a computerized female voice announced. I pushed the button and the pod dropped at a quick and controlled speed. "Welcome to Galaxy One Alpha. Proceeding to Grand Central Station. The temperature on the main floor is currently a comfortable 68 degrees Fahrenheit. Wind speed is 7 miles per hour."

As the mechanical operator finished her welcome speech, the pod stopped and the doors parted to reveal the Grand Central Station. A large archway stood overhead. Underneath were passenger terminals, tram stations and service desks. From here you could arrange transport to any section of the station or charter a passenger starship to another station or planet in the galaxy.

The skyline of Galaxia City was in view over the trams. As you stepped out of the archway of the station brilliant, warm, artificial sunlight illuminates the city. One of the most appealing aspects of the station was the total sense of realism. The city itself was designed to represent the pinnacle of our technological prowess on Earth, with structures of unimaginable beauty, gleaming skyscrapers, and abstract art running along the streets. I knew the city was inspired by New York City, one of Earth's biggest and most popular cities in the United States.

The artificial atmosphere designed for this station was unlike any other. When I looked up at the sky I saw numerous clouds pass overhead. The "sun" created a warm sensation on my face. When I took a deep breath, the air didn't give off the same artificial smell that was on most starships or the external hubs of the station. When I closed my eyes I felt the sun and the wind, smelled the various aromas from the people walking by, and heard real birds chirping. I could be convinced I was on Earth.

The hairs on the back of my neck stiffened and the calm moment passed. I turned to look behind me. I had an odd feeling that someone was watching me. There weren't that many people nearby and those who were close looked focused on their own lives, not mine. I turned my head from left to right slowly, trying to determine if anyone in sight was looking in my direction. Nothing.

To most people paranoia is a nasty trait to have. At times it can be a curse. A few years ago mine was so bad I thought every shadow was someone waiting to attack me. However, with time and discipline I learned to turn it into a strength and a skill that I would be able to use to survive. I learned to trust my instincts.

Instead of taking the long way to my destination, which I originally intended, I used what little money I had to buy a tram ticket. The 'thank you!' the clerk nearly sang was dripping with an abundance of enthusiasm.

The tram itself was a long multi-car transport. It hovered in the air above its track, which was designed with some kind of magnetic device to keep the tram from derailing. Inside each car were a large number of cushioned seats and long benches. I sat on one of the benches closest to the window and watched to see if anyone who got onboard looked suspicious. Nothing. Maybe this time it was simply a case of the aforementioned paranoia.

"Please state destination," said the same voice I heard in the elevator. All at once everyone in my car spoke. It sounded like gibberish when we all said it in unison. Not everyone was going to the same place, but the microphone installed on each car was able to determine all of the individual stopping points and direct each to the navigational computer, which was pretty impressive. The cars lifted a few inches into the air and with a short jolt the tram shot forward.

The Galaxia marketplace was located in the middle of the city and it was the one place you could find anything in the galaxy; from food and drink to ship parts and armor. You could also find a variety of illegal items if you knew where to look. A lot of business transactions on the Starcade ended in the marketplace to acquire payment or items. In order to start or finalize your contract, you would meet in one of the establishments that surrounded the marketplace. These establishments were very reminiscent of clubs, bars, and taverns back on Earth. One of these places was my destination.

When the tram stopped I made sure to be one of the first people off. I jogged a few feet ahead and turned to face the cars letting people off. I wanted to be sure no one followed me. I even went as far as to activate my bionic eye, which sent the familiar surge of pain through my head when I turned it on. I fought back the need to wince and curse as it powered up, and I immediately scanned people. Again, nothing seemed out of the ordinary. My eye scanned over items and found nothing more than manifest and shipment documents, and sale purchase receipts. Some people had sidearms tucked under their coats, but none of them gave me the light of day. I shrugged and turned my eye off, feeling a great sense of relief. I turned and walked down the stairs into the marketplace.

A wide open, stone covered area was littered with carts and booths. The plaza was surrounded by shops and taverns. Saying the noise was loud would be a major understatement. Merchants shouted at the top of their lungs saying whatever was necessary to draw attention to their assortment of goodies. 'We take all forms of payment!', 'Trades allowed here!', 'Shop here and let's work together to mutually benefit!' were some of the things I could pick out. At the same time potential or previous customers were shouting right back at them. Some people were shouting out bids for popular items, while others were complaining about the service or low quality item they received.

Needless to say, I tried to keep out of marketplace business unless I desperately needed something that couldn't be found elsewhere. Every rare item ever heard of somehow ended up here. I was shocked that people weren't selling the empyreus Al told me about. That's how in-depth the retail is here.

The place I was looking for was down an alley which led in and out of the marketplace. Sitting comfortably in-between a weapons depot store and a consulting firm was Neptune's Tavern. I often wondered if the bar's placement was intentional, so that when a consultation went sour people could go to the weapons store, shoot at each other, then finish off with a drink. The entrance was down a set of stairs and before you entered there was a large sign that read 'Weapons belong next door, not here' with an arrow pointing toward the weapons shop. It continued by saying 'All are welcomed, but leave weapons outside'. The owner of the tavern didn't take well to people shooting it out in his establishment. He also welcomed all races, human and alien alike. Neptune's Tavern was known to be a popular neutral location.

Once I opened the door my sense of smell was overwhelmed by numerous scents. A hickory flavor loomed in the air as well as the smell of onions and garlic. My mouth watered and my stomach growled at me. I couldn't remember the last time I had an actual meal as opposed to rations and dry food. Neptune's Tavern was one of the best places in the galaxy for grilled food and exotic drinks. It took every ounce of strength not to pounce on the nearest plate.

Every piece of furniture in the place was mahogany, at least I think that's what the owner once told me. There was a long bar on the far side of the room with twenty stools in front of it. All of the tables were square with four chairs on every side. There was an old fashioned pool table and dart board, which were very popular among the human crowd. There were also a couple alien games, though I never took the time to learn how to play one. The bartender, who was also the owner, was smiling at one of his customers, an alien with grey skin and sharp corners. I wasn't sure, but I think his race was called the Rokor.

Derrick Kenton, the man behind the bar, imported every piece of furniture from his establishment on Earth. Despite the tavern being on a space station he wanted it to feel like home. When he saw me his expression went from inviting to grimacing. He excused himself from his customer and walked to the opposite side of the bar, nodding me over. I took a deep breath and walked over to him.

"What are you doing here Danny?" His voice was low, with the rasp that would accompany a heavy smoker's voice. I couldn't stand the name Danny because it sounded like a child's name, and that was what Jason called me when we were younger. By using that name for me, he was telling me that he was talking down to me like a parent would to a disobedient child.

"Derrick," I said, my voice breaking slightly. "It's good to see you!"

He raised his hand to me.

"Save it, you know you're not welcome here, at least not until the large sum of money you owe me is settled."

I winced. He continued talking before I could even think about it.

"Not to mention you have made a lousy reputation for yourself which could potentially hurt mine!"

He wasn't wrong, though I didn't want to admit he was right. Derrick had helped me get on my feet when I first came to him looking for jobs. He showed me the system that was the Starcade and how to use it. Over the years he provided me with small loans of money, which I would in turn pay back to him after completing my jobs. The problem wasn't that I didn't complete my jobs, but I didn't do everything that was required of me during said job.

"Listen please," I said quickly. "I know I've botched a couple jobs, but I wasn't willing to kill someone."

"You do whatever you damn well are ordered to do!" He barked at me. "If your employer wants you to eject someone out an airlock, if your employer wants you to vaporize someone, or if he says stab them to death, then you better damn well do it!"

At the word stab my mind became infected with images and memories of a bloody bed, a slender, lifeless figure with multiple stabs wounds in her abdomen. My heart pounded and my hands trembled. Derrick made a grunt of disgust then walked away from me as unwanted images continued to invade my mind. I tried to think of something else, anything else, whether it was a happy memory or a terrible one, but nothing could close the floodgates.

Derrick reappeared a moment later, placing a small drink in front of me. I took it and quickly drank it all. The liquid burned my throat as if it was engulfed in flame and continued down into my stomach. I let out a violent cough. Whatever I just drank consumed my entire being. All I could think of was how much it burned, but then later realized that it managed to make the unwanted memories disappear. When I opened my eyes Derrick and the bottles and decorations behind him appeared to be swimming.

"Flux!" I coughed. "What was that?!"

He didn't respond to me, at first. Instead all he did was spit where the glass previously sat.

"You're pathetic Quinn. You're a lousy merc and a terrible customer. Get out of my sight."

He walked off without another word. I made one more attempt to stop him.

"Derrick wait!" He stopped. "Let me just say one word about what I found. If I'm right, you of all people should know what it is and what can be done about it. If you've never heard of it, then I will leave and never return. Even when I manage to pay you back, you'll never see me again."

He stood there thinking it over. I wouldn't have been surprised one bit if he shook his head, walked away and that was the end. I hoped that curiosity would get the better of him. After a moment of consideration he leaned forward and muttered, "Try me."

That was all I needed. I leaned into him until our noses were a mere inch apart, and whispered to him, "Empyreus."

Derrick's left eye twitched, and without any movement from his neck or head, both eyes began surveying everyone surrounding us. His posture eased up and he poured himself a drink of the same stuff he gave me. The man didn't even blink after he swallowed.

"Take a seat in the back," Derrick said to me, his voice surprisingly soft. "If you can pay for a meal, you're welcome to one. I'll be along to talk to you."

Without another word he turned and walked into the kitchen. I signaled Derrick's one and only waiter over and gave him my order, paying up front as a sign of good faith. Then I stood up and, still under the effects from the drink, stumbled and wobbled my way past the bar and into a narrow hallway. On the other side was a small, darkened room with three tables. This was infamously known to be the place where Starcade and other operational discussions took place. The walls were soundproof, and there was no electronic devices allowed due to the possibility of conversations being bugged or recorded.

No one else was there, so I sat down at the far table and waited. Minutes felt like hours. When Derrick finally entered the room, he carried a tray of food in one hand and a large glass of soda in the other. A large slice of beef, pink and tender, and a serving of french fries was placed in front of me. I'm not going to go into details of what happened next. The scene wasn't pretty. Suffice to say I destroyed and devoured the food until nothing remained. Derrick sat across from me the entire time watching me eat. I would have said it was awkward, but my hunger at the time didn't give a damn.

"Do you ever think about the past?"

I gave him an inquisitive look as I wiped away the salt and grease from my face. The corner of his mouth turned up slightly.

"I'm an old man," he continued. "When I was young, living on Earth, governments had just passed the bill to construct starships. If you ask a child living in the here and now why our people traveled to the stars, he would tell you that mankind was looking for the next great adventure, the future of human evolution. I don't know where they get that shit. You lived on Earth didn't you Quinn?"

"Yes," I said quietly. I don't remember Derrick ever opening up to me before.

"You probably don't know the truth as much as I do, as young as you are. Building starships and launching into space had nothing to do with evolution or seeking adventure. It was about power, and who held the power? Anyone who had the wealth and the land, that's who. For years every nation fought for money and power, smothering the entire Earth with war and destruction. Eventually on Earth nothing mattered but the conquest of your adversary. Outer space was the only logical place humanity could expand so we didn't suffocate or destroy ourselves. Setting out into space . . . it was an escape. There was nothing majestic about it, and now, those same problems are beginning to rise again. We have an entire galaxy to explore, yet the same groups of people are out here with us now, building armies and gaining territory. And to do this, they need the power, and the resources."

Derrick looked up into my eyes at that point.

"Do you have any idea of the implications of what you know? How dangerous it is to hold information like that? You must have foregone the Starcade. I doubt you'd still be alive at this point."

"I have reason to believe it's been compromised," I said to him, neglecting to mention the part where I probably would have posted it had the ESA not interfered.

Derrick tried to restrain a chuckle, putting his hand to his mouth and trying to feign it as a cough. He reached into his pocket and pulled out a long narrow pipe and a case of tobacco. He stuffed the pipe full then used a lighter from his opposite pocket to light it, then took a slow long drag, expelling the smoke from his mouth towards the ceiling.

"I don't know why, but I'm not surprised at all. Just as well . . . you wouldn't want that kind of attention."

"That's why I'm here Derrick," I said to him, leaning in close even though the room was empty. "I know our relationship is strained right now, but there's no one else in the galaxy who I could talk to or trust with this information."

His upper body twitched for less than a second as I said that. I didn't understand what it was at first, but then the cogs in my head turned. The unbelievable change of tone in his voice and the fact that he didn't ask how I found out about empyreus all pointed to one thing. Just like I had recently done to Sarah King, Derrick was stalling, waiting for something.

The door behind him opened and two absurdly large men were standing there. They both crossed their arms which were the size of tree trunks, looking tough enough to lift a shuttle and toss it three city blocks. They were staring daggers right at me. I muttered a curse to myself and turned to look back at Derrick. His expression was apologetic.

"Never trust anyone son. The information you have is priceless, and you're not the only one who owes debts."

I closed my fists and raised my arms up in a combat stance. Both of the giants smirked at me, clearly amused. It wasn't hard to deduce they were here to rough me up, and at the time I had to force myself to believe I didn't care. They blocked the only exit and I wouldn't go down without a fight. I pushed my fear as far to the side as I could manage and gave them a smirk of my own.

"Sorry boys, didn't anyone tell you this was a private meeting? Invitation only?"

They didn't move, nor did they blink.

"I can guess why you're here, and I'm telling you now that I'm tougher than I look." Still nothing. "What's the matter? Scared to get your massive hands dirty? Let's go!" With that last statement I advanced towards them. That's when they reached behind their backs and pulled out plasma blasters, pointed straight at my head. My courage and anger dropped into my stomach, and I let myself go, shoulders hunched and head hanging down.

"I'm guessing you missed the sign out front that said 'No Weapons'?" I said to them in defeat.

"Quite the contrary!" The voice came from behind them, rich and baritone. An elderly man wearing a dark blue business suit stepped in between them. His head was either shaved or bald and he had a delightful expression on his face.

"They saw the sign Mr. Quinn, but at my command they ignored it."

"My name is Raymond Erebos," the old man said. He joined me at my table along with his two cohorts. Derrick was excused by Erebos. Apparently whatever debt he owed was settled. Derrick Kenton intimidated me and *he* was intimidated by Erebos. Suffice to say, I was not comfortable in my current situation. I wasn't given the names of the two giants sitting on either side of me, but I didn't care to know. Their unbelievably close proximity to me combined with their overbearing body odor was enough. I named them smelly one and smelly two.

Everyone was staring at me. I guess I was supposed to introduce myself as well. Erebos already knew my name. If he was aware of that, how much else did he know? Did Derrick give him my name? Did he look it up in a database? Who knew?

I trembled. I didn't want to look like a wimp, but when you have two men twice your size staring at you like they want to make painful physical alterations to your body and their boss who seemed to be studying my very soul, well, I think anyone would be a bit creeped out.

"So," I finally said. "Have you tried the food here? It's amazing! And Derrick has some kind of drink that can clear out your sinuses in seconds!"

I know, not the most intelligent thing to say. Erebos arched an eyebrow at me, and folded his hands on the table.

"You don't like confrontation, do you Mr. Quinn?"

"Captain, actually..." I found myself spatting out. "Captain Quinn."

"Yes of course," he said, one corner of his mouth turned upward in a half grin. "Captain of the Kestrel Belle. An old model cruiser. If I'm correct there are only a handful of them left roaming the stars."

I had a hunch that he was correct. The way he carried himself and spoke, the way his cohorts sat still like statues focusing their guns on me despite full attention on him, told me this was a man who got what he wanted whenever he wanted it. I couldn't think of anything else to say except to answer his original question.

"I don't have a problem with confrontation," I said.

"Don't you?" he quickly asked. "I would think a man in your situation would start by asking the important questions, such as Who am I? Why am I here? What do I want with you? Instead you attempt to use humor and sarcasm to diffuse your tense situation, very poorly I must add."

Erebos was beginning to crack the remaining shell I kept over my fear. He was so calm and collected; so sure of himself. I wanted to know who he was and what he wanted with me, but I didn't want to outwardly admit that I was letting him walk all over me. As nervous as I was, I needed to stand my ground, or in my case sit.

"Is that all? Should I piss my pants in your presence as well? Maybe you would like me to squeal like a terrified animal?"

My entire core rumbled with nerves as I waited for his reaction. Maybe he would decide I wasn't worth the trouble and would just put a plasma round in my brain here and now. To my surprise, and relief, he smiled. The smile was warm too, not devilish or evil. He held up his hands in submission.

"That will not be necessary Mr. Quinn. I am pleased you don't break under a little pressure. You have courage, but feel fear. Smart." he said.

Now he was paying me a compliment for being afraid?

"Did you know fear is actually an endearing quality?" He asked. "If you stop and think about it, fear acts as a warning system assisting us in being rational during dangerous situations. Without it, humankind would rush to their demise without a second thought."

He paused for a moment, studying my reaction to his words. So far I had succeeded in keeping a straight, slightly bored expression.

"Additionally, you can use fear to control."

"You don't say," I said. His grin grew wider.

"You see, with a simple nod to my associates, they would break both of your arms. If I wanted, I could end your life and the lives of every other person in this establishment with one simple order simply because I make sure my employees fear me."

I would have thought smelly one and two would have argued over being afraid of their boss, but they stared at him with intense loyalty. I even swore I saw one of them shudder at the mention of the word employees. Suddenly I thought of Derrick and his conversation with me only moments ago. I had been convinced up to this point that he was stalling for Erebos and I was sure that still held true, but could he have been warning me at the same time? All the talk about control, power, expansion, and here I sat in front of a man who I assumed wanted all of the above.

"Is that your intention? To control me through fear?" I asked him, barely containing a stutter.

"That is up to you," he said. "You are a mercenary are you not? Maybe it's simply a matter of hiring your services. What would you say to that?"

"I suppose that would depend on the job and payment," I replied. "I can't guarantee I will accept, but you're welcome to explain it to me."

"Can you afford to do that?" he asked me, leaning back into his chair and lifting his eyebrows. "I'm sure you've surmised by now that I've done my research on you Mr. Quinn. In the last three years you've failed a handful of jobs you were hired for. Your reputation is less than favorable to any employer in the galaxy. At this point you would be lucky if you could get hired to escort a waste disposal barge." He paused to let me think on it. Unfortunately all I could think at the time was 'he's right'.

"So why would you trust me with your job?" I asked him. He nodded at me as if that was the right question to ask.

"Because you have what I want. Information. You have discovered possible coordinates for empyreus and I want it. More specifically, I want you to get it for me. If you are willing to do this, I will pay you a substantial fee. In addition, I will also wipe your slate clean off the Starcade."

The offer was incredible, I couldn't deny that. A brand new start? A large sum of money that I could use to live comfortably for years? It's everything I wanted, everything I hoped for when I landed on the station. Sure, I wasn't terribly interested in finding the empyreus myself, but wouldn't it be worth it? All I had to do was deliver one of the galaxy's most powerful sources of energy to the most mysterious man I ever met, a tycoon of sorts who was bent on controlling whatever he wanted. If he held the power of empyreus, who's to say he couldn't control everything.

I decided to play along, regardless of what I thought.

"That's very tempting. What if I refuse to sell the information and my service to you?"

Erebos didn't answer right away. He didn't blink, nor did he flinch. He let out a soft sigh and his mouth pressed into a hard line.

"Mr. Quinn, I'm not an unreasonable man, but when I want something I get it. I am kind enough to let you personally help me and reap the benefits. If you choose to refuse my genuine offer, then I will let my associates here have their way with you and I will strip your vessel piece by piece until I have recovered the information I require. The choice is certainly yours."

That was it. The conversation was over, at least that's the impression I got. Supposedly I had a choice, but if I 'let his goons have their way with me,' would I even survive it? Then I thought of Al onboard the Belle, being taken apart piece by piece, bit by bit. At the same time, what if they found out what Al was and chose to utilize his advanced skills. What the hell was I supposed to do? Did I have any choice but to agree to his terms to stay alive and keep Al safe?

Maybe the answer didn't have to be so simple. It seemed like Erebos would allow me to retrieve the empyreus for him. If I took the job, depending on the location, I could have enough time to figure out how to stay alive and keep it out of his hands. At this point I really didn't see any other way out of this, so I stuck my chest out in an attempt to hide my deep breath. Then I answered him.

"I'll do it."

"Splendid!" Erebos exclaimed, his charming personality returning. He gave both of his goons a look and they stood up and moved away from me. I relaxed a bit and sighed.

"Now that you are officially under my employment, you may use your own discretion as to how you will proceed just as long as it brings back results," Erebos said as he stood up and buttoned his jacket. He turned to leave, but stopped short of the door.

"Of course, your initial hesitation is somewhat troubling. I hope you don't mind that I send along an insurance policy to make sure the job gets done."

"What-" before I could finish my question he opened the door and a woman stepped into the room. She had a slender figure, her eyes an amazing shade of blue. They were so radiant they could have been glowing. She wore a dark red battle suit that hugged her form closely. At her shoulders, chest, and thighs, metallic armor was attached to the suit, and last, but certainly not least she carried a long blade sheathed at her hip, curved like an ancient samurai sword.

"Captain Daniel Quinn, meet Cessa. She will be accompanying you on your voyage."

As I stood up to greet her I tried to wipe my perspiring hand on my pants. My stomach tied itself in knots as she walked up to me her eyes looking into mine, her face smooth, and her lips lush. As I reached my hand out, she swiftly pulled out her sword and swung it at my arm stopping mere centimeters from cleaving it. The butterflies in my stomach exploded.

"Pleased to meet you Daniel," she said, her voice the sound of music . . . dark, brooding music. "Disobey Mr. Erebos or look at me the wrong way, and I will cut you."

FIVE

The blade. It sent a shockwave of recurring emotions through me. Fear, pain, and despair all attacked me at once. Before any memories could surface I fought them back. At first, I didn't think I was in control of it, but the awkward position Erebos put me in helped me keep my focus on the present. Before the scene could fade to black, I stared hard at Cessa concentrating on every facet of her.

"So . . . Cessa right? Like . . . as in Cessation?" I asked her as my voice fluctuated. Raymond Erebos and his goons had already taken their leave. My testosterone level dropped to zero. I watched as her lips formed a soft smile while her left hand was wrapped around the hilt of the blade

"Simple and to the point, wouldn't you say?" My body shivered with the seductive tone she spoke in. She was a predator. If she found a weakness she would exploit it. If she felt threatened she would attack. I was definitely out of my league here, but I could only assume she was going to be on my ass from here until the job was done.

"Well, we're wasting time I suppose. Let's go," I said, suggesting she go first. I would like to say I did so because she was a woman, but I didn't really want her behind me with that sword. In the end I didn't really get a choice, as she stepped behind me and gave me a gentle shove toward the door. As we left the tavern I checked the main room for Derrick, but he was nowhere to be seen. If I survived this, I promised myself to return here and punch him in the face.

The two of us stepped back onto the streets of Galaxia City. The bright artificial sunlight temporarily blinded me, and I stood still with my hand over my eyes as I waited for the effect to diminish. Cessa made sure she was attached at my hip. If I stopped, she stopped, where I moved, she moved. I was tempted to start skipping around the marketplace just to see what she would do.

"I need to get some provisions for my ship," I said to her. *Like maybe an escape pod, some tranquilizers and extra strength antidepressants,* I thought to myself.

"Not necessary. Mr. Erebos is providing you with everything you will need, including food and fuel."

Wow, what a nice guy. You'd think he had a stake in this adventure we were about to embark on. With a simple nod I turned in the direction of the Tram and walked my way back to Al and the Belle. I was nervous that I couldn't warn him before we got back to the ship, and I really didn't want Cessa knowing he existed. Of course, Al was a state of the art intelligent system so I could only hope that he would stay silent while she was onboard.

We were walking through the alley that led into the marketplace when that bad feeling returned, the feeling of being followed. Someone was watching us. This time I was absolutely sure of it. I stopped in the middle of the alley, turned to look around, but at the time we were alone. Cessa tried to push me forward again, but I turned to her and gave her a stern look.

"Stop!" I whispered loudly to her. Her eyes widened in fury and her hands clenched together. I quickly followed with, "I think we're being followed."

Cessa tensed and turned her head toward the way we came. Her hand wrapped around the leather hilt of her sword and she stood in front of me. We both watched as pedestrians walked by, but only a few of them turned their heads to look at us. None of their expressions led me to believe they were intentionally following us. Just as I was starting to feel better, two pedestrians turned into the alleyway. They differed in height, one short and one tall. Both wore long coats over their outfits.

As much as I wanted to raise my fist in the air and shout 'Ha! I knew someone was following me', I restrained myself and instead activated my bionic eye. The pain that followed was sharp but manageable. I locked my sight onto them, and my eye scanned their figure inch by inch. It told me that the tall one was 6'7'', that the short one was 5'4", a man and woman respectively. Their coats were made of leather, but after looking over their boots and pants, my eye told me the one thing I didn't want to see. They wore the standard uniform of an ESA agent.

"What do you want?" Cessa asked the two of them. I found myself slowly backing away. The two agents made no aggressive movements toward me, but advanced on us until they stood only a couple steps away. The taller one took something out of his jacket and flashed it in front of Cessa. It was his ESA ID. My eye zoomed in to confirm what I already knew. He was from the Echelon.

"Ma'am, we're ESA agents from the starship Echelon. The man you're accompanying is a dangerous fugitive. We are charged with taking him back to our ship."

Cessa turned her head slightly in my direction, giving me a view of her side. She smiled slightly.

"Him? Dangerous? You're an amusing fellow now aren't you?" She laughed at the two agents. I wanted to grab her by the shoulders and ask if she was insane. They were two highly trained operatives who no doubt were carrying weaponry, most likely plasma guns.

"Ma'am," the man continued. "We are taking him. You can move out of our way, or you can stay where you are and we will arrest you for protecting a criminal. The choice is yours."

I'm not sure if the agents noticed her the way I did in that moment. Without moving her entire body her feet shifted slowly, all her weight towards the front. Though her hand was on her sword hilt this whole time, I noticed her fingers clenching tightly against it. She was contracting herself like a locked spring, and I didn't have to guess what was going to happen next.

"Oh I do love it when I get to make my own decisions!" With that she sprung, moving quickly towards the two of them. Both agents in well trained fashion threw off their coats and reached for their guns. Neither of them took their eyes off Cessa as she approached. I tried to retreat back, but tripped over a crack in the street and landed on my ass. I was completely unprepared for what happened next. The two agents had their guns pointed at her, and I could see them pulling the trigger, but before they fired, Cessa spun sideways. Her sword came unsheathed and sliced through the man's weapon just as she lifted up her right leg in a roundhouse kick that sent the other gun flying out of the woman's hand. I don't think the man even realized half of his gun was missing. For a split second after her blade cut, he stood there still pulling the trigger. By the time he noticed his gun wasn't working, Cessa brought the hilt of her sword up and thrust it right into his forehead. He fell instantly, knocked out. The woman backed away to retreat, but Cessa dropped to the ground and swept her leg under the agent. She fell and her back smacked against the ground causing her to cough out a breath. I watched in astonishment as Cessa walked up to her prone body and placed her foot on top of the woman's chest.

There was no warning, no last words. The two of them looked at each other, the woman fearful and Cessa victorious as she raised her sword straight up, intending on running it through the woman's midsection. All at once my vision blurred and instead of me being in the alley with a sore ass, I was back in the small, familiar room staring at a lifeless body, fatal wounds on her chest with blood everywhere. I trembled.

No, this isn't real. You're not here right now. Snap out of it damn it, I thought to myself, and my vision returned me to the alley just before Cessa's sword finished the job.

"Cessa! Stop!" I screamed as loud as I could. The blade stopped just short of piercing flesh and Cessa turned her venomous gaze toward me. I stood up and ran to her, just in case she made a second attempt at taking the woman's life. People walking by in the streets turned their heads, wondering what all the commotion was. I assumed what they were thinking with two ESA agents on the ground and a messy looking man and swordswoman standing over them.

"What in hell's wrath are you doing? Cessa asked furiously. "These agents are pursuing us, and that cannot be allowed. They must die!" She raised her sword up again.

"No! We are not killing them. Come on, we have to go! Someone is bound to contact security if they haven't done so already. Let's go!" I ran away and hoped she would follow me. My feet carried me to the other end of the alley. Just before I turned into the street I looked back and saw both agents were still alive, on the ground, but my eye detected movement from their chests. They were still breathing. I deactivated my eye and continued to run. Cessa followed behind me, her expression hateful, but I would deal with that later. We avoided the crowded tram station since guards regularly patrolled that area and headed for the port on foot.

We passed city streets, businesses, and retail shops until we saw nothing but green grass and a forest in the distance. In order to reach the docks we would have to run through Grand View Park. It's so named because of its sheer size, almost taking up as much space as the city itself. If you walked along the path built into the forest you would find a lake filled with clean water and aquatic life. Likewise the forest held many of Earth's forest animals. I was relieved knowing our route wouldn't pass by the public walking grounds or the children's play area. As we stepped onto the grass, there were less than a handful of people in sight.

Behind us was a different story, a story told by a barrage of footsteps and loud voices. I turned to look and saw six station security guards with an additional three ESA agents, one of them the woman from the alley despite the fact that I saved her life. Cessa took notice of her instantly.

"You idiot. If you would have allowed me to kill that girl we wouldn't have so many people chasing us, if any!"

I didn't respond, but instead tried to push my legs a little harder. In that moment I couldn't help but feel that my entire life revolved around running away from something. Did that make me weak? Was I a coward? These were the things constantly crossing my mind, but in truth I felt that sometimes you need to run away to survive and that's what this was about right now, survival.

"Stop or we will open fire!" I heard someone scream. I didn't have to look back again to know they had their guns trained on us. I tried to remind myself that it's hard to shoot at a moving target, even harder if both you and your target are moving, but throw in crowded forest with hundreds of trees to zigzag through, and your chance of hitting your target is slim. At least I hoped that was the case.

Only a minute passed before I heard the first shot. More followed, but I wasn't hit. I didn't chance looking for Cessa because I didn't want to take my concentration off the path in front of me. Come to think of it, I wondered why I would even look to see if she was still with me. Wouldn't I prefer to get her off my back and get off the station alone?

Splinters smacked into my back as I rounded a tree. Had it not been there the blast might have gone right through my skull. I shuddered at the thought and kept moving. The shots never stopped. A few more hit the trees I used as cover and some hit the ground behind me. It was only a matter of time before one went straight into my back.

Without warning thick drops of rain fell from the sky, followed by hail the size of a fingernail. Both clouded my vision and if I wasn't running for my life I would have stopped to wonder what the hell was happening. Instead, I slowed my speed so I didn't run face first into a tree. A noise to my left indicated someone was catching up to me. Cessa appeared and ran directly alongside me.

"Keep going," she whispered loudly. "This weather is meant to help us."

Erebos had influence over the weather control system? The man wasn't kidding when he said he always got what he wanted. I couldn't be ungrateful to him now as much as I wanted to be. Thanks to him we cleared the forest and were now on the outskirts of the park. I couldn't see the docking office at all, but the elevator shaft lights acted as a beacon. My breaths were short and I couldn't tell if it was sweat or rainwater streaming down my face. My clothes felt heavier the longer we were out in the rain. Finally the two of us ran under the archway blowing past a crowd of people who were no doubt wondering why the weather system had malfunctioned.

There was a large commotion from the way we came. Men were shouting and feet were scurrying.

"Where are they?!"

"I can't see a damn thing!"

"Restrict elevator control!"

The elevator doors opened and a large man with a long beard stepped off, a bag of supplies hung over his shoulder. Cessa grabbed him by the shirt and yanked him past us and at the same time turning, unsheathing her sword, and slicing the rope that held his numerous items. As we stepped onto the elevator I saw countless trinkets, canisters, and more litter the ground.

"Who is that? Stop or we will open fire!" I heard the guards shout towards the noise. I never got a chance to see if they opened fire or not. I hoped the man was alright.

"Men are such pigs," Cessa muttered. We were finally on our way up to my ship. I closed my eyes and counted the seconds as we climbed, hoping that the commotion was hindering the guards' attempt to remotely halt our ascent. I could hear Cessa breathing heavily and stole a glance. Her hair was clinging to her head, drenched. The water caused her face to glisten. Her mouth was parted and her chest was rising and lowering. She was beautiful.

Hey down there, I thought to myself. *She is an assassin, outwardly said she would kill you, and she almost sliced up two people only minutes ago!*

My brain knocked some sense into me and I turned my concentration back towards escaping. The doors opened to the familiar docks I had left earlier and a wave of relief washed over me as I saw my ship. I took a deep breath and ran as fast as I could to her knowing it was only moments before the station would go into full lockdown, if it wasn't already. People loading and unloading their ships stared at us as we ran by, but didn't make any motion to stop us. When we reached the ship and stepped on the bay door, I laughed. Cessa and I both hunched over, putting our hands on our knees. I watched the drops of sweat and water hit the ground.

A quick survey of the room told me we had taken on some cargo. I wanted to ask Cessa about it, but out of the corner of my eye I saw the elevator open and the Galaxy guards racing towards us. I pointed towards the left side of the wall, where the large lever stood surrounded by a taped yellow border.

"Hit that! It will close the bay doors. I have to get to the bridge and get us out of here."

I didn't wait for her answer but hoped she heard me. I ran towards the ladder and climbed up into the main corridor. The ship vibrated and gears squealed as the bay door closed. I crashed right through the bridge door and leaned back into it to shut it. There was no time and Cessa would be heading this way.

"You sure do like to make an entrance sir," Al said. Hearing his voice lowered my stress level from bat-shit crazy to only shit crazy.

"Al, there's no time. Initiate passenger protocol and let's get the Belle out of here before they lock us in."

"Acknowledged."

Passenger protocol was designed to protect Al from being discovered. Anyone who understood what he was capable of would try and take him for themselves. I could only imagine the kind of damage someone like King or Erebos could do with Al. So for the duration of the protocol, he would keep quiet when any passenger was within a certain distance of the bridge and the only way I could communicate with him was by messaging him through the computer terminal.

The engines roared and the screen in front of me read: BAY DOORS SEALED. ENGINES ONLINE.

I set my coordinates for the Space Port doors and sent my authorized code to the signal tower, indicating I was departing. As the ship soared through the docks the doors opened, indicator lights flashing around them. The Belle flew back into the vast reach of outer space and we were free from the station.

"How the hell did we pull that off?" I said to myself.

"Please tell me you're not that stupid," Cessa said behind me, nearly sending me out of my chair. I didn't even hear her come in, but had no time to turn and face her as the proximity sensor alarmed me to an incoming ship.

"We escaped because they let us. It's time to see if your piloting skills are at all superior to everything else I know about you."

"How many ships are there?" Cessa's voice dripped with frustration and contempt. She leaned over my shoulder and attempted to get a good look at my sensor readings. The screen relayed the information that my sensor received every five to ten seconds. The red screen was solid, except for a small blip drawing closer to the center of the screen towards our position.

"Just one, could be Galaxy One patrol or ESA, I don't care to spend time scanning the damn thing," I told her, though I didn't mention how odd sending out one ship was. Maybe they only had time to prep one ship to follow us or maybe they were attempting to track my route. Either way I had to lose the bastard.

I input a command into the computer to fly the ship around the station, keeping a safe distance from it and the ship following us. The maneuver bought me little time to think up a plan, but my options were limited. I could plot a course using slingspace but if I engaged the engines now my pursuer would be able to analyze the trail that we would leave and lead them right to us. Additionally I couldn't risk depleting my fuel tanks by jumping multiple times like I did to escape the Echelon.

"You are an idiot," Cessa said, her lips an inch from my ear. "You should have let me kill those agents."

"Right, because no one would have noticed the blood, or the sword, or the potential screaming of the victim." I said sarcastically

"I knew what I was doing. They could have been disposed of. Instead you had us weaving in and out of trees like cowards. The memory makes me sick."

A lot of memories make me sick, I thought.

That's when an idea sprang to mind and I looked back toward my sensor screen. With a small transfer of power from my environmental systems, I was able to send my sensors out into a wide arc and I found a way to evade my pursuer. Cessa still paced behind me and told me how much of a coward I was. I spun around in my chair and gave her a stern look of my own.

"Do me and yourself a favor and strap yourself into that seat over there. This ship gets the job done but it's not exactly operating at recommended efficiency. If you want to get out of this alive, then sit down and shut up."

To my surprise Cessa said nothing, but turned to sit in the seat I indicated.

The ship was starting to overtake us, and though I assumed their orders were to take us alive, I still wanted to stay out of their firing range. I spun back around to the helm and plotted a course away from the station, straight towards a nearby asteroid field. Behind me I heard Cessa buckling her harness.

-AL, DEACTIVATE DISPERSION FIELD, I typed into my console.

-I FEEL IT IS NECESSARY TO REMIND YOU THE DISPERSION FIELD IS WHAT SHIELDS US FROM SMALL SPACE OBJECTS SIR. DEACTIVATING IT WOULD ALLOW ANY SUCH OBJECT TO POTENTIALLY PENETRATE OUR HULL.

-UNDERSTOOD. DEACTIVATE IT ANYWAY.

-I DETECT YOU ARE ON COURSE WITH THE OMEGA ASTEROID FIELD. THIS SOUNDS LIKE A TERRIBLE IDEA, NO OFFENSE SIR.

-YOU'LL HAVE TO TRUST ME ON THIS. DEACTIVATE NOW ON MY AUTHORIZATION!

- . . . ACKNOWLEDGED, Al responded.

At the top corner of my helm an indicator light blinked and signified the dispersion array had been shut off. Normally while active, the array would send out a field of energy that would deflect any nearby space junk or debris. Flying into the asteroid field would have been ten times safer if I left it on. The problem with this was anyone following me would essentially get a nicely paved opening for them to fly through. Now I was going to have to fly around each and every one of them, just like I did with the trees in the forest. The agent following me would have to do the same with his ship. I could only pray that I was the better pilot.

With one hand held firmly on my navigational sphere, the other was tightly clamped to the thruster control. I watched the readings from the enemy ship, mostly to judge his distance in an attempt to match his speed and keep a consistent length away from him. Our speed increased as he tried to accelerate to catch up to us only to fail when we did the same. Ahead of us, the asteroid field was within viewing distance. From here it looked like tiny specs of rocks.

"You're not seriously considering taking us in there are you?" Cessa asked.

"Yup."

"So now you're just as insane as you are stupid. Please tell me you have a deflection device?!"

"Of course I do, but it's turned off."

She didn't say another word, though I thought I heard a smacking sound one would hear when a palm impacts on a forehead. I allowed myself a smile before I took a deep breath and stretched out my fingers. We were approaching the belt.

"SPACE CRAFT, THIS IS THE ESA SHUTTLE CESARO. WITHDRAW YOUR COURSE TOWARDS THE ASTEROID BELT. THIS IS YOUR ONLY WARNING. IF YOU DO NOT COMPLY WE WILL OPEN FIRE!"

The speakers buzzed with electricity as the high pitch man gave me his demands. I only had one demand to give him back.

"Shove it!" I reported back to him and with that I pushed my thrusters forward to maximum, and the two of us were jolted back in our seats as the Belle took off into our escape or possible destruction.

The first layer of the belt was smaller than my ship, but if any asteroids made impact at this velocity they could still cause some damage. I jerked the helm left, right, turned us upside down, and basically used any maneuvers I could think of to avoid the rocks on my sensor screen. My stomach hated me right now. Cessa sat behind me cursing and gritting her teeth as the ship swung from one side to the next. The gravitational settings on the ship never worked perfectly. If I kept the ship straight on course you wouldn't feel a thing, but moving in circles and pitching right and left was really playing tricks on our equilibriums. If neither of us vomited after this was all said and done I'd be surprised.

So far we were a little over a quarter ways through the field and I had only hit one of the smaller rocks while moving to avoid a bigger one. My damage control screen didn't show me anything of consequence so I counted my blessings and continued on. The damn ship behind me still kept up and now the screen flashed a warning that his weapons were arming. As if avoiding countless asteroids wasn't enough to stress me out, let's add some missiles!

I couldn't concentrate on both his ship and mine, so I kept a watchful eye on the sensor screen every now and then while the majority of my attention was on my path through the belt. A minute or two passed before the first missile launched straight at my ass. I altered my maneuvering strategy so that with every rock I passed I put it directly at my back, hoping the missile would hit one of them instead of me. Minutes passed and the signal faded. Two more missiles came at me and with some clever driving and a very sick stomach I managed to pass a larger asteroid that took both rockets and caused an explosion behind me.

Suddenly I got an idea. I messaged Al and told him to prime the engine reactors for slingspace. I checked my screen for another large asteroid and set a collision course with it. An alarm sounded throughout the bridge.

"What the hell is that sound?" Cessa asked. I almost forgot she was here, she was so quiet. Now her tone of voice was restricted, almost fearful.

"Don't worry about it, just hold on."

The Kestrel model of star cruisers was designed with weapons both at bow and stern. I often wondered if someone on drugs designed the weapon systems. The ones at the bow, two plasma lasers, were located at the eyes of the ship. The weapon at stern, well I'm going to let you guess where that was placed. Unfortunately I didn't have any missiles, but my plasmas in front were charged. I locked onto the asteroid in front of me and hit the execute button.

I watched from my shield window as two beams of intense plasma shot out to the asteroid, causing an explosion and sending a vast number of debris right at us. If there was a divine power watching over us at that moment I'll never know, but I managed to fly the ship through the debris while only taking minor damage to the Belle. The pursuing ship was another story.

My sensors showed the ship's velocity slowing and eventually stopping. There had been multiple impacts, but I didn't know where or how bad.

When we cleared the belt I spun the ship on its horizontal axis so I was facing the belt and powered down the thrusters. I didn't see the ship, nor was it in my sensor range any longer. If it had been destroyed I would have been able to scan the overload of the shuttles engines, but there was no signature of it. He most likely had been damaged too much to continue pursuit.

I looked back to check on Cessa. Her eyes were closed, her hands tightly wrapped around the hilt of her sword. Was it for comfort? With her sword being reminiscent of a samurai, would she have fallen on it if the escape hadn't worked?

During the downtime I asked Al if he had succeeded in determining a potential course to find the empyreus.

-YES CAPTAIN. A COURSE IS AVAILABLE. WOULD YOU LIKE ME TO APPLY IT TO NAVIGATION?

-YES. GOOD WORK AL, I typed back.

I activated slingspace once the course was plotted and let out a deep sigh of relief, much like one would if they had been holding their breath for minutes. My hands were shaking and my vision began to blur. The cheeseburger I had eaten earlier was battling my stomach to regurgitate itself. In all the excitement and built up adrenaline, I didn't realize until now just how worn out my body was. I typed out a quick message to Al to take control of the ship. Autopilot wasn't unheard of in starships and cruisers, so Cessa wouldn't question it.

When I stood up and turned, Cessa was at the door staring intently at me. The way she moved, so quiet, was creepy. She studied me for a moment and then muttered a single word.

"Impressive." She left before she could see my jaw drop in shock. Had she seriously just complimented me?

After confirming via the sensors that Cessa had found the crew quarters and retired there I trudged my way to my own room, locked the door, and dropped onto the bed. Sleep took me quickly. Instead of dreaming my mind played twenty questions with me, asking things like "where are we going? How long will it take to get there? Did we really get away from the ESA?" And most importantly, wherever we *were* going, what would we find?

Empyreus was the next thing that passed through my mind. What was it exactly? And how would I transport it back to Erebos? Should I? The whole deal made me feel sick. If I succeeded in my mission would he be true to his word, pay me the money he promised, and help my reputation, or was it all a farce? Too many unknowns were in my future, and it made me uneasy. I didn't want this deal, but what choice did I have? I'm already being pursued by the ESA. Did I really want my name added to another hit list?

After that my brain was too tired to continue. I saw and felt nothing for the duration of my respite. For once there were no nightmares. For the first time in days I wasn't running from someone anymore. Of course there was a catch. I had a professional assassin onboard who would kill me the minute she detected any deceit.

SEVEN

My head screamed at me when I woke up. I was convinced there was a tiny little man inside it pounding a hammer into my skull. I rubbed my temples with my middle and forefingers hoping to massage the pain away, but it only helped to slightly alleviate it.

Without a change of clothes I stumbled to the bridge which was in full operation, the sensors scanning out into space and the star charts updating our location every few minutes. When I shut the door Al's voice nearly knocked me on my ass, the pain in my head intensifying with the sound of his voice.

"Captain." The sound drummed its way from one ear to the other. "Our passenger is out of range. May I speak to you openly?"

"Whoa, Al...lower your voice please and turn the lights down 50%."

The illumination receded in the room and most of the light now came from the panels and screens on the consoles. I sat in my chair and closed my eyes taking a few deep breaths.

With the headache I almost forgot Cessa was onboard.

"Yes, Al. Proceed with vocal communication. There's no way I'm looking at the damn screen right now. Just keep an eye on her."

"Acknowledged sir. I wanted to express my reaction to your escape through the asteroid belt. The maneuvers were adequate. By the time any reinforcements arrive at our last known position the signature left by our engines will have dissipated."

Adequate? He continued his report.

"Our course is set for an uncharted section of the galaxy, previously marked as Orion 035. We will arrive in its solar system in 1 week, 3 days, 12 hours, 9 minutes, and 57 seconds."

"Over a week?" I thought about spending ten days confined with Cessa. "Al, could you just open the emergency airlock and let it suck me out?"

" . . . Sir, was that sarcasm?"

I found myself hesitant to answer, but ultimately said, "Unfortunately, yes."

Military time was standard onboard a starship except that now it was called SEMT, or Standard Earth Military Time. The clock still turned in 24 hour increments, but to be honest if felt strange when the clock would strike noon and all you could see out the window was the endless dark of space.

Three days passed.

Cessa and I managed to avoid each other despite being the only two people onboard. While I kept mostly to the bridge and my quarters (which I firmly locked each time I went in), she stayed in the crew quarters and occasionally visited the cargo bay. With plenty of time left on our voyage, I was able to take a closer look at the boxes and supplies that had been loaded onto my ship. There was no threat as far as I could tell, but all the same I asked Al to do an internal scan.

"Five of the boxes carry mechanical equipment, nothing that matches any schematics in my database. The other seven read as empty sir. If I may make an assumption, I would say these are for the excavation and transfer of the empyreus."

I didn't know what to think of the boxes, or whether I should ask Cessa about them. Normally I didn't take any cargo on my ship that I didn't inspect myself, but this time I didn't get to decide if they would come with us or not. We were in somewhat of a hurry getting off the Galaxy space station.

A couple of hours later my headache mostly subsided despite staring at monitors all day checking the sensor sweeps. I knew we were safe, but that nagging paranoia in the back of my mind convinced me to keep an eye out for any unusual readings. I returned to my quarters and did a short workout, a combination of jumping jacks and push-ups to stay in shape. I won't say how many push-ups I actually accomplished . . . because I'd embarrass myself. Afterwards I walked into my small closet-sized bathroom and splashed cold water on my face, then went to the mess hall.

In addition to the cargo that had been brought on my ship, my fridge had also been stocked with organic foods and vegetables. The first time I laid eyes on all of it I almost fainted. Eggs, butter, wheat, beef, chicken, and more filled the cold space. The options would make any man drool. I helped myself to a cup of milk and grabbed a couple of eggs to scramble over my stove, but I was interrupted when a hand grabbed the back of my head and slammed it into the refrigerator door. The cheap shot wasn't meant to be lethal because I could have been thrown into it a lot harder, but it still hurt like hell. I was on my ass and I could see stars *inside* the ship. I turned around to see Cessa standing over me, her arms raised in a fighting stance.

"Get up," she said. Her teeth were visible and her brows contracted inward. She wasn't wearing her sword, but her black clothing looked flexible as it hugged her body. I tried to say something to her, but before I could speak a syllable she threw her right foot into my ribs knocking the wind out of me and sending a sharp pain up my side.

"Fight back, damn you," she snarled. Once more she threw her leg into me, but I managed to block it with my forearm. In response I tried to catch her off guard by tripping her with an outstretched leg, but she saw it coming and jumped back. I wasn't surprised. My move hadn't been designed to hurt her, but give myself some breathing room. With the left side of my ribs aching I stood up and took a step back.

"Cessa, what the hell are you doing?" I coughed out.

She didn't waste time and leapt for me throwing her right fist into my jaw. I didn't see it coming fast enough so I couldn't block it, but I did turn my neck in the same direction her punch would've sent it anyway, and that eased some of the blow. Out of the corner of my eye I saw her left arm following with an uppercut, which I managed to deflect by swinging my left hand down to intercept it.

I may have been a crappy mercenary up to this point, but I'll be damned if I didn't have at least some combat training. It had been years since I utilized what I learned, however I was sufficient enough to block a majority of her blows. The occasional punch or kick did get through, but she wasn't satisfied with that alone.

"Fight back! Fight me! Stop running from everything! From everyone!"

She screamed now, her motions weren't tactical anymore, but a flurry of uncoordinated attacks. Eventually I didn't even have to predict her next move. She was just slapping at my chest, her eyes glazing over, but no tears fell. I moved out of range but she didn't follow up with another attack. She just leaned on the counter with her head down. The only sounds were the humming of the ship's engines and Cessa's breathing. I sat down at the table and stretched out my left side. My ribs were sore, but I didn't think she fractured any of them.

To my disbelief, she followed the attack by working on the breakfast I had been preparing. She took the eggs, milk, butter, and scrambled enough for the both of us.

"You come in here, attack me without provocation, and then you expect me to just let it go? Give me a damn good reason that I shouldn't throw you off my ship," I said while holding my stomach. The pain lessened into a dull throb.

Cessa didn't respond, which either meant she was ignoring me or called my bluff. Galaxy One Alpha was the closest station. If I wanted to be rid of her I'd have to return, which wasn't an option. She kept her back to me, cooking the food. When she finished she brought two plates and forks to the table and sat across from me, immediately digging into her food. I studied mine and wondered if she poisoned it in some way.

"You deflect," she said to me without looking up. Her voice wasn't angry or frustrated, but soft and concerned. "You deflect everything. You fail to act, to stand up for yourself." Her eyes met mine. "Eat."

"Ummm . . . was that escapade supposed to help me with that?" I asked.

"You allowed yourself to be manipulated by Raymond Erebos. You refused to fight or let me kill the ESA agent that hunted you. Instead you ran like a coward. I threw punches and kicks to see if you're at least willing to fight for yourself and your ship, but instead you stood there only making attempts to block me. You deflect, hide, and cower. It's disgusting. Eat."

"Sometimes you need to run away in order to live on," I said to her, trying to defend my actions.

"That's not living. Eat!"

What did I get myself into? Cessa was crazy, a woman with obvious personality shifts. One moment she was yelling at me, another trying to fight me, and now she sat across from me like some kind of concerned parent.

I humored her. The eggs were more overdone than I would've cooked them, but they were hot and delicious nonetheless. As I finished my plate, her words played on a loop in my mind. I'm a coward. I deflect, not living. Was I really that fearful? I always thought I was just doing my best to stay alive, but a part of what she said really got to me. This really wasn't a good way to live, and I think somewhere deep down I knew it.

"Have you ever killed anyone?" She asked me. The question came out of nowhere, startling me a bit. I opened my mouth, but closed it. She nodded at me, knowing the answer before I said it. "Those two ESA agents wanted you for something. I don't care what, but you refused to let them be executed when in fact you should have been the one executing them."

She spoke so matter-of-factly it scared me. I could only imagine the upbringing she had that she could be so heartless and manipulating. She looked at battle as if it was a sport and killing her adversary was the ultimate goal. Just thinking about it sent a cold feeling throughout my body and unpleasant images to my mind. I tried to shake it off.

"I don't want death surrounding me," I told her. "If I had killed those guards I would be a murderer. If I had fought back just now I might have hurt you."

That last sentence caused her to laugh, her head tilted back.

"So what now, you're protecting yourself from me because I'm a woman? You are disgusting and you're lucky my job is to keep you alive!"

My face felt increasingly hot, and I gritted my teeth together in frustration. Of the two people on this ship I really didn't think I was the crazy one, but she was damn sure going to make it seem that way.

"Listen to you," I spoke out, suddenly speaking everything I was thinking. "Do you even realize how insane you are? What the hell did Erebos do to you to screw you up so much?"

As soon as the words left my mouth I regretted it. Cessa stared back at me expressionless, but I could see her eyes glisten. She stood up and turned from me before I could see one of the tears fall.

"Cessa, wait," I said to her. She stopped at the open doorway and turned her head slightly.

"Don't ruin this moment. You actually showed some strength. Even though it wasn't physical, it will do for now." She walked out and left me with another confused look.

I had moments when I wished my ship had a brig so I could lock her up. Her personality was so damned peculiar. At the same time something about her seemed so . . . I don't know . . . vulnerable almost, as if this tough-girl persona acted as a shell of armor. I saw the look on her face, the words that she used when we came out of the asteroid belt unscathed. I impressed her, but the look on her face was fear. She thought we were going to die and that terrified her.

I knew people like her years ago. I mean not exactly like her, but similar principals. They were so dedicated to the job and to their superiors that it made it seem like a master and pet relationship where they blindly followed any order given to them. In a way they almost lived on autopilot and let other people control them.

Cessa told me that running and avoiding was cowardice. Maybe in some ways she was right, but those actions were caused by pure emotion, the will to survive, and the need to stay alive. I had a feeling that she didn't feel the same way. She had a job to do and that's all that mattered to her. Now that I thought about it like that, her actions on this trip almost seemed reasonable. She's been living without emotion or self-control for so long that in order to feel any emotion she had to take extreme actions, whether with arguing, fighting, or even killing. I wondered if this was the key to break through her emotional armor.

The next few days passed without incident and Cessa continued to avoid me. She spent most of her time in the crew quarters training with her sword. I left her alone. We were here to do a job, not be friends. She moved throughout the ship parallel to what I did. If I was in my room, she was in the mess hall or on the bridge looking at the monitors. I wasn't worried when she was there alone. Al had all my previous databases and logs locked out.

I was in the mess hall having breakfast on the fourth morning when a large buzzing sound echoed throughout the entire room.

BBBBBZZZZZZZZZZTTTTTTTTTTTT!

I took one last bite of my eggs and made my way to the bridge. I knew this was Al's way of getting my attention. There wasn't a warning alarm on the ship that sounded like that.

"Al, what's up?" I asked after I firmly locked the bridge.

"Sir, if I may say so, your relationship with that woman is . . . intriguing."

"To you and me both my friend, but is that the real reason you wanted me?"

"Negative Captain, I wanted to inform you that just moments ago this ship was scanned."

In seconds I was sitting in my chair checking over the sensor readings for the last hour. Go figure something would happen while I was away from my station. Everything looked normal. There was a gaseous anomaly, a small moon, an asteroid, but as I ran my finger down the time chart, at time index 07:57 there was feedback along the sensor signal. The asteroid we passed over must have been some kind of satellite or probe. This entire time our sensors had been moving in a circular motion and after the second pass the probe activated its own beam to send back towards us. From what I could tell, it wasn't harmful in any way, but that meant someone knew we were out here.

"What do you make of it?" I asked my computer.

"The sphere shaped probe is metallic in composition. There are traces of iron, but the other elements are not in my database."

"And the signal? Where's that transmitting to?"

"Judging the trajectory of the beam that's scanning us to the beam that is relaying back its data I am certain that it is coming from the fifth planet in the solar system ahead of us. Coincidentally, that is the same planet we are on route to."

I stared at the monitor into the open space in front of us. Currently there was nothing to see but stars, but somewhere out there some type of advanced civilization kept watch out here, and now they knew visitor's would soon be arriving. I often wondered what Cessa and I would find when we landed on the planet containing the empyreus. Now I had my answer.

Life.

To be honest I wasn't sure what to think. I suppose it would have been stupid to assume the planet that held empyreus would be uninhabited. I'd been spending most of my time on the ship trying to figure out our passenger. At the same time, inhabited or not, we were going there, but I had thought and hoped we would be arriving without any prior knowledge of our arrival. What kind of welcoming party would these aliens throw us? Would there be starships coming to intercept us? I asked Al to do a specific sweep ahead of us, looking for signs of any ships.

"I detect no other vessels in range, however I cannot scan far enough to reach the planet itself. It is possible there could be ships in orbit around it. Captain, shall I initiate first contact protocol?"

I couldn't remember the last time I was in a first contact situation, though with Al being a computer he didn't have the ability to forget or really understand the passage of time. The first contact protocol dictates that once an alien species is discovered, we halt our course and send out a broad general transmission. Vocally we use every language known to man including any alien languages we've learned. We also send out a written message with language, mathematical equations, sometimes even music, basically anything that will show the aliens we mean no harm and are interested in making contact with them.

The Kestrel Belle wasn't exactly an appropriate ship to make contact with. She was inadequate in every way, except for Al who wasn't an original part of this ship. Meeting new races meant having the equipment for diplomacy if a truce was reached, or defense if they turned out to be hostile. Not to mention the only two humans onboard were not exactly made of diplomatic material.

Like Derrick said, humanity ventured into the stars not for exploration but for conquest, expansion, and escape from the planet that we had suffocated. Racism and prejudice were still in effect on Earth and now it had even spread into space, and that was just with our own race. Some gangs and radical people out there attacked aliens just for *being* alien. For every human who accepted life beyond our planet, another human would murder and abuse to keep their homes and streets 'human only.' I didn't agree with that way of thinking, but I couldn't be sure where Cessa stood on the subject. Time would tell.

"Do not initiate first contact Al. Continue on course and keep us at alert level two. If you come into range of any starships activate the shield coils and notify me immediately." I paused for a moment, scratching the heavy stubble on my chin. From here on out I would be a nervous wreck with no idea what we were getting ourselves into.

"Also," I continued. "Make sure the weapons are charged and ready, including my rifle. I don't care for that damned thing, but better to be safe than sorry. How long until we reach the fifth planet?"

"The ship will pass into the solar system in 7 hours. Total time to the planet is 16 hours, 4 minutes and 21 seconds."

I left Al on the bridge after I told him my plans for the next few hours. I walked throughout the ship to find Cessa. She was downstairs in the cargo bay again, sitting on the floor cross-legged, staring at the containers Erebos brought onboard. To me it seemed like she was in some type of meditative state. I stood at the top of the stairs looking down on her.

"What do you want?" She asked me. Nothing but her lips moved.

"I thought I would let you know that we are less than a day from our destination. We . . . I mean, I also detected an alien signature scanning our ship."

She stood up immediately and walked towards me. That certainly got her attention. For a moment I was worried that I messed up when I said 'we', but she seemed to write it off.

"I know you consider yourself a badass and you're eager for something to happen," I continued. "But I strongly suggest you get some sleep. In sixteen hours we will be sailing into the unknown."

Nothing happened for a moment as she processed the information, but then she looked in my eyes and nodded in agreement. I turned around to take my own advice, but at the same time I felt a sense of pride wash over me. I felt like the true

Captain of my ship, giving a speech to my crew. If anything, now is the time that Cessa and I would have to put our awkward relationship aside because we were the only two people between whatever waited for us out there and the empyreus we were charged to collect.

EIGHT

"What should we name it?" I asked.

The two of us stood on the bridge staring out the window. The planet came into view about thirty minutes ago and I don't think either of us moved an inch since. Even Cessa with her unique personality and attitude couldn't deny the sheer magnificence of a brand new planet. Like Earth and many other planets we inhabited, the overall color was blue, though it had a green tint to it, almost a turquoise color. Though I was somewhat tense waiting for some kind of welcoming party to intercept us, the sensor readings were completely clear. There were no ships or even any satellites in their atmosphere. The scene in front of us was peaceful and beautiful.

"What do I care what we call it? All I require is the empyreus," Cessa said.

I rolled my eyes at her and told her to buckle up. Our descent to the planet was going to be bumpy from here on out and I had to find a suitable spot to land. The scans from the planet were highly unstable due to the extreme energy output the planet was giving off. There was no easy way for me to tell if there were villages, settlements, or even cities.

Assuming the lowest energy readings were the least active areas, I chose a spot that held a wide radius for the Belle and initiated landing procedures. At the same time I made sure Al kept his figurative eyes looking out for any signs of trouble. My heart was pounding and I found myself smiling from ear to ear. This was why I came out into space, to explore the unknown.

The ship slowed down to standard orbital velocity as we entered the upper atmosphere. There was a slight hesitancy on my part as I was of half a mind to stay in orbit for another half a day or so and collect data. It's always best to be prepared for any given situation, but the ship was beginning to feel smaller than usual. Tensions were at an all-time high and I was having trouble controlling my nightmares with the medication I had. I wasn't sure my sanity would make it another day, so I made a judgment call. The time had come to be the first humans to land on this world.

The thrusters ignited and the ship was veering down into the atmosphere. I felt the floorboards vibrate as the temperature of the outer hull began to rise exponentially. In minutes we flew through the troposphere, surrounded by oxygen. I leveled the ship out as we passed through the familiar white clouds that were identical to Earth's. In the display screen land was finally visible and I was surprised to see that the turquoise color that covered the majority of the planet from space was endless fields of grass. Earth was 70% water, but that didn't seem to be the case here.

The main screen on my console relayed that all systems were operating efficiently and the landing gear had dropped. I held onto the navsphere so long my knuckles were white. The last part was tricky. As the ship dropped within five hundred feet of the ground, I fired the bow thrusters and then the stern thrusters until we hovered, then I synced all four so the ship could lower and finally land.

My chair jerked as we touched down and I quickly deactivated all thrusters and engines. The core powered down and within a minute the ship was quiet. I clapped my hands together and shouted out cheerfully. You never fully appreciate a docking station and the signal that allows your ship to automate landing procedures until you've had to manually land your ship on solid ground.

"We're here! Safe and sound," I said to Cessa as she unfastened her harness. Her eyes were wide open and she was breathing heavily. I'm guessing she didn't expect me to actually land without any incident. Of course it amused me more to think she was scared. I wouldn't mention that to her though.

"Yes," she said softly while walking towards the display screen to look outside. "But where is here?"

"Ha! You're the one who didn't want to name the planet!" I thought about the amazing view from space, then the sky looking down on this new land. Every step we took and everything we saw would be for the first time in human history. Naming the planet was easy.

"Dawn. I'm going to enter in the ship's log that this planet is now called Dawn."

Cessa looked at me as if asking, 'seriously, that's your name'?

"Take an hour to prepare. We'll exit the ship after I've confirmed levels of oxygen and carbon dioxide. We'll meet in the bay."

"Whatever you say," she said solemnly, walking towards the door. I was so happy from the landing and the thought of being on this new planet that I couldn't stop myself from responding to her.

"Whatever you say . . . Captain!" I suggested.

She scoffed at the comment and slammed the door. She still couldn't ruin my mood. I knew I was just on a high and it would end eventually, but I let myself enjoy it while it lasted.

I spent the next half hour sending out a low level bio-scan and got a lot of results, such as forests, plant life, and some minimal life signatures most likely from animals, but I didn't see anything that resembled a humanoid life form. It's possible I landed in an uninhabited area. If so, it made me feel a little bit safer. I wasn't quite ready to meet any new species yet. One thing at a time.

"I am most impressed with this planet, sir." Since we landed the only other thing Al said to me was, 'congratulations on an average landing', but he was as dumbfounded with the readings as I was. In his dictionary, 'impressed' was the same thing as 'dumbfounded'.

"The scanners are not detecting any alien life signatures, except for local animal life."

There was a possibility that they were masking their signature from us. They knew we were coming and the ability to have a deep space relay satellite meant their technology was at least as advanced as ours. Whether or not there were any humanoids around us we had a job to do.

I didn't know how long it would take us to survey the area. Depending on what we encountered and whether or not we could find the empyreus easily, we could be away from the ship for a couple of hours or even an entire day. I checked the security camera to see if Cessa was in the cargo bay and sure enough she was. She was well armed, but I couldn't zoom in to get an accurate description. What really interested me was the box she was carrying towards the doors.

"Al, while we're away make sure you do regular sensor sweeps and take another look at our passenger's boxes. I find it hard to believe they're empty."

"Acknowledged sir. While I have no human emotion to be concerned for your well-being, I will wish you good luck."

"Thanks Al. Keep the ship in one piece while I'm gone."

I took my leave of the bridge and hustled to my room. Once there I grabbed everything I needed including a change of clothes, sleeping bag, water jugs, and the pills which helped to calm my mind. Lastly, I stopped in front of my secret compartment and grabbed my tactical suit. I stared at my rifle for a couple of minutes, but ultimately decided against bringing it. Scanning our surroundings didn't reveal any danger and if we did happen to make contact with an alien I didn't want to look aggressive.

The suit is a lower grade of armor than most soldiers wear. I dressed in a black, skin tight mesh that was resistant to certain ammunition such as bullets and plasma. Over that I attached various pieces of grey colored armor including a chest piece, shoulder pads, forearm guards, and gloves. My legs had similar armor pieces and all were designed to shield my body from various dangers including plasma blasts and intense heat. The outfit wasn't the most comfortable thing in the world, that is, until you realize that it raises your chance of survival by 100%.

When I reached the bay Cessa was sitting on the same box she had carried toward the door. Now that I was up close I could see that she was wearing her comfortably tight armored suit, metallic plates covering her upper arms, chest and thighs. It was the same outfit I met her in, but it looked even more impressive now. Her sword hung at her side and she had also equipped small daggers in her belt. I stood next to her and took a quick look around my ship.

"Where is your weapon?" Cessa asked me. "Please tell me you have one."

"Ha! Of course I have one. I just chose not to bring it."

I think she nearly fell off the box when I said that. Cessa stood and walked up to me. Her chest was touching my arm, her face centimeters from mine.

"Don't be an idiot! How do you plan on protecting yourself? How do you plan on handling any potentially hostile natives?"

I looked right in her eyes and replied, "Isn't that why I have you"?

After that she folded her arms and said nothing. I took the moment of silence to inquire about the box.

"Beacon indicators," she muttered. "We can use these to mark our journey and not get lost."

"Smart," I said, then walked over to the door lever. I put my hand around it then turned back to Cessa.

"Ready for this?"

She stood up straight and loosened up her arms, placing her hand around the hilt of her sword, which was apparently her standard pose.

"Are you certain we won't require masks or helmets?" She asked.

I shook my head, "Multiple scans were completed of the environment outside the ship. The air is going to be a little lighter than what we feel on Earth, but gravity and oxygen levels are very similar to what we're used to."

I threw down the lever and the doors grinded against the hull as it lowered to the grass. I immediately felt a gust of wind and inhaled it. The aroma was wonderful. The air smelled like a spring morning, standing in a flower bed after a light rainfall. The temperature was warm and the wind comfortable. I moved slowly off the ship and onto the boarding ramp. To my right the sun was shining a brilliant golden light.

As much as I wanted to explore the planet and go looking for the empyreus, I also wanted to get a look at my ship to discern the damage from the asteroid belt. There was a lot of paint damage and some dents in the wings of the ship. I didn't see anything that needed immediate repair, which was fantastic. I walked back to the bay and initiated the closing sequence. Within seconds the Belle was secured and Cessa and I were completely on our own.

"Do you hear that?" I heard Cessa mutter. Stopping to listen, I didn't hear anything but the wind, at least at first, but then I did hear something far off in the distance. Was it animals or bugs, like a bunch of noisy crickets? As I focused on the sound the answer was neither. The sounds that Cessa heard were music. Some sort of melody was playing on the wind, the sounds reminding me of a flute or piccolo. I had to strain in order to hear it, but it was beautiful. For a brief moment I considered activating my bionic eye to get an extra sense of perception, but I wanted to take this time to enjoy the moment of being here. Sure, I was still uncomfortable with the terms of my journey, but you couldn't deny the brilliance of moments like this no matter how you got here.

To my left, Cessa pulled her sword from its scabbard. She bent her knees and wrapped both hands around the hilt, taking a stance of caution.

"What are you doing?" I asked her. "Put your damn sword away."

"We have no idea what's out here . . . we need to be ready." She kept looking from side to side, moving her sword to match her direction.

"Didn't I just tell you that this area was scanned multiple times? Not only is the planet environmentally safe, but it detected no signs of humanoid life. Nothing is going to happen to us, we are completely fine."

That's when I felt a sharp pinch in my neck. I tried to feel the area with my hand. I thought I felt something stuck in it, but immediately my hand went numb as did my feet. I heard a *thump* beside me and turned to see Cessa on the ground, unconscious. When I tried to take a step my legs failed me and I hit the ground too.

The music grew louder as my sight got darker. My head felt like it had been completely separated from my body. I couldn't feel a thing. Eventually I lost complete control of myself and my eyes closed to blackness.

The nightmares were so numerous that I questioned whether they were actually real. For brief moments I recall lying on my back looking up at the night sky. The stars above were foreign to me, but that didn't mean I couldn't appreciate them just as much. I could hear music all around me, some of it soft and tranquil and some more aggressive.

Seconds later I was somewhere else. Two heavily armed guards dragged my body down a corridor. The back of my head throbbed in pain as if someone struck me with something hard. As the guards turned left, then right I realized the sights around me were familiar. I was on a starship about a week after I departed Earth for the first time. I tried to speak to one of the guards. My words came out a jumbled mess, but I felt like I knew him somewhat. Maybe he could tell me what was going on.

"You need to shut your mouth right now Quinn," he said to me with his teeth forced together and a look of hatred about him.

I didn't argue or say another word. Something had gone horribly wrong and I knew that, but my head was swimming and I couldn't focus on the events of the past few hours. The three of us entered a large octagonal room where each wall held a smaller room encased in thick, impervious glass. The guards opened one of the smaller rooms and dropped me there, then locked me in. It was a brig. I was a prisoner.

None of this made sense. What was I doing in the brig? I stood up, but became lightheaded very quickly. I put my hands on the glass wall to steady myself and that's when I noticed my hands. They were both covered in blood. My heart raced as I searched my body for wounds, but then my memories resurfaced. The blood wasn't mine. Memories attacked me, showing me things I didn't want to see, a body in my room, the blood spattered everywhere. I ran to the body and fell to my knees screaming a name I couldn't comprehend.

Screaming. There was so much screaming. When I woke up to the starry sky, I screamed. When I blacked out the memory replayed over and over and ended with my screams. During the night I woke up shivering and sweating at the same time. A warm hand covered my forehead, but I couldn't see who it was. I could only see stars above me. I could only hear music playing.

At some point my nightmares continued past the screams. I was still in the brig though my hands were clean. The doors to the main hub opened and a woman stepped in. She approached my cell and stopped just short of her nose touching the glass. I stood up and saluted her.

"Commander King," I said, my voice hoarse.

She didn't tell me at ease, nor did she say anything for a good while. She just looked at me in a way that made me feel like she was considering her options.

"You've murdered a member of my crew, Daniel."

I murdered? No, I didn't remember being the one who committed murder. I found the body in my room. I wanted to say something to her to try and convince her that I didn't do it.

"Don't speak," she said while holding her hand up to me. "You will be taken to the nearest space station and be placed in a holding cell until you can be put on trial. It is the Captain's and my recommendation that you be sentenced to death."

My entire world fell apart in a matter of hours. She turned and left me there, screaming her name, telling her to come back. I didn't commit murder and I couldn't allow myself to be placed in holding on a station. Somehow, someway, I had to escape.

The memory slowly faded away and my consciousness returned to reality. The starry sky had been replaced with bright sunlight and the air was cool on my face, but my body was covered with something. I moved my hands and felt a light, soft cloth that ran from my chest to my feet, a blanket. It took a while for my mind to process that I was finally awake and the nightmares were over. I sat up and found myself lying on a cot . . . in a cell.

This wasn't any kind of cell I'd ever seen before. For one thing, there was no roof. That explained how I saw stars before and the sun now. The cell itself looked square shaped with a soft curve in each corner. The walls were cream colored and solid, though on four sides there were open gaps. I walked up to one of them, which began above my feet and ended a foot above my head. There was enough space to comfortably look through, but not nearly enough room to squeeze through and escape.

My prison stood in a meadow of bluish grass. A forest of rich brown bark with branches covered in leaves of red, gold, and blue stood on the opposite end. I squinted at the ground toward the border of the forest and counted a couple of dirt paths leading into it. I assumed my captors would be entering the area from one of those paths.

Someone screamed. At first I wrote it off as something that was in my head, just a figment of my imagination from the nightmares. When the screaming didn't stop I focused on it. A flurry of words followed the primal screams.

"Let me out! Now! I swear on each and every one of your lives that I will end you!"

Cessa. I quickly sidestepped to my right until I found the next set of gaps. Beside my cell was a second cell where Cessa was being held and she was angry. I could see the foundation of the cell trembling. Every couple of seconds I saw a womanly figure rush back and forth past the gaps, presumably slamming herself into the walls to try and breach them. I could hear her labored breathing. She had been at this for some time.

I couldn't help but feel a sense of comfort knowing she was alive. I was taking this imprisonment a lot better than her, but that didn't mean I was comfortable. I tried to remind myself that the two of us were aliens to whatever life form existed on this planet. I pressed my face into the gap as much as I could then whispered loudly to Cessa.

"Daniel?" She gasped. She ran to the opening opposite mine.

Besides her hair being messy from the running and sweating, she seemed okay. Her eyes were wide in a look that could have been terror or hatred. I couldn't be sure which.

"Are you okay?" I asked her.

"Do you have brain damage?" She was on the verge of screaming again. "No I'm not okay! I'm trapped like an animal! They took my sword! They are vile, loathsome, bastard freaks!"

She must have seen them already. I turned to give her a moment to breathe and cool off and noticed that like her sword, my equipment was missing as well. The only thing in the cell that belonged to me was the suit I wore and of course, my bionic eye. Whoever they were they had my bag, my clothes, my medical supplies and with that, my medication to control the nightmares. I muttered a curse to myself, but quickly got control of my own temper. If the roles were reversed and these aliens landed on Earth they would be going through a lot more trouble than the two of us were right now.

Despite our imprisonment being relatively comfortable, that didn't stop Cessa from continuing her assault on her cell. I now saw what she was like in captivity. It wasn't pretty. She was acting like a crazed animal, shouting, screaming, and attacking the walls in various ways, testing their durability. In the open world she was a predator, but inside a cage she was a victim.

I became distracted from Cessa's aggression when sounds carried on the wind towards us. The sounds were those of music again. I looked out all four openings but saw nothing. Maybe there was a village through the forest. As time passed, I thought I could hear the music grow louder. The trees across the small meadow rustled and I pushed my eye against the gap in the cell to look. Two of the aliens . . . no, the natives, walked into the meadow and gave me my first look at this new alien race.

They were taller than me, much taller. With a twitch of pain I activated my bionic eye and within seconds I had details of their heights, 7'2'' and 6'5'' respectively. Curiously, when my eye scanned over the clothing I received unknown readings and errors. Whatever the material was made of it wasn't anything known to man. The clothes made me think of ceremonial robes. The skin on their hands and faces was a modest shade of lavender. Their heads were longer and more oval than the average human. They didn't have eyebrows or ears, but instead on each side of their head had two indents with various openings. Their eyes were twice as large as a human's, golden irises surrounding dark brown pupils. The mouths were similarly shaped to ours except they had no lips. I counted three fingers and an opposable thumb on their hands. Everything else was covered by their clothing.

As they approached us they were speaking to each other, gesticulating with their hands. I tried to concentrate on what they said until I realized that the music I'd been hearing was coming

71

from *them*. They spoke in musical intonations. My knees became weak and I almost fainted from the beautiful melody, but this presented a problem. How was I supposed to establish communication with them? I didn't expect them to speak any human languages of course, but I hoped it would have been something I could have learned to translate. I had no idea whatsoever how I would translate their musical speech patterns.

The two of them first stopped in front of Cessa's cell. From this close up I could see that their shoulders were very broad, but one alien's shoulders were square and the other's were curved. The curved alien's chest was slightly bigger than the male's, supposedly her breasts, but they were higher on the chest than a human woman's.

"I'll kill you! Where's my sword you bastards?"

Cessa forced her face as far through the opening as she could. From my point of view it looked ridiculous, almost painful. They stood in front of her a moment watching her reactions to their presence. Then both of them, in sync, turned toward me. My stomach erupted in a flurry of butterflies. I quickly deactivated my eye hoping they didn't notice the soft glow the pupil made while active. Goosebumps formed on my skin as they took position directly in front of me.

What was I supposed to do? Should I say hello? Wave to them? My mind was a completely blank slate. If there was one sure thing, it's that I wasn't a diplomat and I only knew the basics of the first contact procedure. What would I want to know if I captured an alien creature and had no idea of its intentions? I would probably want to know that it wasn't a threat. I had no idea what they considered to be a sign of friendship so I did the first thing that came to my mind. Slowly extending my right hand over my heart I bowed to them. They looked at each other and conversed, their musical speech mesmerizing. The change in notes was quick and precise.

The male looked back at me and leaned in. He sang something to me, but I obviously couldn't understand him. The music itself sounded somewhat unsure of itself like a progression of notes in a minor chord. I shook my head and decided now was as good a time as ever to let them hear my speech as well.

"I am sorry, but I do not understand you."

He retracted his head and looked to his associate or partner. There was more musical speech. This species walked and talked with their own personal soundtrack and that astounded me. I could only imagine what Earth scientists would think about this.

The two . . . Dawnians? I had to come up with a name for them at some point. They turned to walk away from me and my shoulders dropped. I hoped my sincerity would somehow read in my expressions, but with the lack of communication there was no way to be sure what they thought of us or what they would do with us.

I could still hear them singing. They hadn't left the area yet, but they had moved out of sight. I pressed my face through a couple of the openings to try and see them through my peripherals, but that didn't work. I tried listening, which was difficult thanks to the variety of curses Cessa was still spouting out. She only made the situation worse and I wish she realized that. On the other hand maybe I was being too calm about it. We were locked up, which I was no stranger to. Who knew what they were going to do with us?

The male Dawnian returned with a strange device held in his palms. The female stood behind him, paying close attention to the scene in front of her. The device looked similar to a motherboard from a computer console. What caught my eye were multiple charges and pulses of blue and gold emanating from it like a visible electric current. He moved the device to his upper chest and attached it there, though I didn't know how. He tinkered with it for a minute then sang towards it. I heard a buzzing sound and he played with it some more. After his third alteration of the settings I almost lost all feeling in my legs and fell.

"Comprehend?" He spoke. He actually spoke to me, in English no less!

The whites of my eyes must have been as big as dinner plates. Whatever the device was, it acted as a translator. He sang his song; the device recorded it and then transformed it into human speech, but how? I completely froze, shocked. He stood there waiting until he again spoke to me.

"Comprehend?" He said again.

Come on Daniel. Your brain is working. Use it. Talk to him!

"Y-y-yes, I understand you! Uh, I mean . . . comprehend!"

My fears and hesitation slowly dispersed. If we could establish consistent speech patterns between each other there might still be hope for this mission and more importantly, my life. The two of us stared at each other. The scene was eerily quiet. Even Cessa was rendered speechless.

"*Personal situation?*" He asked.

This would take some time to perfect I could see. I wasn't sure what he meant by personal situation. Maybe he was asking how I was feeling. It was as good a guess as any.

"Very well," I said as I placed both of my hands flat together in front of me. "Thank you."

In truth I was excited and terrified at the same time. I wanted to get out of this cage, but I didn't want to give them a bad impression. I did my best to hide my fears and act as friendly as possible. The Dawnian seemed to understand what I said. We both looked at each other awhile longer and it occurred to me that he was probably feeling just as curious and excited as I was. Maybe he was having trouble finding the right words to say.

"My name," I said patting my chest. "is Daniel. I am Daniel."

". . . *Laraar,*" He said after thinking over a moment. He moved his hands towards his female associate and said, "*Idza.*"

I repeated their names to them. "Laraar . . . Idza . . . ," And he nodded his head to me, saying mine.

"*Daniel.*"

I waved my hand toward Cessa and told them her name. When the male looked at her his eyes narrowed and if I could have guessed, he wasn't happy with her. They knew she was unhinged and a threat without the need for communication. Of course her actions up to this point didn't help her cause any.

Laraar sat on the ground and motioned for me to do the same. I wasn't sure why we were sitting until hours passed like minutes. The two of us ended up talking for hours. For the most part he asked me the questions though I wouldn't go as far to call it an interrogation.

Where was I from? How did I get here? What is my home planet like? He coincidentally ignored crucial questions like 'what was my mission' or 'was I dangerous?' I got a momentary wave of deja vu as I recalled Raymond Erebos saying something similar to me.

I saw no reason to lie to him or speak untruthfully. I hoped he would return the favor so I could learn about him and his world. More importantly, I wanted his trust. If I wanted to find the empyreus on this planet I was sure I'd have to go through them.

I told him about Earth, though I didn't mention the poverty, crime, and warfare that plagued half the planet. Instead I focused on the other half, the goodness that still remained and the people trying to make a difference. After a while I felt like the two of us were sitting together at a table, conversing with each other as if we were close friends. It wasn't until he nodded at me and stood when I remembered where I actually was.

"*Gratitude,*" he said, inclining his head in a small bow before turning to leave. I pressed up against the opening of my prison.

"Wait!"

He slowly turned back to me. "*Time . . .*" The two of them turned and walked back into the forest, their songs mirroring each other. Cessa and I were once again alone as the golden sun lowered past the horizon covering us in darkness.

"You talk about the dumbest things," I heard her say. She was back to her good ol' self.

I rolled my eyes and ignored her. Nothing and no one could take away the excitement I was feeling. Yes, I was still caged like an animal, but the natives were interested in me. There was no poking or prodding, no experiments to test our biology. Instead they chose to sit and talk. The level of relaxation and calmness they expressed was the last thing I would have expected. In less than a day I felt like I was already forming a bond with Laraar. I wasn't sure what to think of Idza. She stood behind us the entire time watching, listening, and seeming to concentrate on our interaction. The two of them must have been their race's version of scientists.

At the same time there was some other part of me, call it the pessimistic part, which wondered if this was only the first stage in a line of interrogations, experiments, and research. Just because they were kind and respectable today didn't guarantee they would be the same way tomorrow. There was a possibility that we were simply lab rats in the total equation.

No, I couldn't think of it like that and that's not at all what it seemed like.

"They seem peaceful and curious," I heard myself say to Cessa. "If you can keep yourself from screaming and overreacting, we might be able to establish some kind of peace between our races."

"Go ahead and try Daniel," she said. "But if they let me out, the first thing I'm going to do is kill them for imprisoning me in the first place. Then I'm going to find my sword and kill whoever took it. All that matters is the job, not these disgusting aliens. We get out and find the empyreus. That's all that matters!"

I dropped my shoulders in defeat and walked over to my cot. The day spent talking to Laraar was enough to tire me mentally and there was nothing to gain by talking to Cessa. I stared up at the stars as I drifted off to sleep and when I woke up the next morning there was no cold sweat, no tremble in my body or remnants of disturbing images in my mind. I felt good, refreshed and ready to live. Of course living would be difficult inside a cell, but one thing at a time. I was just happy I managed to elude my nightmares for a night.

The morning air was cool and the sun was just beginning its ascent when I smelled the rich aroma of smoked meat. My stomach seized up and growled at me like a vicious lion. I saw movement from one of the paths in the forest and stepped up to my opening to see a large metallic curricle hovering towards us. Laraar was moving behind it with a small pad in his hand that I assumed was a remote control device. He had a stern look on his face. I waved at him hoping to convey a welcomed greeting, but his expression was unmoving. Maybe he wasn't looking forward to our second meeting as much as I was.

As Laraar approached I caught sight of another figure coming through the forest, a different looking Dawnian than

Idza. The form was very masculine, muscles clearly defined. His eyes were glaring at me and his mouth was set in a tight frown. He carried a long staff that curved at each end. Tribal markings covered its smooth center. The material didn't match the color of the trees, but instead was a rich, glimmering black.

The new Dawnian strode past Laraar and the curricle, straight to my cell. He raised both arms up, held his staff high and swung it forcefully into the cage. The attack caused the walls to tremble. As I watched the staff make contact I threw myself to the ground, half expecting it to go straight through the cell and hit me.

What followed was a sharp and out of tune musical pattern that was rushed and angry. I met his eyes and felt his hatred. I looked as his hands wrapped around the staff so hard I thought it might shatter. There was no doubt in my mind that this Dawnian wanted to kill me.

TEN

No matter which wall I backed into, the Dawnian would stride over and swing his staff into the wall. Eventually I just stood in the middle and he paced around me, taunting me, shoving his staff in between openings to try and hit me. I avoided each hit where I could and stood my ground. There was nothing I could do. Provoking him even more wouldn't get me anywhere. Besides, Cessa was doing most of that for me, screaming for him to come and attack her and then throwing out a bunch of harmless curses that they couldn't comprehend anyway.

I noticed a crowd forming just inside the tree line and counted six other Dawnians including Laraar. Most of them remained still and watched the interaction between us, but two of them were throwing their arms around and their song was louder than the rest. I had a strange feeling that they were egging their friend on, encouraging him to continue.

Laraar raised both of his hands up and a loud, thundering pitch erupted from his vocals. Everyone stopped, including my staff-wielding friend. Laraar lowered his voice and spoke out to everyone in the area. Within minutes the three aggressive Dawnians looked furious, huffing and puffing their breath out and pointing at me. Whatever Laraar said to them didn't sit well. The one in front of my cell sighed and threw his staff into my bar one last time then moved off with the others. Laraar put his hand on the Dawnian's shoulder as he passed, but it was shaken off.

As my new friend and savior approached my cell I bowed to him much the same as when I met him. I saw that he was wearing his translation device so I thanked him vocally too. He simply nodded in return and moved toward the curricle. He pressed his fingers onto a panel and the top of it opened up. Though I wasn't tall enough to see what was inside it, my stomach instantly recognized the scent of food. I leaned against the front side of the cell. I felt like a caged animal with a slab of meat dangling in front of me.

Laraar produced two containers that were grey in color and brought one to me. He turned it vertically and slid it inside my cell and I hastily grabbed it. Heat emanated from it and I looked for the clasp or button that would open it.

When I finally figured out how to get it unlocked I stared at the items in front of me. An enclosed cylinder with purple colored liquid was accompanied by a bowl holding a mashed substance, somewhat reminiscent of potatoes but the consistency was more like pudding. Last but not least there was a piece of some sort of meat, very brown in color and covered in what looked like fat. Honestly it looked more like something I would see in a bathroom than on a dinner plate and the thought almost made me heave. I looked at Laraar and he gave me an almost pleasant smile.

"Ingest."

He carried the other container to Cessa who refused to take it. With a sigh and a frown that spoke disappointment to me, he lowered himself to the ground and set the food inside her cell where she completely ignored it. Assuming she was as hungry as I was her stomach must have been cramping terribly. The thought occurred to me that not only did I have to set a good example for Laraar, but I needed to do so for her.

Without utensils, none that I could find anyway, I placed my finger in the potato pudding. I forced my eyes to stay open and tried to keep an open mind as I put my finger in my mouth and sucked the food off of it. The taste was bitter like biting a lemon, but when the sensation faded what was left was a taste that reminded me of green vegetables such as peas or cucumbers.

The meat was soft and didn't alleviate my previous thoughts of it looking like shit, but thankfully it didn't taste like it . . . not that I knew what shit tasted like. It was lightly salted, but beyond that very bland. I tried my best to not grimace as Laraar stood there like a statue watching me eat. After I finished the meal I washed it down with the drink, which wasn't that bad. If I had to guess I would say that I was drinking their version of milk. The purple liquid was thicker than water and was neither sweet nor sour. I drank half of it before I set the container away from me and placed my hand on my stomach. Though my stomach was satisfied with the intake, the taste was at best average.

Laraar clapped his hands together and smiled like a giddy school boy who had just been given a new shiny toy. I obviously pleased him. Go me.

I gazed over in Cessa's direction, turning a corner of my mouth up and raising my eyebrows, essentially saying, 'There! I did it, I'll bet you can't'! She got the message right away and gave me her famous look of death before stomping over to her box. If Laraar was the giddy school boy then Cessa was the fussy toddler. As she finally ate, she showed absolutely no hesitancy in letting Laraar know how disgusted she was with her food. She gagged, spit, and threw half of her meat outside the cage.

I was amused by her behavior, but our host was not. He walked over to pick up the wasted meat and took it back to his curricle placing it in a side compartment that might have been a waste bin. He reached into the curricle again and I hoped to the stars above that Laraar wasn't presenting us with dessert. He didn't. What he pulled out was worse.

Laraar approached me with Cessa's sword. She grew frantic, slamming into the wall and shaking her cell hysterically.

"Give me my sword you alien piece of shit!"

Ignoring her he unsheathed her sword, running his finger slowly over the edge of the blade. He looked at me quizzically.

"*Intentions*?"

Eventually we would have to explain ourselves and the reason we traveled here. It seemed like that time had come. I could have given him multiple explanations, but I wanted to keep it simple for now, something he would easily comprehend. The weapon was Cessa's and I knew what she intended to do with it, but I figured it wouldn't hurt if I altered the truth slightly. Whether he chose to believe me or not would be another matter.

"Defense. Protect," I said to him, which was true enough. Cessa was technically sent to make sure I accomplished my mission.

He seemed to ponder over it a moment, looking at the blade. He held it in various positions, even swung it a couple times in the air testing its motions. Once he was finished he sheathed it again and sat on the ground, laying the sword on his lap. I sat in front of him and waited for him to say or do something.

"*Daniel . . . Reason . . . Defense*," he said to me and I was astonished at how well he understood me. The translation wasn't perfect, but so far we seemed to be in sync with each other and our expressions.

"We were unsure of the danger," I said, repeating myself a couple of times emphasizing *unsure* and *danger*.

"*Not . . . threat?*"

"No threat. Curious. I want to learn about you and your world." I reached my arms out wide letting him know I was opening myself to everything he was willing to teach me and I found myself nervous about what would happen next. The two of us seemed to be making a lot of progress in getting to know each other and maybe it was a fool's hope, but I wondered if he might trust me enough to let me out of my cell. I was starting to grow restless. This wasn't the first time I had been locked up, as my nightmares often reminded me. I had been doing a good job of keeping those thoughts behind closed doors despite not having my meds, but there was a lot of weight and pressure against them and they could burst open at any time.

Laraar stood up and returned the sword to his curricle then touched the controls, activating and sending it on its way back to what I assumed was their settlement.

As the curricle disappeared into the trees another group of Dawnians came towards me, though I couldn't tell if it was the same people grouped together as before. Laraar welcomed them with a short note then walked up to my cage and unlocked my door. I couldn't believe it. Had he read my mind? Immediately I felt relieved that I was being released. That's until the group surrounded me and two of them grabbed onto my shoulders.

"Laraar? What's going on? Explain," I said.

"*You . . . curious . . . want . . . learn*," he sang, then paused a moment. "*Earn.*"

They led me into the forest, with Cessa behind me screaming to let her out and not leave her behind. I looked back towards her and her eyes were wide and gleaming with tears. I actually felt sorry for her. No matter what we went through, her expression wasn't anger, but fear and desperation. The only thing she didn't want more than being locked up was being locked up alone. As the two Dawnians continued to drag me along, I wondered if I would prefer to be back in my cell.

She was out of sight within a minute and we were fully immersed in the forest that surrounded our holding area. The grass was tall, surrounding the path we walked along. I saw now that the path itself was outlined with sticks and branches. As we walked deeper into the forest I couldn't help but stare in awe at the trees and plant life. Every other tree was a different shade of brown and grew in varying directions. One of them stood as tall as a statue, its branches hanging down to the ground creating an umbrella effect. Another one grew completely sideways, but strangely didn't look strained as it hung above the ground.

Small animals were running through the brush and up the trunks, not all that different looking from the animals on Earth, with the exception of a couple extra limbs. They squeaked and chirped and bugs buzzed all around us, though they were too fast to see or describe. I could have sat on the ground and immersed myself for hours just watching the sheer beauty of it all unfold.

I activated my bionic eye as we continued and the discomfort was light. I tracked the route we were taking as the path forked. We followed it to the right. My eye detected more movement farther in the forest, and registered that we were now over 33 meters from where they kept me locked up. Up ahead of us outside of the forest, a large number of signatures registered in my sight. My counter went past one hundred and I grew restless as I heard a group singing a tribal chant.

The group of Dawnians ahead was standing in a semi-circle around a ring of gleaming sand. The sun literally caused it to sparkle as if covered by diamonds. In the middle of the ring was my friend, the one who egged me on by smacking my cage with his staff. Beside him were the two that were encouraging him from the forest border. Everything suddenly made sense. He had come to my cage this morning to size me up and intimidate me. I knew now what Laraar had meant by earning my place among their people. I was about to be tested, but how and to what degree? There was one of me and three of them. Surely they wouldn't force me to fight them. I almost wished Cessa was here. With all her pent up rage and anger she would have been helpful in a fight.

The hundreds of Dawnians stared at me as I approached the ring. Some were taller than others, fatter or skinnier, but all were united in song, melodies and harmonies mixing together to create a soundtrack for this event. My competition looked unbelievably bored in the middle of the ring.

"They're awfully sure of themselves aren't they?" I said to myself, trying to stay collected.

The hands holding my arms finally released me, but another hand rested itself on my shoulders. Laraar stood behind me.

"*Chorta*," he sang to me, indicating my friend in the ring. I finally had a name for him. The other two, I learned, were named Horku and Grent. Laraar moved his arm around me, pointing to the three of them. "*Choose . . . Horku . . . Grent . . . defend Daniel, and earn . . .*"

Um, what?

Laraar squeezed my shoulder gently then stepped back. I turned to look at him, but he was lost in a crowd of Dawnians when they extended their company into a full circle surrounding the four of us. I was frozen, standing there without any weapon or understanding of what I had to do. I suppose Chorta grew sick and tired of waiting. After a couple minutes of me muttering 'oh shit oh shit oh shit' to myself, he touched his staff to the one on his left, Grent I think. Chorta and Horku stepped into the crowd.

Grent did some kind of martial art exhibition which I have to admit was impressive. He shouted a long flat note that drew laughter from the crowd. I was shaking, nervous, and terrified.

Don't let that get to you and don't let them get to you. You're fighting for your freedom and possibly your life, I thought to myself.

It wouldn't be the first time I fought for my life. I stretched out my arms and stood in a fighting stance. It seemed that this was meant to be a duel, but to what end? I didn't have any more time to think about it as Grent growled at me and charged, his hands clenched into tight fists. I didn't know their fighting style and my eye couldn't tell me much, except that there was a 75% chance he would charge me until I thrust at him only for it to be deflected by his left arm. No matter what kind of match this was

I didn't want to kill him, especially in front of all his brethren so I fell to my right and kept my left leg extended, hoping to trip him. He saw that coming and jumped over it turning his midsection quickly after and swinging his right fist at my head. I barely had enough time to raise my forearm to block. It wasn't a good block and he managed to hit my jaw.

I rolled out of the way of his large foot and jumped to my feet before he gained too much advantage. I tried alternating swings to his midsection and fortunately he moved to block my right swing which allowed my left to connect with his ribcage, or what I thought was his ribcage. The hit knocked the wind out of him momentarily and I used the opportunity to attack again. He held his hands out to block another attempt at his midsection, which I ignored. Instead I threw my leg up and around his defense, landing an agile kick across his face.

Grent backed away as an abundance of sweat built on my face and underarms. As I stood there breathing heavily I realized I was smiling, enjoying this. Maybe it was because I forgot that I had some skill in fighting or maybe it was simply a matter of Chorta and his men underestimating me. In fact, there was a small part of me that was confident I could win. That is until Grent stood up straight, took a deep breath, and smiled. Either he healed astoundingly quickly or he had been feigning his injuries. He charged at me again, shocking me with the increased quickness in his steps.

Round two was a joke. In the blink of an eye Grent threw his elbow into my leg, the pain caused me to drop to one knee. His arms were so quick they looked like a blur as he thrust his fist into my stomach and I fell to my knees and hands. I couldn't see what he did next, but the impact felt like he clamped his hands together and threw them down on my back like a sledgehammer. I was now flat on the ground, the pain soaring through my limbs. I felt like such a fool. The entire time I thought I actually stood a chance.

Despite the pain, Grent's taunting, and the cheer of the crowd, I got to my feet and raised my hands again. The noise quieted as everyone looked at me. I tried to take a deep breath, but the previous hit to my stomach had knocked the wind out of me. Grent narrowed his large eyes and snarled as he came at me again.

I tried depending solely on my bionic eye this time, letting it absorb his movements and giving me a counter move. He jumped at me with his foot in the air, but I sidestepped in time to avoid it. That's when he compensated by swinging his left arm into mine. I moved to block, but in doing so I made the same mistake he made earlier, leaving my opposite side completely wide open. With amazing agility and flexibility he threw his leg into my side. The hit took me off my feet and I hoped the crack I heard was my imagination. In less than a minute I was on the ground again.

My mouth tasted like blood and sand, my back throbbed, and my side hurt badly. There was nothing wrong with giving up at this point, at least in my opinion. But this wasn't just any ordinary fight. These people had brought me to this ring to fight with one of Chorta's associates only for him to feign most of my attacks. My blood boiled at the thought of being played with. I was tired of it. Once more, I stood up and faced my enemy ready for whatever he was going to throw at me, even if it was death.

Just to irritate Grent one last time, I turned my mouth up in a devious smile and invited him to try again. He got the message loud and clear, and he clenched his fists so hard I expected to see blood running from his palms. He bent down, arms up and I spread my feet and straightened my back.

"*OOOOOOOOOOOOoooooooooooooooooooooOOOOOO OOOOOOOO*"

The booming sound came from the crowd, and I turned to see three Dawnians enter the ring. These three were dressed differently than the others. Two of them, smaller than the one in the middle, were females. Their sleeves were infused with gold rings, and they wore neck and ear jewelry. The male wore a golden belt and a crown-like head piece. The first thing that came to my mind was that they were the authority over these people. They stood in front of Grent and me with their hands up, indicating we were to stop the fight. I wasn't about to argue.

The three of them sang out to their people. The male's hands pointed towards me, then spread out wide. The women followed him like a physical echo. Their movements, like their voices, were flawless and in a consistent rhythm.

Someone stepped up behind me. I turned to see that it wasn't Laraar as I had expected, but his companion I had met that first day, Idza I think her name was.

"*Masters sing your honor . . . Daniel,*" she sang to me. The speech that her device translated was leaps and bounds over what Laraar could produce.

"My honor?" I asked her, hoping she would explain.

"*Authority required . . . test . . . quality of your life force.*"

My ribs were aching and I was still trying to catch my breath so it was a little more frustrating to try and deduce the meaning of her translation. I deactivated my bionic eye to help me think more clearly. Somehow, just from watching me fight they were satisfied that I was a man of honor. I was confused more than anything, but if the fight put me in their good graces I wasn't going to say anything else about it.

"What did I do to gain honor?" I found myself asking before my brain could play catch up. I had to restrain myself from clamping my hand over my mouth.

"*You fought . . . courage . . . no fear,*" she said quickly, as if she knew that was my question.

She escorted me out of the ring and back into the forest, looking at me the whole time.

"How is it you talk so well?" I asked her. She thought over her answer for a moment.

"*Studying. My job requires understanding you.*"

"What about Laraar?"

"*Laraar studies . . . all . . . everything. No time for specific.*"

So I wasn't wrong about Laraar being some sort of scientist. Right now what I needed though was a medic. I was in pain from top to bottom thanks to Grent's attacks. I wanted a shower, a change of clothes, and maybe a steak. I wondered what the chances were of the Dawnians allowing me access to my ship to grab some of the food stocked in the refrigerator.

"*Healer will treat wounds,*" Idza said to me as I grunted in pain and limped along back towards my cell. Laraar was nowhere to be seen when we finally reach the holding area. I spotted Cessa sitting against the left wall from the opening in front. Her arms were around her knees and she was looking at me. There was no expression of anger on her face, but she didn't care to show remorse for the way I looked or felt. In my cell, however, a new Dawnian waited.

"*Donos*," Idza said to me, pointing to him.

She motioned me forward and I hopped and limped onto the cot. As I sat there Donos scanned me with some sort of medical device, trying to determine my injuries. He took out a bowl and mixed herbs in it, adding a touch of thick liquid along with it. He brought it to me and motioned for me to drink it. I did, but couldn't hold back the gag reflex after I swallowed. Whatever it was, it tasted terrible.

"*Mixture will help immediately,*" Idza said to me in an amused tone, but then her features changed to something more sincere.

"*Being caged . . . cruel, yet necessary. When sun greets us, you will be free to walk among us. Your friend too . . . should you choose.*" The two of them gave me a low bow then Idza locked my cage and walked away, leaving Cessa and me alone once again.

Neither of us talked that night. I found myself staring up at the stars trying to draw new constellations in my mind. I always made a habit of looking at the stars, whether on land or in space. Centuries ago men who sailed on Earth's oceans used the stars to navigate. When flying in space among them, you could chart your own course. That led me to think of the Dawnians and the situation they put me in. I was going to be free and I was excited, don't get me wrong, but they left Cessa's fate in my hands as well. This was my biggest concern at the moment. Did it have to be a concern though? All I had to do was let her stay in her cell while I gained the respect of the natives, but what kind of person would that make me? Was it possible for her to remain calm and neutral once she was free among the people who imprisoned her and stole her precious weapon?

By tomorrow morning there was a choice to make and I had a bad feeling that no matter how I decided, some part of me would regret it.

ELEVEN

The sky was still dark when I opened my eyes from a restless sleep. Something in the meadow had awoken me, a noise of some sort, but I was too groggy to pinpoint it. I rolled onto my back and pulled the blanket high to my neck, the night air colder than usual. I wish I knew what time it was or for that matter what day, but there was no way to tell.

"Daniel," a soft womanly voice whispered. I blinked. Cessa's voice woke me up, her tone soft and sad out in the darkness.

"What?" I grumbled, wincing at the dryness of my throat as I swallowed. I heard a deep breath and something else too. Was it crying? I leaned up and tried to concentrate on the sounds Cessa made, but if she was crying it was too hard to tell.

"I just wanted to say . . . I'm sorry. I haven't helped to make this mission any easier. My actions seem to get us into more trouble. I . . . I hope you realize that I am just doing my job, or t-t-trying to at least. Finding the empyreus for Mr. Erebos is all that matters to me, but I admit I could have done things differently."

At this point I sat up and leaned over to the opening next to my cot, the same one that faced her cell. She was standing, her hands placed on the borders of the gap. She shivered in the cold. Her mouth was parted and her eyebrows raised. She looked sad, but a couple of days in a jail cell could do that to you, I suppose. Still, this was the first time she had opened up to me.

"Why do you work for him?" I asked her. I thought it was a personal enough question that, if she was remorseful, would be answered. She looked away from me, but I couldn't tell if it was due to shame or deflection. I waited for her to say something, but it took a couple of minutes.

"Working for a man like him wasn't something that required a job application or a training operation. When you work for him, it's because you owe it to him. He owns you and he doesn't let you forget it."

"Can I ask what you owe him?" Her saddened face hardened.

"No," she said quickly, sounding more like the Cessa I thought I knew. I cursed at myself for losing what might have been a bonding moment with the Cessa underneath all the baggage. She took a deep breath and let out a long sigh, frozen air expanding from her lips into the wind. "Will you release me? I overheard the native talking to you, t-t-telling you that I could be free if you chose it. I c-c-can't promise I won't lash out, but I can promise I'll try. Please don't keep me locked up like an animal," she pleaded.

This was going to be the million dollar decision apparently, one that would refuse to let me get anymore sleep tonight. On the one hand, I could let her out and she could wreak havoc on anything she comes into contact with, but maybe there was a small chance she'd behave herself. Of course if I kept her locked up, I would be safe to explore the land and bond with the natives, but once the job was finished I would either have to face her wrath once we departed or leave without her and face the potential wrath of Raymond Erebos. No matter what direction I walked in, there was still a pile of shit for me to step in.

I sat up and ran my hands through my hair. For a second I considered pulling a few out to distract myself from the problem.

"If I let you out, I swear Cessa, no matter what our feelings for each other are, you have to keep your anger and frustration at bay. No harm can come to these people. They were simply protecting themselves. Anyone on Earth would do the same if aliens landed on our planet."

"As I said, I promise to try."

"And one more thing," I said. "I know you're here to make sure I get the job done at any cost, but I'm confident if we play our cards right and earn their trust they'll be willing to tell us about the empyreus. With that said, we do this *my* way. No rushing, no screaming, and no loss of patience from you. Agreed?"

She took longer to answer this time, but after a couple of minutes she finally agreed to my terms.

"Thank you Daniel," was the last thing she said as she moved away from the opening and back to her cot. I lay back down too, but as expected my sleep fluctuated. For a while I would be awake, staring at the stars, but then at other times my eyelids would be too heavy to keep open. Every time I was awake, my mind talked to me saying only one thing.

I hope you know what you're doing . . .

When the morning came, so did our hosts. If I had a watch or a way to tell the time I would guess they were consistently on the same schedule each day. I looked towards Cessa's cell where she was standing and waiting too. She met my eyes and with a genuine smile, nodded to me, reaffirming her promise from the night before. Idza and Laraar both walked up to my cage and Laraar unlocked it for me.

"Congratulations . . . honor . . . earned," he said, and it felt like a huge compliment coming from him. Idza may have the job of being our main translator, but I felt like Laraar and I had developed a connection.

I stepped out of the cell and was not only pleased there were no guards to drag me along, but I also felt fantastic physically. All the pain from the previous day was gone. There was no soreness or tenderness in my body. Not only that, but I thought about the fight itself, how my bionic eye was less painful than it normally was when activated. Their food and drink must have some kind of medicinal properties. Whatever I ate yesterday morning must have numbed the pain somehow and the medicine I took last night reacted in such a way that I felt like I could run a marathon.

"Time has come to join us," Idza said, zoning me back in from my inner monologue.

"Will she be joining?"

I allowed a few seconds of second guessing myself, but ultimately decided that Cessa didn't technically do anything wrong to deserve rotting away in her cell. I just hope she didn't have her fingers crossed when she told me she would do no harm.

"She will be joining. Yes," I said, less than sure of myself, but they nodded to me and Laraar walked over and unlocked her cage. Cessa slowly walked out and smelled the morning air as if it was different outside the cage than in. She stretched out her arms and legs and I'll admit I had my hands clenched, wondering what her next move would be. Surprisingly, she took her place at my side.

"So, where are we going?" Cessa asked, simply curious, no form of malice or contempt in her voice. Maybe she would hold true to her promise after all.

Idza smiled at both of us and summoned Laraar to her side. Both couples gave off very different dynamics. Laraar and Idza were very comfortable with each other. Both touched each other on their shoulders, smiling. Cessa and I stood apart. We didn't touch nor did we make very much eye contact if any.

"Friends, much you should see . . . come . . . see village," Idza said to us, intertwining her arm with Laraar as they turned and led us into the forest. Cessa tried to be silent and still, but I noticed her eyes darting from tree to tree, from grass to plant. Every now and then her lips would part then close up again. She was amazed by the sights just as much as I was. She was just better at hiding it from everyone else.

The four of us walked past the path that branched off to the sand ring and after about sixty meters I could see various structures hidden behind the tree line. Humanoid figures moved back and forth throughout them all. Even with the small preview from the forest, I was completely unprepared for the amazing sight that was the Dawnian's village. I will admit now I can't do the view justice. Houses and buildings were circular in design. The roofs were domed and the entire structure seemed to be built out of wood. Nothing was painted or covered so the walls looked completely natural to the environment. None of the openings had doors on them. People were free to come and go as they pleased. I couldn't imagine what the winters here would be like, but then again maybe they didn't have winter.

The ironic thing was, for how pre-industrial the village looked it flourished with technology. Every five or six houses surrounded a main computer console, and even inside some of the openings I could see machinery of some sort. I saw no wires or connections, which meant it was either buried in the ground or this society was completely wireless.

If the technology was wireless, then how were they connected? Could it have been the very energy source we sought? If the Dawnians powered their tech using empyreus, then they would know and could potentially tell me how to harness it. Of course I just had to figure out when and how I should bring it up to them that I wanted their energy.

Cessa and I were led to a large building where many Dawnians were entering and exiting, a pleasant aroma filled the air. Inside I was reminded of a buffet style restaurant back on Earth as various seats and tables were placed around a large serving area with large quantities of food. Four Dawnians walked up to us with plates and gave them to us. I took some of the items Laraar and Idza took and hoped they had good taste.

I recognized the meat and the potato pudding-looking stuff from my imprisonment and I avoided those. I grabbed an orange colored slaw and pasta of some kind. The only drink that seemed to be available was the purple milk stuff. I couldn't be sure, but I thought I heard Cessa gagging every few seconds as she surveyed the food.

Laraar and Idza waited for the two of us to finish selecting our meal and led us towards an open area of grass and dirt. They sat down on their knees, placed one hand palm up to hold the plate, and proceeded to eat with the other. Reluctantly I did the same, hoping to show them I was eager to learn. Cessa couldn't care less and sat cross legged.

We silently sat there and ate. The food hadn't really improved any from what I previously sampled, however the pasta was well seasoned. Idza smiled at me as I finished all of it.

"*You enjoy Rax?*" she asked. I just stared at her, not knowing what rax was. She picked up on it and looked toward the ground, thinking of another word. "Shredded animal," she followed up with, and my stomach twisted a little. I didn't really care to know what part of the animal, but the cold and chewy texture led me to believe it was raw.

"Delicious," I said. A little white lie never hurt anyone right?

"*You ate little . . . skin shavings,*" she said as she pointed to my slaw, and I almost gagged and vomited. I shook the feeling off and coughed a couple of times, feigning an itch in my throat.

"Same animal? This rax you spoke of?" I asked her, indicating both food items.

"*Not same. Rax land animal, Quer air animal,*" She said.

Great. If their animals were anything like ours, I just sampled shavings of bird feathers. Ick. Laraar sang to Idza, waving his arm over the area we sat. He wasn't wearing a device today, so I didn't know what he was saying.

"Laraar asks how you ingest?"

"We cook meals, food, for ourselves. We use metal utensils for transferring it from our plate to our mouth to eat it." I hoped I explained it well enough. If they wanted to know the specific anatomy that allowed us to digest food I would have to decline, but she seemed satisfied and relayed my answer to Laraar.

"Our . . . people come here to ingest . . . to eat. Food all created here. Nowhere else."

I asked her if that meant their version of families, or anyone for that matter didn't eat in their specific home. She confirmed this. If anyone wanted to eat they had to come here for their breakfast, lunch, and dinner, which I learned was separated throughout the day in multiple meal times. Instead of three meals a day they ate nine times, from sunrise to hours after sundown. I felt fatter just thinking about it.

When I asked them how they managed to provide so much food and drink throughout the day, they told me that their food doesn't spoil for days even in an unrefrigerated environment. Their food was also rarely ever cooked. The animals that were sacrificed to become nourishment were pure and untainted by products and ailments.

Cessa sat with us and listened the entire time, barely touching her food. I tried to get her involved in the conversation but she would only answer with one word, mostly yes, no, or maybe. I wasn't sure if she was acting this way because she still held hard feelings towards them or she just wasn't in the mood to converse.

Three days passed with a sort of schedule governing our time on the planet. It started by being let out of our cells, going to get our first meal, and spending the rest of the day exploring the village, learning crafts and hobbies of the locals, and listening to the melodies and harmonies they sang. Their music, the tasks they set for themselves, and the village around them all existed in a synchronized manner. Watching it was like watching an orchestra on stage perform flawlessly and as such, when I listened to them, I felt my own emotions and feelings matching the tempo and feeling of the music itself. The only time their music was out of tune was when Chorta tried intimidating me in my cell.

Every night we were led back to our cells and locked inside, which grew a little frustrating. I just told myself that in a matter of hours they would let us out again, but it was another job entirely to make sure Cessa didn't fly off the deep end or act irrationally, something I worried about every day. I guess I hoped after days of behaving ourselves they might give us open lodgings.

On the fourth morning after our first breakfast a horn sounded in the distance and everyone stopped eating and conversing and stood up, including Laraar and Idza. We followed suit and watched as Dawnians exited quickly. Idza was particularly pleased, clapping her hands together as she looked at us.

"You are to see something amazing!" She said excitedly. I picked up my plate to empty my leftovers into whatever they considered a garbage disposal, but Laraar put his hand up to me and then to the ground. I assumed he was telling me to leave it, as that's what they did. I obeyed, and with Cessa we once again followed the two of them.

Outside everyone was converging into one line moving outside the village, elder and child alike. I kept pace with them until Cessa grabbed my arm and held me back until we were a few Dawnians away from Laraar and Idza. No one around us wore a translation device.

"We should sneak away from the group now and search for the empyreus," she whispered to me.

"Are you serious?"

"When will we get a better chance than this? The village is emptying out and you know as well as I do that they have access to the empyreus. Did you see how seamless their technology worked?"

"Yes, of course I did, but I am not deceiving these people. We are finally starting to earn their trust. Besides, even you can't be blind to the fact that two humans, or aliens in their eyes walking away from the crowd wouldn't be suspicious. We are going to keep moving with the group."

"Fine then," she said. Somehow she held back calling me a coward, though she had it written over her face. "I'll do it myself," she added. This time I grabbed her arm.

"No! You will not. You are free because I told them to release you and I am responsible for whatever happens between the two of us. You agreed that we do this my way!"

I didn't hear a word from her after that. I let her arm go, though I did look back every few steps to make sure she didn't wander away. I wasn't focused on how far we walked, but I started to tire. When we finally slowed down to a stop, I peered out to the side to see where we were going.

Hundreds, maybe even thousands of Dawnians were entering some sort of pavilion. A wall of tree trunks separated into a wide archway where we entered. More trunks were lying flat on the ground acting as benches where people sat. I noticed all of them were facing a sand ring, just like the one I had been forced to fight in against Grent, except there was a makeshift stage erected at the far side of the ring where a number of other Dawnians already sat.

"Please tell me I don't have to fight again," I said to myself, but Idza heard and laughed.

"*Your place is earned. Now we witness a joining.*"

I wasn't sure what she meant until I took a closer look at the people sitting on the stage. They were all women. Furthermore I saw two rows filled with male Dawnians in front of the ring. I guessed that we were about to witness some sort of mating ritual. How open were these people with each other? How much were we going to see? That's all I could think about as the remaining Dawnians took their seats and quieted down.

Nothing happened for a couple of minutes. Everyone just sat there looking towards the stage. I glanced over towards Idza, but she placed her hand up to her mouth gesturing for me to keep quiet. That's when I heard a beautiful soprano voice coming from the stage. Just one. In the second row to the right, the woman was singing her song towards the men in front of her. I never thought of myself as sentimental, but I was moved by her song, and even felt my eyes grow misty. I felt as if she were intentionally causing me to feel this way, longing for someone, lonely that I was alone. I wanted to stand up and go to her, hold her, and tell her it was alright. Someone beat me to it. A man on the right stood and walked to her, joining in her song. Their voices melded as one and the feelings I had previously stopped. It left me confused for a moment.

The ceremony went on; one by one a woman stood up and sang to the men in front of them. Every single one of them had a different impact on me. One of them made me depressed, only to be healed by their love. Another one embarrassingly aroused me, but each time after the man stood up and joined their woman the moment stopped and I felt like myself again. After nearly two dozen pairings were created, I felt like I had just laughed, cried, sang, fumed, and more all in a matter of minutes. There was so much pressure in my head, but then a gentle hand on my shoulder helped to ease it. Idza was next to me.

"Forgive . . . Male's not of age or already paired do not feel effects. I was unsure how you would react, not of our people," she said reassuringly.

"Apparently I was of age," I said, trying to shake off the dizziness. "That was an amazing ceremony. What do you call it?"

"It is Urar-Viara, you might name . . . Soul Song. Males and females, once of age come together to find Urar-Nika . . . Soul Mate I believe you say . . . Female expresses feelings of want and desire . . . Male answers her call depending on how the song affects them. They are forever bonded." It took Idza some time to tell me this. Her translation was really improving.

"What? No dating or friends with benefits?" Cessa spat out with disdain. Her head was resting on her palms and her eyes drooped. I guess romance wasn't her thing. Then again, I reminded myself who I was talking about.

During the ceremony, one of the songs recalled the fondness I had for space and my ship in particular. I really needed to return to the Belle at some point soon. I guessed that a week had passed since I had left the ship and I didn't know what Al would think of that. Was he waiting for me in stand-by mode? Was he actively using his scanners trying to find me or did the

Dawnian's technology allow them to access the ship? Was it now under their control? I shuddered at the last thought.

"*Daniel,*" Laraar said to me as he stepped around Idza. He was now wearing his translation device. "*Suns . . . moons pass . . . we reveal many things . . . we give you trust . . .*" He stopped as he tried searching for the words, but Idza stepped in.

"*Laraar is right. It is, how you say, your turn to trust us to reveal many things. You will show us your vessel you traveled with and you will tell us why you are here.*"

Looks like I wasn't going to have to wait long to get back to the Belle after all.

TWELVE

We weren't even given a day and night before Cessa and I led the Dawnians to my ship. Laraar and Idza followed us along with two of their companions, Ortu and Druga. None of them talked to me or asked me questions as we made our way back to the Belle, but Cessa was more than willing to speak to me most of the walk.

"Have you noticed anything strange about these aliens?" she whispered to me.

"Like what?"

"While you've been running your mouth over the last few days, I've been watching them and listening. Don't you think it's a little unorthodox how they've acted and treated us?"

I thought about it for a moment and shrugged my shoulders.

"They've treated us well enough, even you can't argue that," I told her.

"That's the point Daniel! They have treated us well, more than well even. When we're not sleeping in our cells they practically treat us like we belong. I wasn't going to complain, but you have to admit how unusual it is that they let you out, and then me as well simply based on conversations and a small skirmish."

I wanted to argue against what she thought of as a small skirmish, but her words were a fuel that kicked my mind into gear. She had a good point. I shuddered at the thought of what scientists on Earth were ordered to do to any invading aliens, no matter what the reason. Aliens would be imprisoned much like us, but then things just got darker from there. Experiments, interrogations, and terrifying medical bullshit would be the least intrusive operations. Only after an intense research and identification process would the alien be allowed to walk freely among us. Even then I was pretty sure that they were watched and surveyed during their stay. If the aliens were deemed a threat, well, I didn't even want to think of what happened next. Our government would just say humanity takes pride and protects its own, but I felt like fear was more the instigator in those types of situations. There was already enough trouble on Earth. The last thing anyone wanted was outside interference.

The Dawnians caged us, sure, but after only speaking to me for a couple of days they decided to let us out and invited us to witness a very intimate ritual. Don't get me wrong, I was grateful and thrilled to have them put their trust in me, but the more and more I thought about it, it didn't make a lot of sense. They released Cessa who had been insanely angry and did her best to intimidate any Dawnian who passed by her. Yet at my word they set her free? And now, we were returning to the Belle and neither of us were tied or cuffed. No guards escorted us. Ortu and Druga were engineers of sorts, interested in studying the ship itself. Did they really trust me so much that I wouldn't take Cessa, flee into my ship, and take off? Did they not care or did they assume we wouldn't leave?

All of these questions ran through my mind as the Belle came into view and my heart leapt out of my chest, like two best friends seeing each other again after a long separation. The Kestrel Belle never looked better. For a moment I did consider running to her and taking off. Ortu and Druga caught up to me as I briskly walked to her, smiling from ear to ear. Cessa backed off, most likely satisfied that she had planted the seed of uncertainty. Both Dawnians sang to me in turns. The two of them had supposedly been doing their own study of human speech, and wore translators similar to Idza.

"*What powers . . . ship?*"

"*Where . . . crew?*"

"*How . . . you reach us?*"

I felt like a ping pong ball as each of them asked question after question, not even allowing me to answer one. I let them get it out of their system as we walked up to the starboard side of the Belle and then to the cargo bay door. I input my code and the sound and motion of the door dropping brought another smile to my face. Nothing had been messed with as I took an assessment of the bay. Cessa's cargo was still here, but a grimace on her face told me something wasn't quite right.

"Where's my box?" Cessa exclaimed. Her outburst confused me until I recalled she did have a box she carried outside when we landed. The box was the only thing missing.

"*Safe . . . Rest assured,*" Idza said, and the look Cessa gave her put all other looks I've seen her give to shame. Her eyebrows dug into her wide eyes and her mouth was a hard frown.

"I want it back," she said, gritting her teeth together. Idza smiled and nodded. Was that a yes? I had no idea, but everyone besides my human counterpart turned to me as if saying, 'Your turn to talk'.

I didn't see what choice I had and I didn't think anything bad would come of giving the Dawnians information on my ship and our race, so I told them what I could. Humans started to explore the stars over twenty years ago. Our ships were powered by what was known as a fusion reactor, which produced an energy output greater than a nuclear blast. Unfortunately neither of my engine cores were powered by renewable energy. Depending on the type of ship you traveled on, you would need to dock at a space station or refueling platform every six months to a year. Of course the more you used slingspace, the quicker the fuel depleted. The Belle, for an old ship, was very conservative with her energy because she was small and nimble.

The Dawnians understood some of the things I talked about, but others required a little more explaining. Things like different factions, multiple starship classes, and operating certain stations of the ship were some of the topics I had to elaborate on. All four Dawnians were entranced by what I was saying. They stood so still, like statues, as I told them things I felt could be comfortably discussed. When Ortu again asked about a crew for the ship, I broke eye contact and shrugged.

"I don't feel like I can bear the responsibility for the safety of others. I kind of have a bad luck complex. Bad things happen around me."

"No kidding," Cessa muttered. I rolled my eyes at her.

If only, I thought.

A flashing light near the bay door latch caught my eye. Everyone turned to look at it.

"Proximity alarm," I said to them. "I have to go to the bridge to deactivate it, otherwise it will consider us intruders."

Al you genius, I missed you too.

"*Proceed . . . allow an escort?*" Idza asked me. I would have preferred to go myself so I could vocally communicate with Al, but the request didn't surprise me. I agreed and climbed to the main corridor with Druga behind me. When we got to the bridge he spent most of his time looking at screens and controls. His expression was vague, but if I made a guess I would say his interest in the ship dropped substantially as he looked over the specifications that were available to him.

I took this time to key into the main screen in front of my chair and typed a message to Al.

- AL, I MISSED YOU BUDDY. EVERYTHING OKAY HERE? I asked him.

- SYSTEMS ALL OPERATIONAL SIR. NATIVES HOSTILE?

- NEGATIVE. I'M SORRY I HAVEN'T BEEN IN TOUCH, BUT I NEED YOU TO STAY ACTIVE. I WANT THE SHIP TO BE READY, THOUGH I CAN'T SAY FOR WHAT. THE LONGER WE'RE HERE THE MORE I FEEL SOMETHING IS OFF, I told him.

- ORDERS UNDERSTOOD.

I waited as Druga finished his analysis of my bridge. He didn't study the computer systems as much as I thought he would have, which was a relief to me.

"*Weapon capabilities . . . vessel?*" He asked me.

"Two plasma lasers at the bow and a missile tube stern," I told him, and then had to explain the terms bow and stern to him. I tried to explain the humor of the designer when placing the weapon ports, but Druga didn't seem to get it, or maybe it wasn't as funny as I thought it was.

Druga finished with his study and we walked back toward the bay. He seemed genuinely disinterested as I gave him a small tour of the ship on our way back. The rest of the gang was still in the bay waiting for us. Druga sang something to the others which didn't translate and the three other Dawnians all nodded to him.

"*Daniel,*" Laraar said to me. "*Tell us . . . your reason . . . why here?*"

I thought about how I would approach it. I looked at Cessa, but she turned from me, clearly not interested in being a part of the conversation. I wasn't sure how they would react or even understand what I was going to tell them.

"We came here for what we call empyreus . . . it is a great power source. After much research we discovered that it exists on your world. We came here to see if that was true."

"*And take it?*" Idza asked. How honest should I be with her? It wasn't exactly an easy answer. I could have said anything from 'yes' to 'only because a powerful madman wants it for his own personal gain', but with Cessa here and still dangerous in my eyes I chose something a little less descriptive.

"My mission is to find the empyreus and if possible, retrieve it. If you know what I speak of, I want you to understand I am not trying to deceive you in any way. I have no interest in taking it from you, but instead I wish to negotiate a deal that will allow us to mutually benefit both of our people."

I waited as they stood there listening to me, then looked to each other and conversed in their native song. I heard notes of varying degrees, some minor, some melodic. There were soft sounds and loud ones. They knew exactly what I was talking about, but unfortunately I couldn't read their facial expressions. If anything I noticed some disagreement between Druga and Laraar, but I based that off the intensity in their eyes and their quick songs back and forth.

As I was about to sit down, my feet still sore from the trek to the ship, Laraar moved forward and waved his hand toward me.

"*Follow me,*" he said, then looked at Cessa and said, "*She stays*".

"I don't trust these people with my equipment anyway. You go. Don't screw anything up."

I rolled my eyes at her and left the ship with Laraar, hoping Al would keep an eye on things. The two of us walked about thirty degrees left of the trail back to their settlement. In the distance I saw movement, a lot of it. About 45 meters in front of us, a group of large animals traveled in a pack. I jogged closer to get a better look. Their skin was a light brown and from here looked somewhat leathery. I wasn't sure if they had hoofs or paws, but the ends of their legs were covered in a black fur.

Horns protruded from their jaw bones, and they slightly resembled a hippopotamus in the facial area.

Laraar startled me from behind as he let out a loud siren call and I watched in awe as the lead animal raised his head and responded in a similar sound. None of the beasts seemed to be bothered by our presence as we closed in on them. They simply continued to graze.

"Unbelievable," I muttered. "Can you understand them? Talk to them?"

"*Understanding . . . very simple,*" he responded.

I kept my eyes out for additional animals as we continued across the field and entered a forest that looked similar to the one by our camp, but little variations told me it wasn't the same one. I heard chirps and cricket type sounds, but couldn't see anything. I tried activating my eye, but the pain was too difficult to bear. Whatever had numbed it the previous day had apparently subsided, so I shut it down and simply enjoyed the music and sounds of the forest.

I wish I had gotten a chance to look at the landscape from the air, but at the time I was too focused on landing. The environment was very repetitious. We either walked through a busy forest or over a wide open field. I assumed Earth was at one point very similar, but on our planet there were numerous mountains, rivers and deserts. I had only ventured a short distance on this planet, but even far off in the distance all I had seen so far were either open fields or busy trees surrounding me.

Laraar hadn't spoken since we saw the animals which he called 'Irinx'. I was curious as to what he thought of my ship, of Cessa and me, but he didn't seem interested in sharing anything. In a way it upset me. I felt like the two of us were bonding after we first met, but then he downgraded himself to an observer while Idza took over for all the translating. Maybe he needed someone to talk to him.

"What did you think of my ship?" I asked him.

"*Adequate.*" Coming from him I took it as a compliment. He could've said 'sucked'.

"None of you seemed surprised by it. Even when Druga overlooked the consoles on my bridge he didn't seem terribly interested in what he was seeing. If anything, he just wanted to know the tactical capabilities of the ship."

"*Star . . . travel, not unknown to us,*" He said, and completely threw a figurative curveball at me. I almost tripped over my own foot when he said that.

"Your people have traveled through the stars? I didn't see any ships. Do you have many? What are they like?" I bombarded him with questions much like the engineers did to me.

"*Travel no longer . . . it is . . . unnecessary.*"

"But why?" I asked him.

"*Everything we need . . . right here,*" he responded.

That was the end of the conversation concerning space travel and it irritated me. There was so much about these people that I didn't know. In some ways they reminded me of humans, but in other areas not so much. They were easily as advanced as us if not more so. They were curious, but it never lasted very long. A question here or a comment there and that was the end of it. They were too easily satisfied.

We never left the forest, but kept walking for what felt like a lifetime. My feet were beginning to get sore when we arrived at a mountain side within the forest itself. At the base of the mountain I spotted an opening which led into a deep cavern. Inside was a soft golden glow, not unlike the color of the sun in this star system. I thought it was fire at first. Maybe this was an active volcano or something due to the comfortable heat the mouth of the cave was giving off. The two of us entered.

The walls were lined with crystal like structures protruding from the walls. I heard myself gasp at the sight. I couldn't even begin to count them, there were so many. The glow came from afar and reflected so brightly I had to put my hand up in front of my eyes. The other hand I used to touch the crystal structures themselves. Neither warm nor cold, they were hard as rock and smooth as marble. As Laraar walked farther ahead than me, I could see a warped version of him through the crystals, which were transparent as glass.

The cave tunnel was a little difficult to navigate, as the crystals were various shapes and sizes. Some ended in a point, while others were square shaped. They led us to a wide open cavern that was completely covered with them, but as amazing as they were, that wasn't the most amazing sight I found there. On the hard surface were machines, conveyer belts, smelting stations, and other devices that I couldn't really label.

The entire system was automated as there were no other Dawnians in the cavern with us. Two automatic hands reached out to the mountain and cut the crystal with some type of beam attached to the fingers. Then they placed the broken piece on the belt which led to the smelting station. Once the crystal was melted or processed, it was simply dumped into a stream of gold that flowed out the other side. I walked up to the stream and took a closer look.

The golden liquid was littered with streaks of blue, like small diamonds floating in the stream. Each blue diamond left a trail behind it. I finally decided to activate my bionic eye, grunting a bit at the pain. The sight of the stream completely blinded my optic adapter for a moment and I fell back onto my ass.

Laraar just stood next to me watching. I sat still for a moment clutching my head as my eye reset and once again activated. I tried to keep from looking directly into the stream, but it seemed to adapt to the overload and filtered out some of the brightness. Scanning the area told me 68,503 crystal structures grew in this cavern alone. The machines were made of an unknown metal, though it did recognize a small concentration of iron, just like the probe in space. I took one more look at the stream, moving slowly over it to prevent another overload and the power readings were completely off the charts.

"Empyreus," I whispered.

"*Yes . . . power . . . life,*" Laraar said to me.

Something else in the cavern caught my eye. A large sphere of metal covered with antennas sat at the far end on the opposite side of the cavern. My readings displayed the metal as human in origin, specifically an ESA model.

The ESA probe . . . the one Al discovered . . . that led us here.

I ran over and studied it. There was definitely some damage, but it was still intact. I remember Al telling me how it was still

105

sending back readings, but they were erratic most likely because of tampering. Then I fit the pieces together.

"That's how you can translate . . . you used parts from this probe to build your translator didn't you?" I wondered how the hell they managed to learn to translate human language so easily. They must have been able to access files on the probe itself!

Laraar nodded.

"*Always good . . . to be prepared. Come friend,*" he said as he led me back along the path of the stream. He took us through another tunnel with the same obstacles as before. When we emerged into the open, my heart stopped, my hands and jaw dropped as far as they were allowed. There was no forest or field, but a giant lake of empyreus, fed by the mountain and its processors.

The lake was illuminating the night sky with its golden glow. I wanted to pinch myself as if it were some kind of dream. Laraar told me that the lake itself was the one and only method of harnessing the empyreus. After the processing device in the cave melted the crystal, the stream of golden power flowed out to the lake to be collected and transported back to the village. They used empyreus for everything in their daily lives.

Truth be told, this lake was so big that every single Dawnian living in the village could fit in it at the same time. Hell, I could even land the Kestrel Belle in it. I could only imagine the kind of power my ship would absorb from coming in contact with the lake.

"*You . . . first outside to witness,*" he sung softly to me.

My bionic eye was figuratively in a bad mood, giving me a small headache. After making more discomforting noises, Laraar grabbed my arm and led me down to the . . . I guess, empyreus shore line. I wanted to ask so many questions but my mind was blanking out on everything except one detail.

Despite being sent here against my will, I made first contact with an alien race, earned their trust, and was the first human to lay eyes on the supposedly mythical energy source we call empyreus. The last five years of my life had been less than ideal. I had a ship, which was great, but to keep her afloat and live my life, I needed work. I took what jobs I could and put my name out for every opportunity that presented itself to me using the Starcade. Mercenary life was a lot harder than I thought it would be. Most of the jobs I took were either accomplished unsatisfactorily or required violent means of action, which I wasn't willing to do. As the years passed, my name and reputation cascaded into nothing. Now no one could deny what I accomplished. I wouldn't deny that I had help. Al, and in her own way Cessa, helped me get here.

I was speechless, shocked and excited all at the same time. I stood in front of what was most likely the most powerful energy source in the galaxy, possibly the universe.

"Why is this so powerful?" I asked Laraar. There was a slight strain in my voice as each sound only hurt my head more. I was about to shut down my eye when Laraar stopped me.

"*Stop . . . remain active . . .*"

He knew about my eye, which I suppose wasn't a huge shock. With their technological prowess I knew there was a chance they could discover it. Laraar knelt down and placed his hand directly over the liquid. I moved to stop him, thinking it was something dangerous like fire or lava, but he thrust his hand in and . . . nothing. He turned to look at me and smiled.

"*Daniel . . . Try,*" he said to me, nodding toward the empyreus.

Kneeling down, I couldn't help but take a couple of deep breaths. I was nervous. I reached out toward the warm golden liquid, my hand trembling. Before I could psych myself out, I plunged it in just like Laraar did. The best way I could describe it would be like inserting your entire hand into pudding slightly above room temperature. The texture was thick, but I could easily move my hands through it. Oddly enough, the longer I held my hand in the better I felt, physically and mentally. Aches and pains that nagged at me dissipated and even my headache lessened some. I shrugged it off, thinking maybe the relief of stress was the reason. That's when Laraar removed his hand, cupping the empyreus in it. He took a step closer to me and put his other hand around the back of my head, gently pulling on my hair so I was looking up.

"Laraar, what are you doing?" I asked him, struggling to free myself.

"*Stop . . .*" He said in a calm, soothing voice. He brought his hand up over my head, specifically near my eyes. I closed them shut, but he insisted I open my bionic eye. I refused at first, but then he said something to me.

"*Daniel . . . I trust you . . . Trust me . . .*" The moment I opened my eye, he let a drop of empyreus fall into it.

I flailed around, backing away from him. The sensation was a mixture of intense burning and pinching all around my optic receptor.

"What the flux?" I cursed, then cursed some more, but as I tried to wipe the liquid away from my eye, I found that it had completely absorbed into my skin. My eye twitched as the burn receded into an itch.

I couldn't tell you how long it lasted. I felt like it was hours, when in fact it was probably closer to a minute. When the feelings subsided, the results were . . . impossible at the time to convey.

I felt amazing. The fatigue and strain in my body from traveling were gone. The pain in my head ceased to exist. My bionic eye was functioning at full capacity and everything I looked at was in a high definition of clarity. I shut the eye off. No pain. I turned it back on. No pain. I even knocked on my head a couple times with a closed fist, but there was no irritation or pain whatsoever. I could almost feel Laraar beside me and I could sense other life forms far beyond us. The empyreus was more than energy and power. It had the capability to induce biological organisms with healing properties and enhance their senses.

"What the hell just happened?" I asked.

"*Sorania,*" he said. "*That is name . . . to us. Sorania. It . . . powers us all . . . machine . . . every living thing that contacts it. Every machine it powers . . . strong . . . connected. Your eye . . . machine . . . now you.*"

"What do you mean, now the eye is me?" I looked around more, closing my left eye and focusing with my right. Sure enough, even though the eye still scanned my surroundings and reported statistics to me, it felt just like a real eye, the same as my other. "Are you telling me that this liquid fused my mechanical eye with my biological body?"

He nodded.

Things started to fall into place, whether it was due to the empyreus in my system or my brain just putting everything together. Not only did I feel healthy and invincible, but I also felt unbelievably relaxed, like I didn't have a worry in the world. Time itself didn't even matter. Why would it? With the empyreus I had everything I would ever need.

I thought back to when I used my eye against Grent, the food and drink I ingested, then my injuries afterwards, which were healed with the medicine. The Dawnians even infused their food with it.

The possibilities, the potential of being able to harness empyreus for almost anything was worth more than . . . well, it was priceless. You couldn't put a price on something that was compatible with man and machine alike. I could also imagine the various ways that something like this could be used for evil, for lack of a better term. Raymond Erebos could use it to turn the entire galaxy upside down, lead into a new era where he was the ultimate power. Then I remembered my original intel came from the ESA Echelon and specifically Sarah King. If she got her hands on it, no one would be able to stop her.

Unfortunately, the time for revelation was short lived as my gut suddenly told me something wasn't right. The hairs on the back of my neck stood up on end, similar to the same feeling I get when someone is watching me from afar. I turned toward the opening of the cave and I couldn't see anyone, but my bionic eye easily detected a third set of footprints at the mouth. I ran up to it and zoomed in for a closer look. There was one set of Dawnian footprints and two sets of human boot prints, one noticeably smaller than the other.

"Flux! Cessa!" I muttered as I ran back into the cave, my guard up and ready. Maybe I was delusional, but I thought I moved quicker than before. I put on the brakes as my eye revealed something terrible.

"*Daniel?*" Laraar called out as he ran up to me. I was looking down at the ground, right next to the processed stream that led out to the lake. The smaller set of footprints turned towards it, then the right foot dragged back, followed by a small indent in the ground. Her knee. I imagined Cessa somehow managed to follow us here. With all the cargo on the ship it wasn't hard to assume she brought a collection device of some kind with her. She went to the opening leading to the lake, and made sure we were engaged in discussion, possibly while Laraar was giving me the empyreus. She ran back to this spot, dropped to her knee and collected some of it. Flux.

"We have to get back to my ship now. Cessa has the empyreus."

We ran the entire length back to my ship. I hoped that with my increased speed I would catch up with Cessa, but I didn't. That either meant she used it on herself or she wasn't heading back to my ship. Either way that's the first place I had to check. How the hell had she escaped from Ortu, Druga, and Idza? Somehow she got away and possibly with some type of collection device. I had no doubt she had the empyreus, but why? What was she going to gain by taking it from behind my back? It just didn't make sense.

I wasn't breathing hard or perspiring during our run back, which was impressive, but didn't matter once we returned to the Belle. When we reached the bay door Laraar let out a howling cry of despair. Ortu and Druga were dead from multiple slash wounds. How the hell was that possible? Cessa didn't have her sword! I looked away before the scene could cause an invasion of disturbing memories into my brain, but strangely enough I felt calm. That was odd and I knew right away the feeling wasn't natural. As Laraar sobbed over his fallen friends I realized that empyreus didn't just enhance my physical abilities, but my mental ones as well. It affected me like a calming agent, keeping my head level and unresponsive to the carnage around me. Suddenly I understood why the Dawnians chose to trust me so easily.

I tried to focus on the anger and betrayal I felt towards the woman I brought here, the one I released from her prison. After all the hurtful words and actions, I thought she had finally opened up to me and cracked her shell of ice, but it was all for show. Thinking about this over and over built a strong sense of frustration and annoyance. I wanted to find Cessa and make her pay for this crime. So where was she? Al wouldn't have let her take the ship. She didn't seem to be here anyway. That's when I noticed that over half of Cessa's cargo boxes were missing. Something wasn't right here. Looking around the room, I saw things that weren't there before, specifically scratches and marks along the bulkhead next to Ortu and Druga. I scanned them and found the marks on them and the wall were a match, almost like the clawing from an animal. I needed information.

"Al, what the hell happened here?" Nothing. "Al? Al! Say something."

The damn passenger protocol. I never turned it off. I cursed myself and the empyreus running through my veins for not thinking of that earlier.

"Al, disengage passenger protocol on my voice authorization and tell me what the flux is going on!" The speakers squealed and grumbled with static, then finally Al was with us.

"Sir, I am here. Attack alert red, sir. The passenger attacked the two natives shortly after you left. She appeared to be looking over her cargo, then opened the boxes which contained the mechanical devices. When she activated them, the cube shaped machines morphed their structure until they appeared to be animalistic. They attacked the two natives as she commanded. The third native ran away as the others were being slaughtered. Afterwards your passenger ran in the direction you left with her five canine machines.

"Automated mechanical devices shaped like canines. So you're telling me she has robotic guard dogs that can kill."

"Affirmative sir."

Both of my hands were clutching onto my hair, ready to pull it out. That's why she wanted the empyreus. She now had a number of super-charged robotic animals.

"Has she returned to the ship?"

"Negative sir, though she passed into my sensor range minutes before you returned."

I turned to Laraar, who seemed oblivious to everything that was going on, including me talking to an ominous voice in my ship. I grabbed the cloth on his shoulders and pulled him up to me.

"Can you read a map? Can you understand an overhead view of your land and surroundings?" He thought over the words for a moment and nodded. I dragged him up to the bridge with me and pushed him into the chair by my tactical station.

"Al, bring up a map and coordinates of known location of Cessa and her robotic creatures."

A blip on the radar changed and suddenly an overhead view of the surrounding area was placed on the screen. Trees, grass, and mountains were etched out as the signal closed in on Cessa's location. I had a terrible feeling I already knew where she was going. When the signal stopped, my suspicion was confirmed. Laraar's shoulders hunched down.

"*Village,*" was all he said. I buckled him in and jumped into my seat.

"Al, set course for her location and take us directly in." The journey from the village to the ship was about two hours, and even running there wouldn't save much time. "See that my weapon is fully charged and ready for deployment."

"May I inquire what you are going to do sir?"

"I'm going hunting. Top speed to the village, now!"

THIRTEEN

The trip took us minutes, but the horror taking place in the village could be seen from the sky as soon as we took off toward it. My blood was boiling, and I could only sit there and hope that there weren't too many casualties. This was all my fault. All I could think over and over again was how this was all my fault.

"Al, land directly outside the village. We don't want to crush any buildings."

"Acknowledged."

The ship landed softly and I turned to Laraar.

"Let's go!"

He didn't move, didn't make a sound, but just sat there staring down at the floor. The Dawnians outside didn't have time for me to shake some sense into him so I left the door open and ran to my quarters. Inside the locker my assault rifle was fully charged. I was never a huge fan of guns because of their ability to easily kill, but I was able to modify mine to shoot out a variety of projectiles, including electro-magnetic pulse rounds, stun rounds, and yes, I did keep the lethal plasma rounds active as well. I didn't ever want to use it, but there's always a chance that my life could depend on it.

"Al," I said, about to open the door. "I need to know what I'm up against. What can you tell me?"

"There are five of the devices moving throughout the village sir. Their energy output has somehow increased dramatically."

I figured as much. Unfortunately I had no idea of the effects empyreus would have on machines. I hadn't gotten a chance to examine the Dawnian computer consoles throughout the village. One could guess that their armor would be a lot stronger and their movement a lot quicker.

"Captain, sensors are detecting a signal emanating from the center of the village. Some of the equipment matches components that were carried on this ship. I believe she is creating a communication device of some kind, judging by the wavelength and type of signal."

The box Cessa was looking for . . . oh flux, I thought.

"She's calling Erebos . . . son of a bitch. She's going to

bring the bastard here! Can she do it?" I asked Al quickly.

"If I take the percentage of power that was raised after the machines were infused with empyreus and apply that to the communication console . . ." Al cut out a moment to process the equations. "Sir, the passenger will have enough power to contact anyone in the galaxy."

"Well, flux . . . I'm going to try and stop her and not get killed in the process. Lock and restrict all ship operations. Understood?"

"Yes sir, good luck."

I threw down the lever and the bay doors opened to terrible, screeching sounds. I brought my rifle up, held it against my shoulder and moved forward into the village. To my left a 'dog' was inside one of the houses tearing it apart and I heard someone singing a shrieking cry. I ran to the entrance, checking my flank and caught sight of a couple of bodies on the ground. I would have to check on them later, my first priority being to protect those that were still alive and in danger.

A section of the home's wall was completely torn out and I saw movement inside. My eye scanned the body and a holographic image appeared in my sight. The dog was four feet tall and long, sharp blades extended from his paws. There wasn't much of a face, just a cone shaped head with a signal responder, which was probably the way Cessa was controlling them. There was a chance that simply disconnecting the head from the body would deactivate it, but at the same time if they were doused with empyreus, then most likely their bodies would go on an uncontrollable rampage. My best bet was to find Cessa and force her to power down the robots remotely.

I ran to the front of the house to try and take the dog by surprise. When I stepped up into the home it was tearing at a barricade of furniture, which the trapped Dawnian must have made to defend him or herself. Smart. I turned off the safety, activated the EMP and looked down the sight. My bionic eye targeted the dog and I pulled the trigger. A flurry of bullets hit the target, with a few flying above him as my gun recoiled. I watched as the bullets caused an electrical discharge throughout the dog's systems. Its body shuddered and dropped to the ground . . . then stood back up and turned to me.

Shit.

I unloaded more ammunition into the damn machine and again, after a momentary fluctuation it completely recovered. The only other choice was to use plasma rounds on it so I switched over, but not before the dog leapt right at me. If I wasn't wearing my armored suit my ribs would have been crushed as it landed on me. Instead, I just got the wind knocked out of me, which was still a problem. As I tried to inhale oxygen I saw a large multi-bladed paw about to slice through my face. Then I realized my gun was pointing right at the dog's midsection and I opened fire. It jumped off me, the plasma barely scratching the surface. I quickly sat up and unloaded countless rounds into it, screaming curses at the machine. I watched as many of the blasts dented the frame of the beast, but finally as the plasma's charge ran low, a few of them punched through its head and neck. The dog keeled over.

I took a moment to lean over and breathe. If I had that much trouble with one, how would I deal with four more? I doubt they were all conveniently separated and distracted.

"You're okay! Stay there and you'll be safe!" I screamed toward the barricade and the Dawnian behind it. I knew there was little to no chance they would understand me, but I thought maybe just hearing a voice instead of the clawing and scratching of the machine would put them at ease.

I ran outside and toward the center of town. Bodies lay in the streets and I tried my best to let them be for now, but with my eye now working without pain or irritation, it could pretty much scan over anything it wanted, and it analyzed the wounds on the lifeless people, stabbing wounds from the blades on the mechanical beasts.

Suddenly I was thrust back into that dark room, the blood on the floor, and the girl on the bed, stabbed to death, her lifeless eyes staring right at me.

"No, no, no . . . not now!" I shut my eyes. When I opened them I was on the village street. I tried shutting my eye off, but it wouldn't disengage, so I ran as fast as I could past all the bodies. Sounds of commotion came from one of the other housing areas, and as much as I tried to convince myself to keep moving, I stopped to take a closer look. A group of Dawnians,

Chorta, Grent, and Horku, were fending off two of the machines. They were impressive. More than once the dogs attacked and intended to kill, but Chorta and his companions threw punches, kicks, and used a means of strength I didn't realize they could summon. Even with my suit a physical attack would have hurt me more than the dogs.

I tried convincing myself they had things under control, but the battle was currently a stalemate and the problem was that the Dawnians would eventually tire out and the machines wouldn't. Plus, if these dogs were advanced enough, they could most likely analyze and adapt to the Dawnians fighting style. The three of them deflected attack after attack, and followed with a couple of their own, but couldn't penetrate the dog's armor. I hustled to join them, but skidded to a halt when a thick sheet of glass dropped right in front of me. When I tried to turn around, I was back in my cell onboard the Echelon, my clothes and hands covered in blood. Commander King stared down at me.

"You murdered a member of my crew, Daniel," she said to me, her mouth turned in a twisted frown.

"No, I couldn't have, I wouldn't!" I screamed back at her, but then quickly realized that this was another hallucination.

"Get out of my damn head bitch!"

The sound of a wailing siren pulled me back into the now and I looked up to see Chorta lunging at me with his staff. I quickly sidestepped but the end of his weapon grazed against my shoulder, leaving a burning sensation that hurt like hell.

"Chorta! Stop! I'm here to help!" He didn't have a translator attached to him. Even if he did I wondered if he would listen. His arms moved fast, changing direction from the first swing and coming back for a follow up attack. With my suit and eye operating at full capacity I was able to jump over it, but Chorta bested me in agility even with my advantages. His motions were so smooth I didn't notice them until a second too late. As he missed with his swing, he jammed the end of the staff in the ground behind him and vaulted towards me, extending his leg, and kicking me square in the chest.

I hit the ground and instead of focusing on Chorta I caught sight of his two companions who were ignoring us and focusing on the dogs. Grent was mercilessly pounding his weapon into the back frame of the machine, but as I feared each swing was slower and slower, until finally when he brought up his staff for another strike, the dog simply threw its leg out and pierced his flesh in three places. He was dead before he hit the ground.

Chorta was suddenly in view, throwing his own staff down at my face. I craned my neck sideways before he could leave a permanent mark, but my frustration with him was close to skyrocketing.

"Chorta listen to me! Your people are being slaughtered! Let me help!"

All I could see was his bared teeth. All I could hear was his exhilarated breath, and the smell. Blood, a scent so familiar I couldn't help but walk into my room after a long shift, only to find her in my bed staring up at me, her spring dress stained with her blood. Her stomach was violated by multiple stab wounds. Her death was my fault, just like the attack on this village. No matter where I went, blood followed, and it was never my own.

Shake it off damn it! Get your head together or your blood will be covering Chorta's staff!

I raised my gun toward Chorta, and his widened. He knew my discharge would be faster than his swing. He was as good as dead, or he would have been if I was actually aiming at him. My sight locked on the dog that advanced behind him and I shot one blast. It knocked the dog off balance and caused Chorta to move to the side and turn around. This gave me a wide open view of my enemy, and again I unloaded into the metallic bastard until my plasma bank ran empty.

"Like I said, I'm here to help." I bowed to him, trying to express my submission. He didn't thank me, nor did he continue to try and kill me, but grimaced and turned towards the other dog. With him and Horku together and only one target to concentrate on, I saw them meld into a melody of attacks, striking limbs and pressure points where the armor would be at its weakest. In the end, they managed to smash all the joints, leaving a headless and limbless body. Each Dawnian chose a part flailing on the ground and smashed into it over and over again. I left them knowing they would be okay.

Three dogs were down and two more to go. Now if only I could find a way to keep past images from flooding my mind, I might stay alive. The assault by Chorta left my direction to the town center askew so I got my bearings and leapt into a sprint.

The closer I got to the center, the more bodies I found. Some were still moving, so I held hope that there were survivors, but Cessa was capable of terrible things. To be honest I wasn't sure what I was going to do with her. The time for intimidation was over. She scared the shit out of me when I met her. Her cold, seductive tone and disregard for life made her someone to keep an eye on when my back was turned. Her mistake was betraying me and playing me for a fool. I have a habit of getting pissed off when people do that to me.

I saw the large computer console towering in front of me before anything else. Pressing my teeth together and using my adrenaline to give myself one final push, I rushed the site with my gun armed and ready to fire. For now, stun rounds would have to suffice. My plan involved aiming for Cessa and taking her down with a stun round before she even noticed me. After that I could try and find the deactivation switch for the remaining dogs. The damn things were strong and lethal and most of the people here didn't have the prowess for combat like Chorta and his men. I also prepared myself for the possibility that there was one dog guarding her.

I was wrong. Two remaining dogs stood a meter away from her on each side. Cessa was intensely focused on the control panel. I aimed down my sight and fired a stun round before I finished taking a breath. The bullet flew through the air in her direction. If she went down before the dogs realized what was happening there was a slim chance I could get by them. Instead Cessa, having found her sword at some point during the attack, swung the blade and, I shit you not, cut the bullet in two.

"You've got to be fluxing kidding me," I cursed to myself. I readied my gun to shoot again, but my window for opportunity closed and the last two vicious dogs were on route to kill me per her command. Naturally I did what any Captain of a cruiser would do in a situation like this.

I ran like hell.

Please don't judge, it's just that I didn't care to be sliced and diced by a couple of machines. That just didn't seem right after everything I went through. I couldn't run as fast as them, that much I knew, but it gave me enough time to switch my rounds to EMP. I looked back in my peripherals and had one in my sight. I turned, aimed, fired.

Nothing. The gun was jammed.

I didn't even get a chance to curse at the damn thing. I had all of one second to pull the trigger before they were on me and my time was up. Assuming they would jump at me, I dropped to the ground, and sure enough one sailed right over me, but only one. The other had waited. As soon as I was on my back it launched itself at me, the blades of its paws extended and ready to run me through. Rolling out of the way wasn't an option at this point.

Laraar came out of nowhere and tackled the dog before it could finish me. He grappled with it, throwing punch after punch to various parts of its structure. All the impacts should have broken his hand, but surprisingly they didn't. I attributed this to my lack of knowledge where Dawnian biology was concerned. He threw his leg forward and kicked the machine in its midsection, sending it flying away from him.

"*Finish,*" he said, pointing to the machine which was already starting to recover. I was about to answer him when I saw the first dog running towards him from behind, and pushed him out of the way just in time. I tried firing my EMP rounds again. Still jammed.

"It's not working!" I yelled at him.

He thought about it for a moment, and then sang out "*Sorania . . . empyreus! Find!*"

Of course! The liquid would enhance my weapon the same as it enhanced the machines Cessa was using. Now I just had to find some. I suspected the few houses in the area held some supply of the fuel. I just had to get past the animals to reach them, but that would leave Laraar facing off against two of them. Unless he was some secret martial arts master, he would die. I wouldn't allow that.

"Can you handle one of them?" I pointed toward the dogs. He did well in his first round, but like Chorta and his men, Laraar would tire out over time. He nodded to me, his eyes completely locked with his opponent, knees bent and arms at the ready. I didn't waste any more time and took off towards the first house. I turned to see if one of the dogs was following me and sure enough, one was. I had hoped their mechanical minds would think in mathematical terms and balance the ratio one to one.

I jumped into the house's opening and threw every furniture item I could find in the path of the dog including chairs, tables, and cupboards. There wasn't nearly enough crap to block the enemy's path, but with any luck it would slow it down some. This house was equipped with a main area and three separate rooms. I had only searched one of the three rooms in the house when I heard the dog slashing at the debris. Chairs and a cushioned mat inside the room suggested this was their sleeping area. There was no way of checking the other rooms without being spotted by the dog, so I did my best impersonation of an action hero and leapt through an open window I took notice of. Since I wasn't an action hero, I bumped my right elbow, both of my knees and fell right onto my face. I was not graceful.

From this angle I couldn't see Laraar or his progress in keeping the other machine busy. I had little time before my pursuer realized I wasn't in the house, so I ran full speed to the next one. Their pantry had food in it and I was fairly sure that empyreus was used as an ingredient in their food recipes, but I didn't think rubbing my gun with food would do the trick. I ran to the middle room, which turned out to be their version of a washroom. I cursed and almost ran to the third room, until I realized they didn't utilize water the way we did. I turned and took stock of everything. There was a large round bowl I assumed was a tub, but there were no faucets. A chair, some linen, and other various hygienic items were placed next to the bowl. This didn't make any sense. If this was a bathroom for them surely there would be some way of washing or lathering.

I leaned over the bowl and took a deep breath. That's when my bionic eye picked up irregularities from the bowl's floor. I jumped in and placed my hand on the ground, feeling the smooth texture. Knocking on various parts of the floor, there was a small round hollow spot, but I couldn't open it. I turned my gun around and hammered it down over and over, cracking the marble or granite, whatever the hell the material was. When I broke through, I picked out the pieces to find the rich, amazing

120

glow of the empyreus below me. I almost cried out in joy, but thought better of it. The last thing I needed was to give away my damn position. Besides, the smashing noises I made were probably more than enough.

Not entirely sure of what to do, I mimicked Laraar's movements when he fused the energy into my eye. I took off my glove and dipped my hand in the warm liquid, cupping a small amount and sprinkling it over the entirety of the weapon. I waited, though I wasn't sure for what.

There was a crashing noise from outside and I knew there were only seconds to spare. Not knowing exactly if my weapon had accepted the fuel or not, I switched to my plasma rounds and stood in the opening arch of the washroom, weapon at the ready. In the far distance my eye picked up various Dawnians recovering and running away. Suddenly a terrifying thought occurred to me. What if the dog turned its attention to someone else? Shit. Once again, running for my life may have cost someone else theirs.

My fears were put to rest when the wall behind me was smashed in by the mechanical beast. Pieces of wood hit me and before I could recover, one of the blades stabbed me in the shoulder. I cried out in pain and gritted my teeth together so hard I thought they would break. With adrenaline and empyreus running through my veins, I one handedly brought the gun up to the dogs face.

"Flux you, you piece of shit!"

I pulled the trigger and with a great *BOOM* and recoil the entire top half of the dog was blown away in a flash of intense green plasma. The recoil threw my arm backwards in an awkward position, nearly dislocating it. I was really going to have to brace myself for any additional shots. I allowed myself twenty seconds of leaning against the wall and catching my breath. My shoulder was bleeding, but it was manageable. The wound didn't seem too serious and it only punctured the front side. I could have gone back for empyreus to heal it, but my seconds were up. I had to make sure Laraar was safe and if it wasn't too late, I needed to shut down that communication station.

I ran outside the house and found myself limping slightly.

My ankle must have gotten twisted during the fight. My ankle and shoulder fought each other over which was going to hurt the worst, but I was too focused to pick a winner. I ran behind the houses into the next lot which was a part of the main hub of the village. I saw Laraar still standing, pulling a number of impressive moves against the dog. He wasn't being overly offensive, just keeping its attention and trying to stay clear of its claws. He wasn't entirely successful, as I saw multiple cuts and blood. To my left, Cessa wasn't at the communications station and as much as I wanted to help Laraar, I had to check her progress.

This was the first time I had a chance to look at the alien controls and keys. Two screens transmitted something, but I couldn't make out the symbols or dials. Cessa's equipment was attached to it though, and whatever she brought with her was adequate enough to transmit her script and orders to the alien computer. I searched through the boxes and adapters she hooked up, and finally found a small touch screen display.

The display read, 'Transmission Complete'. I was too late.

"No!" I shouted, and ripped all the attachments from the main console. Sparks and electric discharges ignited in front of me.

"Sorry you missed the show," a woman said behind me. I turned to see Cessa standing over a Dawnian, her foot on his chest. He looked like one of Chorta's companions. I stared into Cessa's eyes, my own shedding a tear for the damage done and lives lost.

"Cessa . . . Why? Why did you do this? . . . All the people . . . you killed them . . . you brought those monsters here on *my* ship . . . how could you?" I was choking up inside and couldn't grasp one single thought. Cessa flashed a grin. She looked so happy, it was disgusting.

"I did what I was told, Daniel. Find the empyreus and send the coordinates back to Erebos. If I were you I would run and flee the system. Take your quaint little ship and go before he gets here."

"But . . . why did you kill? What's the point of murdering, of ending so many lives?"

"Because they're animals! I told them what would come

from locking me up! Besides, Erebos will want to claim this planet for himself. We can't have any native competition giving us trouble."

I couldn't believe what I was hearing. Deep down I realized that I knew all along what she was capable of, but chose to look at the better side of her, to try and reason with her. My hope for her, my attempts to trust her, were all for nothing.

"So you're going to exterminate everyone? Are you fluxing crazy?"

Her grin turned into a scowl. She looked at me with death in her eyes.

"Don't get in my way Daniel or you will end up in the same pile of bodies as these vile creatures!"

With her last words she raised her sword up, pointed the tip down at the guard and thrust it into his stomach. He howled in pain for a moment then drifted off into death. I screamed and raised my gun to Cessa, my finger hugging the trigger tightly. She didn't try and run, nor did she attempt to engage me. She just stood there looking at me.

"Go ahead," she said so softly it was just above a whisper. "Do it. Shoot me. Kill me."

Her smile returned and I tried to pull the trigger. My mind started playing tricks on me and in Cessa's place stood Sarah King. Underneath her boot was the same girl I had found on my bed, stabbed to death. Ashley. Her name was Ashley. I shut my eyes and shook my head violently. When I opened them Cessa was once again in front of me, but now she was laughing.

"You really are a coward, aren't you Daniel? You're unwilling to kill even when it's someone who has killed so many of your beloved animals. You say I'm crazy, but I'm willing to bet you're crazier than me."

I aimed again, jamming the gun into my shoulder so hard it hurt. One click and Cessa wouldn't be any more trouble for me or these people. I looked down the sights, locked on her with my bionic eye, but I couldn't do it. I couldn't kill her.

"If you can't kill me, maybe you should help your friend. Save him for me would you? I promised him *I* would kill him."

I looked towards Laraar and sure enough, he was losing the battle with the last dog standing. I had no idea where Chorta and his other guard were, maybe dead or helping out others who were injured. I turned back to see Sarah King walk off towards the forest. No, that wasn't right, damn it. Cessa was the one escaping. I kept my gun on her and wanted to shout, 'Stop', but I knew she wouldn't listen. I did the only thing I knew I could do, and disengaged her to help Laraar. The dog pounced on him and had him pinned down, its claws seconds away from shredding him. I ran at full speed, ignoring the pain I felt, or the tears I shed. I roared at the top of my lungs and threw my left foot right into the dog's chest. I felt bones shatter, heard my voice screaming, but also saw the dog fly off my friend.

I was on the ground, exhausted, in pain, and close to blacking out. With the last bit of energy I had, I raised the rifle toward the last animal, which was readying itself for another attack, and pulled the trigger. The blast was a little high, but it still seared off the upper half of its head and body. The machine fell to the ground as my arm was bent violently a second time.

As my eyes darkened, all I could see was death, the death of multiple Dawnians . . . the death of the guard under Cessa's foot and the death of Ashley, someone in my past who I cared for very much. I was a harbinger for death. It followed me wherever I went and now I was going to be the catalyst that initiated the potential extinction of an entire alien race.

FOURTEEN

The lines drawn between reality and fantasy were erased, leaving me in a profound state of confusion. As I tried to look at my surroundings I couldn't help but feel like I was in multiple places at once. I felt my feet touching the cool blue grass of Dawn, watching Cessa run her sword down into her victim. Then I stood on a thin line of carpet covering a metallic surface of a ship, looking at Ashley Pierce who was dead, stabbed multiple times on my bed. Next I felt the hot surface of concrete. I was standing on a street facing a small family owned restaurant on the island of Oahu, Hawaii. It took me some time to process where I was, but it eventually came to me. I had just graduated the Star Naval Academy with my friends Jason Hobbes, Benjamin Gregson, and my girlfriend Ashley Pierce.

Every sequence I lived, everything my vision showed me looked, smelled, and felt absolutely real. Then I felt the intense pain of injuries and soreness. I was thrashing on my back, a pair of hands holding me down. I didn't dare open my eyes or concentrate on the sounds surrounding me. I didn't want to see anymore death, but the three other visions would not allow me solace. They came in waves showing me friends lost or killed, Dawnians scattered on the ground of their homes.

Then came the music. A strong, lovely voice pierced through the images and the pain. It sang with a calm fluidity like a soft ballad without words. The song touched my very soul bringing with it a suggestion of peace and relaxation. I didn't even have to try to ignore the images. They simply vanished before my eyes. The pain was still there, but it wasn't suffocating my body as before.

Something inside my head told me I could open my eyes. I slowly drew back the curtain of my eyelids and looked to a beautiful, lavender colored face. Her eyes were sparkling, her mouth lifted into a smile. When our eyes met her shoulders relaxed. Idza was standing over me, singing me the beautiful song.

"*Daniel . . .*" her neck device translated after she sang her melody. "*Relieved . . .*"

Surprisingly I didn't find myself in the cell that had been my home here, but in a small room. The walls and ceiling were a light brown color. I tried moving my hands and feet. They all seemed responsive, but I was sore and even numb in a couple places. My neck felt like it needed a lube job. Every time I tried to turn, it throbbed with sharp pain.

"*Are you well?*" Idza asked me.

I couldn't help but smile, happy knowing she was alright. I hadn't seen her at all during the assault on the village and I feared the worst. She didn't come out of it completely unscathed though, as her left forearm was bandaged and she had minor cuts and bruises all over. She noticed me studying it.

"*When Cessa assaulted Ortu and Druga, I ran for help. Chorta . . . his men came with me, but . . . machines attacked us . . . Cessa ran for village . . . I was thrown . . . injured . . . I am okay now.*"

I smacked my head back against the bed and a painful ringing surged through my ears. It wasn't the smartest thing to do, but the pain distracted me from the guilt that flooded through my conscience. How many total lives were lost? What kind of irreparable damage was done to the village? It was all because of me. I let Cessa out of the cell and I alone gave her the opportunity she needed to attack.

"What happened to Cessa?" I asked, completely forgetting that the last time I saw her, she was retreating into the forest. "Was she caught? Do you have her?"

Idza's shoulders slumped and her eyes closed.

"*I fear not. She evades us.*"

Damn.

"I never should have brought her here. This mission, the empyreus . . . everything started with me. I should have told Erebos and his people to shove it."

I palmed the ring at my neck and held it tightly. The diamond that sat at the top had gone missing years ago, but I would never let it go. It served as a reminder to me of how my actions, regardless of whether or not I knew what I was doing, got people into trouble. It felt like Murphy's Law, anything that could go wrong did go wrong. If I had never set foot into the academy almost a decade ago, would any of this have happened?

That was a dumb question. The world didn't revolve around me, nor did I want it to. Someone else would be in a similar situation. Even if Ashley was spared, someone else would have taken the fall. Cessa would have had someone else to order around and threaten.

"You loved her?" Idza asked, and I about choked on my own saliva. My ribs were hesitant to laughter, but I couldn't help myself after everything that happened.

"Cessa? No! She betrayed me," I muttered over a cough. "I thought that maybe there was a shred of humanity in her, but I was wrong."

"No, not her. You spoke of another. Your sleep was riddled with confession of a time long ago."

She pointed to the ring around my neck.

Ashley? Just thinking her name brought uncomfortable images to my mind.

"Yes," I said softly. "Her death was my fault, just like all your people who were murdered. I'm so sorry." My voice caught in my throat, and my eyes watered. I felt an uncomfortable fluttering in my upper chest and tried to contain it. My head and throat felt bad enough without cascading into more tears and sobs.

I felt a hand take mine and a second wrapped gently around my wrist. Idza knelt down next to me. I couldn't read her face to see whether she was angry or sad. She just stared down at me and it wasn't helping me contain my emotions.

"Tell me," she said to me. *"Share . . . confess. The weight on your life force is great."*

I smiled at her, thinking that her translator was operating a lot smoother. Her voice sounded less like some broken accent. She sat down on the bed next to my waist, folded her hands on her lap, and waited for me to speak. I had never had the chance, nor did I trust anyone well enough to explain what had transpired five years ago. Lying on the bed I still wasn't sure if I should say anything, but before I could consider it any more, tears formed in my eyes and I spoke without thinking.

"Years ago I trained at a naval academy on Earth so I could travel into space. It was a dream of mine. My father was a scientist who worked for the government. He always bragged about his job and how it would help usher in a new era of space exploration. I wanted to be a part of it so I applied to the academy. When I graduated, I was positioned to serve on the Earth Star Alliance's newest flagship, the Echelon."

Idza sat and listened as I told my story. I was in awe of how much I remembered. I remembered the noise and commotion as all the new officers arrived at the docks for boarding. I remembered the smell of the brand new ship. I remembered reporting to my senior officer for my first job. Most of all, I remembered Ashley Pierce.

We had been dating for a couple of years at that point, but almost broke off the relationship after graduation. We were worried that we'd be serving aboard starships on opposite ends of the galaxy. Imagine our shock when the announcement came we would be serving onboard the same ship. As we held each other closely in celebration, I knew I wanted to marry her. I bought the ring just before we left Earth.

At this point in the story I managed to sit up and realized my foot didn't hurt like it was broken. I moved it around a bit and though it was tender, the pain was minimal. They must have mended it while I slept. Idza moved beside me and I almost felt a small smile as I continued telling her about my first few days onboard the ship, getting together with Ashley, Benjamin and Jason, both of whom had also been awarded positions on the Echelon. But the smile quickly dissolved into nothing, my breath felt short, and my eyes watered.

"Ashley and I agreed to get together for dinner and a walk on the ship during our first night off. I went back to my room to change into something nice, something formal for her. I kept the ring with me the whole time, waiting for the right moment."

I started to cry. I had trouble continuing my story, but Idza hummed softly at me, caressing my back. It didn't affect me like her previous music did, but knowing she was there and listening helped relieve some of the stress.

"When I got back to my room, Ashley was already there. She was dead, stabbed multiple times."

Idza made a quick sound that sounded like a gasp. She put her other hand on my arm and squeezed gently.

"Daniel . . . many apologies . . . terrible, so terrible," She whispered.

Idza sat there with me as I allowed myself for the first time in years to break down. I hunched over and let my voice cry out, let my tears fall to the floor. I felt the emotions pour out of me like the fusion exhaust of a starship's engines. Eventually I ran out of tears and had to catch my breath. Idza spoke to me softly again when she was convinced I was ready.

"Do you know? Who killed Ashley?" She asked me.

"Yes," I said. "It was meant to look like I killed her. I was framed for her death and I was supposed to be framed for one other. The Captain of the Echelon, Greg Smithson was supposed to die. Once he was dead and I was secured in jail, a sleeper agent would then take command of the ship, controlling one of humanity's most powerful starships. Luckily, Benjamin and Jason knew me well. They knew I would never kill Ashley, so they helped me escape. Together, the three of us saved the Captain from being murdered."

"That is good news," Idza said to me. I only shrugged.

"Yes . . . and no. I saved Captain Smithson, but in the end they still took control of the ship. Benjamin was killed during our attempted escape. The last time I saw Jason was from a shuttle window as he was fighting off security officers loyal to the new Captain of the Echelon. Her name is Sarah King."

I still remembered that moment just as well as anything. Captain Smithson and I were on the shuttle and I was screaming for Jason to get on, but instead he turned to face a dozen officers running at us. He smashed his hand against the control panel, securing the airlock and launching the shuttle into space.

"Surprised that they did not give chase," Idza said when I told her this. At that comment I allowed myself a small smile.

"They couldn't. They were having a little computer trouble at the time. The Captain uninstalled the mainframe of the central computer core. Navigation, weapons, everything except life support and gravity were inactive."

What I didn't tell Idza was that mainframe was now onboard my cruiser. That mainframe was Al. He was designed by my father. I did give her a vague version of the story.

"My father was in charge of designing many technological systems for the new starships. That's why they intended on framing me for two murders. If they succeeded they would not only have the Echelon, but could lure my father into their trap as well."

"*Your . . . father . . . safe?*"

I nodded to her. He was safe in hiding even from me. I thought about his face and voice, which I had last seen and heard around four years ago.

The room was completely silent for a long time. Idza seemed to ponder over everything I said. I couldn't be sure if she completely understood it all. I told the story without thinking about it too much. I never shared all of those memories before. Al knew some of the story since he was a part of it, but he was just a machine. Talking to him helped me stay sane from being alone in space, but he technically wasn't a sentient body who could feel and react to what I told him.

"*Daniel,*" Idza said compassionately. She sounded so human. "*The weight on your life force is great. The cruelty . . . others bestow upon us . . . not a fault of ours, but theirs. Ashley died . . . terrible . . . unfortunate, but you had no control over it. Your friends . . . my people . . . the actions of Cessa. You can only control your actions. I watch you . . . you always look for the good in people . . . however people do not always show it. Sarah King . . . Cessa . . . these people only reveal the darkness. That is what makes them dangerous.*"

Idza was right about one thing, I always looked for the good in people, but no matter how much good Cessa let slip to the surface her cold attitude froze it underneath. She was still out there somewhere and I had to find her before she could continue causing chaos. That's when I remembered . . . the communication station! She sent out a signal! I quickly straightened up from my hunched form and my entire body warped and coiled itself into one giant spasm of pain. I cursed and grunted, but wouldn't allow myself to fall back onto the bed. I placed my hands on the surface of the bed and pushed hard, straining my body into a standing position.

"How long have I been here?" I asked. My head felt clearer thanks to Idza. Her listening and counseling me helped to alleviate the strain and pressure that plagued me. Now I was ready to get back to work, to repair whatever damage Cessa had done. The only problem was my limbs felt like jelly as if they hadn't moved in a long time.

"You were unconscious for three cycles," She told me. I'm pretty sure cycles were their word for days. So I was out for three days. This was bad. I recounted the time it took the Belle to travel to Dawn . . . over a week. I had no idea how long it would take Cessa's transmission to reach Erebos, but my first priority would be to find out. Erebos and his minions could be days away.

"I need to analyze your communication console. Cessa sent out a message. Her people will be coming."

Idza tried to ease me back onto the bed, but I refused taking a deep breath and trying to ignore the pain. She looked down to the ground, unsure of what to say with a frown across her mouth. There was something else she wasn't telling me.

"What's going on Idza? What aren't you telling me?"

"You are not solely blamed for what happened, yet many feel you are dangerous like your companion. You must stand in front of the Authority . . . answer a blood price."

"What the hell is that?" It certainly didn't sound pleasant.

I sat there and listened intently as Idza explained. In Chorta's rage, he failed hunting Cessa down. When he returned to the village, he demanded permission to kill me in her place. Laraar spoke for me, claimed I protected their people and fought beside them against the machine animals. The two of them stood before the Authority of their race in a battle for my fate. When the Authority could not decide, Chorta demanded something no one could refuse.

"He claimed a blood price on you. What is word . . . brother. Grent is brother . . . he was killed. Chorta will now fight you to the death."

I dropped back onto the bed, not even caring about the pain and irritation that followed.

Oh Flux, I thought. I wish I could say I was shocked or surprised that he took this course of action, but I wasn't. Despite facing death by the hand of Chorta, I could only imagine how he was feeling. He didn't like me from the beginning and now he had reason and even more motive to kill me. As much as I wanted to flee for my life, I felt I deserved it.

"I won't kill him," I said to her. *As if, I have a slim chance in hell,* I thought to myself.

"*He will kill you, Daniel.*" She almost had a remorseful look on her face.

Idza explained how it worked. The entire village or what was left of it would stand in audience as Chorta and I battled in a ring of sand, just like I did before with Grent. Only this time it wasn't a test of honor or strength, but a fight to the death. The match didn't have to be one on one. Chorta could choose to have up to four companions fight with him. The catch was if he chose four I also received four fighters, but I had a bad feeling I was sorely lacking for friends on this planet.

"So what do we do now?" I asked.

"*You will be cleaned, then rest until fit for battle.*"

Well at least I had time to prepare for death. I ran my hand through my hair.

"What about Cessa? Her message? She will have reinforcements on the way."

Idza stood up and shrugged.

"*I will do what I can . . . for now rest.*"

My body was worn down enough to warrant more sleep, but my mind was racing. How long did we have before Raymond Erebos showed up? If Cessa's orders were to exterminate all these people, then there was little doubt he would finish the job when he got here.

What felt like a couple of hours later, two Dawnians came in and helped me out of bed. They took me into another room with a large bowl to bathe in, almost the same as the one I found in the house during the fight. After I undressed they sat me in the bowl and unlatched an opening in the bottom. They pointed to the empyreus flowing throughout and then left me alone.

"Wow. That was ridiculously easy for you," I said to them, recalling that I had to smash my way through the floor to reach it.

For minutes I just sat there staring at it. They used this energy source for literally everything, from cooking to computer consoles, bathing, and even healing. I slowly dipped my hand in it, feeling the warmth. Bringing my hand up to my face, I watched as the gel-like substance was absorbed by my hand. Cuts and scrapes on my knuckles and palm disappeared. I could almost feel it traveling through my veins and repairing damage along the way. No wonder my foot felt a lot less broken when I woke up. They must have used empyreus to mend it. I cupped more of the solution and like soap I lathered it across my chest, legs, and arms. Slowly I felt better and watched as my bruises turned back to my natural skin color. My fatigue disappeared and eventually I sat there with more energy than I had ever felt in my life. A realization came to me in that moment. I felt incredible, like I could take on Erebos myself. I was so sure of myself that I could have gotten up and hunted for Cessa now, but there was more to the empyreus than just the energy. While I felt powerful, I was also compelled to relax, to stop moving forward through life and live in the moment.

Something inside me kept saying, *yes you can do anything you want, but you have all the time in the world.* This wasn't the first time I felt like that. The previous time was after Laraar had fused my bionic eye using the empyreus.

Things I noticed around the village started to make more sense. I called out to the Dawnians. I figured they would stay in close proximity since they were tasked with guarding me. One of them stepped into the room with my tactical suit. It looked brand new. After I finished dressing myself they walked off, motioning for me to follow. That was interesting. They didn't cuff me or drag me, but seemed to know that I would follow them.

The building I stayed in was massive with multiple resting and bathing rooms. This place was their version of a hospital, but I didn't see any doctors. I suppose with the empyreus to depend on they didn't need doctors. The three of us exited the hospital and what I saw was tragic. Multiple smoke clouds rose from the homes, some of which were smashed in completely. Cots like the one in my cell had been placed at multiple points around the village for those who were too badly injured to make it to the hospital. I received multiple glares from people as I passed by them. Every time I stopped to assess the damage of one home or building, my guards would stop, get my attention, and wave me forward.

A wide wooden platform was in our path as we continued through the village. Every Dawnian who had been killed during the battle was placed on top of it with their eyes looking toward the sky. Unlike humans who tended to close the eyes of the deceased, these dead had their eyes opened for them.

At this point, I hadn't even taken notice of the Dawnians who followed behind me and my guards. They were so quiet that their steps could have been simple shifts in the wind. As they caught up to us and stood in front of the platform, a soft and gentle hum began. The dirge was beautiful, clearly a tribute to their dead. I didn't know the notes, but found myself humming along with them. At the very least these people deserved my respect.

"I'm so sorry," I whispered to them. I counted somewhere close to a dozen dead bodies, maybe a couple more. I was so sad for their families and hoped they would find comfort. Maybe my death at the hands of Chorta would be their solace. Time would tell.

Our group departed from the dead. After walking for what I guessed to be ten minutes I saw the ring in the distance. Four Dawnians waited for us there and unfortunately none of them were Laraar or Idza. Instead I saw Chorta standing in the middle of the ring exactly like he did before my last battle. Behind him and grouped together were the three I knew to be the Authority of their race.

The next few minutes played out like a replay of my first visit to the ring. A number of Dawnians arrived and surrounded us in a circle and Chorta gazed at me with a hatred I had never seen before. I imagined that when I looked at Sarah King, I gave her a similar expression. The songs and voices of the many were silenced instantly when the Authority held up their hands. When all was quiet the three of them sang to their people.

"*They speak of the blood price,*" Idza said to me. I startled, having no idea she was standing right behind me. "*They speak of the challenge that is sought by Chorta. They will allow him to make his claim himself then you will be allowed to speak.*"

"Me? Who in this crowd will even understand me? What

do I say?" I whispered back to her.

"Speak the truth . . . friend."

The Authority finished their song and held their hands out to Chorta. He bowed before them then faced the crowd. His song held a mixed pace and rhythm. He sang loud and quick, then slow and soft. He pointed at me a lot and I was the center of attention for many of the Dawnians in attendance. When Chorta finished, the crowd cried out together and I had the feeling they were cheering at Chorta's promise to avenge the dead.

The Authority held their hands out to me and I had no idea what I should say. I walked forward and my stomach turned in knots as I stood right next to Chorta. For all I knew he would snap my neck right here and now. I tried to ignore my gut and lowered myself to one knee. I bowed my head to them for a moment then stood up and faced the crowd.

Speak the truth.

"I know many of you can't understand what I'm saying, but I admit a fault in this tragedy. The woman who attacked your village along with her mechanical beasts, were brought here by me and my ship. I can't express how truly sorry I am for the damage that was done and the lives that were taken. Although I am of the same race as the woman, I do not share her beliefs. This woman has wronged me as well and I want to find her and bring her to justice. The people she works for . . . they are coming here. I do not want to waste time by fighting today, but instead I want to help you prepare for their arrival. We have very little time left and I hope you will trust me when I say that I will do whatever it takes to protect you."

As I spoke I heard a single voice sing out in unison with me. Idza was translating my words. I don't know how much would be lost or gained in the translation, but I felt a renewed hope that some of them no matter how few might believe what I said. When she finished her song, there was silence. Then the Authority sang out again.

"They hear your words and believe in your confidence, but the blood price has been claimed," she said to me.

Chorta sang out again and two Dawnians moved to stand beside him. One of them was Horku who looked just as angry as Chorta. The third Dawnian I didn't recognize, but he didn't look

135

at all interested in this contest. I would later learn his name was Janta.

Chorta chose to make this a team battle. I looked around at the surrounding people, hundreds of them watching us and I couldn't imagine a single one of them would step up to help me. Did that mean I would be forced to fight Chorta and his men one on three?

Game over, Daniel, I thought.

A low bass hum sounded behind me and I turned around to find Laraar entering the ring. I was happy just to see him alive and well. He walked up and stood behind me.

"*Laraar will fight for you, Daniel,*" Idza said to me, happiness in her voice.

"I'm honored, but will the two of us stand any chance against those three?"

"*Not two Daniel,*" she said as she stepped to my side and placed one of her hands on my shoulder. "*Three . . . three will face three. I will be honored to fight for you.*"

FIFTEEN

The Authority raised their hands into the air crying out the beginning of the blood price contest. I understood the hatred that Chorta held for me, but I didn't want to die no matter how much I might have deserved it. Six of us stood there, his group mere feet across from ours. We had no weapons but our fists. I was certain Chorta was the most skilled warrior of his people, twice as skilled as Grent, but I had empyreus running through my veins now. I hoped that would even the odds during the fight.

Chorta must have met with his partners prior to the match. When they began their assault all three of them lunged straight for me. In that instant I froze and would have been torn into three pieces, but Laraar and Idza jumped in front of me and blocked the ambush. The two of them held all three at bay for an instant, but that's all I needed to get my head in the game. As if they knew what I was planning they pushed Horku and Janta to each side, opening a path from Chorta to me. He failed to notice and instead of waiting for him to make his move, I made mine. I bent down low to the ground and pushed off with my hands outstretched like a superhero. My fists connected with his midsection and he flew backwards, but with the elegant grace he possessed he landed on his feet.

I trusted that Laraar and Idza would keep the other two busy, but I checked now and again in case they were overpowered. So far the match seemed even. Laraar and Horku were locked in a bear hug and Idza looked to be egging her opponent on. She kept singing flat notes out to him and each one made him hesitate to make a move. I was relieved that Janta wasn't terribly invested in the fight. Idza wasn't a fighter and I didn't want to see her get hurt.

Chorta, on the other hand, had a fire in his eyes as he rushed at me again. I was sure the worst thing I could do was stand completely still. I imagined him throwing himself at me and tearing the upper half of my body off. My bionic eye analyzed his direction and speed and when he was two feet away from me I quickly sidestepped and threw my right leg backwards in a roundhouse maneuver. The point of my foot smacked right into his chest and he fell to the ground, but he was so quick that he recovered enough to thrust his arm hard into my chin, which hurt like hell. When I brought my foot down I limped and didn't realize Chorta had already recovered, grabbing both of my legs and heaving upward sending me into the air.

Luckily I didn't land on my head, but I couldn't match Chorta's agility and land on my feet either. Instead I landed in between, on my belly and face. I felt blood run from my nose, but I didn't think it was broken. My tongue confirmed that all teeth were still in place. I tried to push up with my arms, but a hand grabbed onto my leg and pulled on me. Out of the corner of my eye I saw Laraar losing his battle. His opponent connected with a backhand to his jaw and he fell. The opponent stood over him.

I dug my fingers into the ground to stop Chorta. When he tried grabbing both legs I pushed my arms straight, digging the bottom of my boots into his midsection. Then I kicked hard forcing him away from me and rolling in a somersault. I stood up and was astounded I could do something so acrobatic, even if it was due to the empyreus. I ran, turning toward Horku as he bent over to attack Laraar. At full steam I jumped up and delivered a surprisingly effective drop kick. He flew sideways, but I lost sight of him as I hit the ground. I looked to see if Laraar was okay. We met eyes for a mere second before he pushed his own feet against me to roll me over as Chorta's foot landed in the spot my face previously occupied.

Chorta's hatred for me was so intense that he completely ignored Laraar and turned for me. Laraar took the moment to sweep his legs out from under him. This was my moment. I got to my feet as Chorta hit the ground, facing upward. My eye scanned over him and told me with a strong kick to his neck I would crush his windpipe and he would suffocate. I actually lifted up my foot over him, ready to strike. One second passed, then another. I couldn't do it. I didn't want to kill him no matter what the rules stated about the blood price.

"*Daniel,*" Laraar said pleadingly. He knew it was my one chance as well. The look of despair on his face told me that he didn't want Chorta dead any more than I did, but if I didn't do it Chorta would eventually kill me just like Idza warned.

Nevertheless I couldn't bring myself to do it and instead looked around the ring. Idza was still taunting her opponent. Laraar was still on the ground, trying to pin Chorta down with his legs. Horku was a few feet away on his feet but breathing heavily.

Standing still the adrenaline faded and I felt my own exhaustion take over. My face and right leg were in a lot of pain and sweat was burning my eyes as it fell from my forehead. I wished more than anything I could just wave a white flag and surrender.

I heard a screeching sound bellow from the ground and Chorta broke through Laraar's hold and tackled me to the ground. The back of my head slammed against the hard ground and my vision blurred for a moment. All I could see was a large blurry shape standing over me. My bionic eye reset quickly and as if in slow motion, I watched Chorta hammer his hand down onto my face. At the very last second a directional reading from my eye saved my life as it told me to swing my head to the left. Instead of smashing my nose up into my skull he grazed the back of my head, which still hurt, but wasn't a fatal blow.

Something had to be done to stop this damn fight, but death wasn't the answer. Still though, my actions would have to be more drastic. As Chorta retracted his arm from the ground I grabbed his upper arm with my left hand and his forearm with my right. I screamed out loud as I pushed with both sides going in the opposite direction. With all my strength, I snapped whatever he called bones. I don't care how tough he was or how much empyreus flowed through him, if he didn't flinch at a broken arm, I would let him kill me and be done with it.

Today was not my day to die. He screamed out and threw himself off me, cradling his arm with his opposite. I took a couple deep breaths before standing up. A wave of dizziness passed over me and I hoped that I didn't have a concussion. Laraar was back on his feet. Idza had her hand firmly on Janta's shoulder. Laraar simply stood in between Horku and me, but Horku didn't seem interested in fighting me anymore.

"That's it!" I screamed out. "This is over! There will be no blood shed."

The crowd stood silent, all eyes on me. The Authority wasn't quite sure what to say either, but the surprised look on their faces told me they understood my tone of voice. I requested Idza translate for me again. I was humbled when Laraar joined her and they both told the people what I said. One Authority member sang out something sharp.

"No blood price . . . no honor," Laraar said to me.

I lowered my voice. Screaming only made my head hurt more. "Is it dishonorable to spare your enemy? I did a great disservice, I admit that, but you need to focus on the true problem and they are on their way here right now! Let me honor you by defending you, by giving your people a chance to survive! Instead of fighting against Chorta, let me fight alongside him!"

The translation took a while. I had no idea what words I said were compatible. Whatever was said to the Dawnians they, along with the Authority seemed to consider it, but some including Chorta dismissed it.

"Listen," I said. At this point I was almost begging. "I know of your empyreus . . . I mean sorania. You use it in your food, for your hygiene, and your technology. I've felt the effects of it and I know how it makes you feel. You feel like you can do anything, but at the same time it makes you feel so good, so overpowered that you don't even care about what's happening around you. When Cessa, the woman, attacked your village you were ill-prepared to defend it. I saw less than a handful trying to hold the machines off from destroying your buildings and killing your people. Those of you who are fighters, like Chorta, are strengthened by sorania, but most of you just live your lives without considering what's going on around you. Not a single solitary person amongst you flinched when I told you that there were more of my people coming. They will be here and they will destroy you and your way of life. My people have a saying that is very ancient, 'The enemy of my enemy is my friend'. Let me be your friend. Let me do what I can and if I can save you then I will leave your planet. If I can't save you then I will die with you."

I had to breathe every few words, my body was so exhausted. I bent over and closed my eyes as I listened to the song Laraar and Idza sang to the people. Based on previous translations I heard they were adding something, their songs taking longer than usual. I waited, closed my eyes and tried my damned hardest not to fall over.

I felt a hand on me, then two. When the third hand touched my back I straightened up and opened my eyes. The three hands touching me were those of the Authority. Idza and Laraar stood behind them, both of them smiling.

The Authority sang out to their people and a weight on my shoulders lifted. Their song made me feel better. My fear, frustration, and even some of my fatigue dissipated. They sang in unison then harmonized with each other in a melody that was soothing and soft, like the current of a tranquil river. The song went on for minutes. When they finished, each one looked into my eyes and sang to me personally. Idza translated.

"Daniel, you have much courage . . . much honor. You show us variety in your people. You . . . unlike the one who caused much death and disgrace. Words you speak resound within us. Blood price is made to avenge the lost with the blood of the guilty. Your life force shines brightly . . . you convince us that you are true in your words."

The Authority sang out loud once more though it took only seconds. Laraar walked over and clasped his hand on my shoulder. I returned the gesture as he told me, *"They speak . . . contest over"*.

At that point my legs gave out and I fell straight to my ass while breathing a huge sigh of relief. I wasn't going to die today. I wasn't going to have to kill anyone to save myself. My two friends sat down beside me as the crowd dispersed, most of them in agreement to the terms of the end. I looked past the Authority who stood over me and saw Chorta still on the ground clenching his arm against his chest. A couple of Dawnians were attempting to help him up. I jumped to my feet, which wasn't a terribly good idea at the time and excused myself from the company around me. I stumbled over to him nearly tripping over my own feet every few steps. My head still pounded.

Chorta looked up as I approached him, and I think I a saw an expression of shock on his face as I extended my hand to help him. He stared at my hand for a moment. Was he hesitant to take it or tempted to bite at it? Either way I kept it extended. Just before lowering it he reached out and grabbed it. I clasped my other hand on his wrist and pulled him to his feet. I hoped he would see this as a truce between us. As my grandfather would say, 'let bygones be bygones'.

The two of us let go of each other and he turned to leave, though he turned and said something to me, the notes low and progression quick. I turned around and found Laraar behind me smiling.

"What did he say?" I asked. I figured he was smiling at whatever Chorta said.

"*Still dislikes you.*"

I laughed and though there was some discomfort, just the action of laughing felt good. Idza and the Authority joined us as we laughed together. Laraar's version of a laugh was very quick high notes one after the other. Hearing this made me laugh harder.

"*Daniel,*" Idza said. "*Authority asks your plans.*"

That was a damn good question. I stood there wiping the tears off my eyes trying to think of what our next move should be.

"Right. I need to get this headache under control." The throbbing and dizziness was starting to piss me off. One would assume vomiting wasn't far behind. "I need to get to my ship. The first thing we need to do is analyze the signal that Cessa sent back home. We should be able to determine a timeframe for when her reinforcements will get here."

"*We?*" Idza sang. I smiled at her.

"I'd like to introduce you to a friend of mine. Come with me."

SIXTEEN

During my recovery a number of Dawnians were placed around the Belle, ordered to stand guard in case I tried to escape or Cessa returned. She hadn't, and with the trust of the people I was let back onto my ship. I took Laraar and Idza with me to the bridge.

"Al, you there buddy?"

"Yes Captain. I am . . . relieved to know you are unharmed."

I might have mentioned earlier that Al wasn't a sentient being, but sometimes he spoke humanly enough. I smiled.

"*Daniel,*" Laraar said. "*I meant to ask . . . how this average vessel comes with . . . advanced computer system?*"

I figured that question was coming. Al had been in full vocal mode when the two of us flew my ship to the outskirts of the village, but at the time Laraar had been too preoccupied by the death of his friends to ask.

"Al was a prototype computer that had been installed on my old ship. Sarah King, my commander at the time, was willing to do anything to obtain it, even murder."

Laraar nodded. He understood, but Idza was the one who could sympathize. She placed her hand on my shoulder and gave me a gentle squeeze. For once I focused on the throbbing pain in my head to distract me from thinking anymore about it.

"Al, Cessa adapted her technology to merge with the Dawnian computer. She sent a message back to our section of space. I believe the message was a beacon of some kind and her people are on her way here. I need your assistance in analyzing it so we can come up with a timeframe."

"Query sir: Dawnian?" Oh right, I never really got a chance to talk to him about them.

"Add new submission to alien database, codename: Dawnian. Two of them stand with me now on the bridge. You may scan them for a biological image." I looked at them to make sure they were okay with the scan. Neither of them seemed opposed. The scan took less than a minute.

"Submission complete sir. I am currently unable to analyze the signal remotely. I will need you to attempt a connection between the console and my mainframe."

That shouldn't be hard, I thought. Cessa managed to install her components to their technology. Theoretically it should work in a similar way. There was just one problem. The size of their communications device was massive. There was no way in hell I could fit it onboard the Belle. I'd be shocked if a hundred of us could even lift the damn thing. I told Al about this, leaving out the curse words. He tends to get distracted when I use them and then inquires about human emotion.

"Wait!" I said, a light in my aching head going off. "What if I use the portable module you gave me? The same one I used on the Echelon?"

"Yes sir, that will work. However, your speech patterns suggest that you need this information quickly. Is that correct?"

"I need it like yesterday, Al." *Oh flux, shouldn't have said that.*

"Captain, I must remind you that there is no current technology within my database that suggests time travel is possible. Would you like to read the information I have stored?"

"No! No, no! That's okay Al, sorry. What I meant to say is, yes, I need this very quickly. As soon as possible would be great."

"In that case Captain, I would not attempt a module connection. The upload would not take long, but processing that much information from such a device would take at least thirty hours. If you want results, what is the expression, sooner rather than later then I require instant access. If you cannot bring the device here, then I suggest you detach my mainframe and take me to it."

I blinked, then again, once for his superb phrasing and again for the thought of removing him from the Belle's main computer core. I wasn't the one who installed him into the Belle and as such I had little knowledge of how to do it. After telling him this, he assured me that with his instructions and the help of an engineer or two from this planet we should be able to take him off the ship and install him into the communications device without any problems.

"If you say so Al, but I'm telling you now if I lose you I don't know what I'll do."

"I will take your word for it sir."

The next couple of hours really flew by. Laraar summoned two engineers, Jortu and Ponta to assist us. Al walked us through everything step by step. He requested Idza use her translator to study the patterns and intonations of everything she said and from that was able to give commands that were most likely compatible with her translator.

Before removing his mainframe, Al had to set the computer to run solely on manual command. The autopilot among other things had been integrated into Al himself and it wasn't possible to remove them without doing damage to Al.

"Captain, I am certain this will work, but in the unlikely probability that something goes wrong with the merger I want to inform you that I have succeeded in breaking through whatever sensor barrier Cessa had on the remaining cargo boxes."

I was literally holding his mainframe in my hands at the time, the only thing connecting him to my computer core were a few wires.

"Uh, I dunno Al, more doggies to play fetch with?"

"Negative sir. Each box contains highly concentrated explosives."

Flux me.

"Wow. Okay, good to know!"

"It would only take one box to destroy the entire ship. You may want to do something about that."

No kidding. I put that on my to-do list and continued to work with Jortu to disconnect Al. When the wires were pulled from the core, his system went offline and I found my eyes misty. Advanced computer or not, for years he was often the only voice I heard and the only . . . thing I could confide in. I don't know what I would do if this didn't work. I tried to tell myself the worst case scenario would just be plugging him back into the Belle, but there was always the chance that something could go wrong. I wasn't exactly feeling like a 'glass half full' kind of guy at the moment.

Jortu and I carried his mainframe down the ship's corridor and into the bay where Laraar had his curricle ready to transport the equipment from my ship to their communication station. We walked down the ramp and a couple dozen feet to the perimeter of the village. Once we reached the middle of town where the station was I noticed that seven out of the twelve houses that surrounded it were missing walls or knocked down entirely. The spot where Cessa stabbed her victim still had a blood stain and it made me shudder.

I mostly stood back and watched over Jortu and Ponta as they connected Al's mainframe. They took a good deal of time studying the circuitry and components on the Belle, and Idza told me they were confident the installation would go well. That still didn't stop me from pacing back and forth like a man waiting to hear if his friend survived a dangerous procedure. While I did, I tried to think of ways to protect the people and village as well as stop Raymond Erebos from getting his hands on the empyreus. My options were few to none.

Cessa. I had immediately written her off assuming that she would lay low until her people arrived. For this reason I didn't encourage anyone to search for her, but if anyone would know how to handle Erebos it would be her. I didn't like the thought of seeing her again, nor did I know how I would react.

"Idza, Laraar," I said. "I need hunters or trackers. I'm going out to find Cessa."

"Daniel, you recall . . . her location . . . unknown to us," Laraar said.

"I do, but I also have something that none of you have." I pointed to my bionic eye, which was functioning at unbelievable precision since the contact with the empyreus. I requested that anyone with tracking skills meet us at the comm station and I also needed my rifle back. I had no intention of shooting her, but I at least wanted to show her I was serious. Laraar walked me to a kind of armory which held a number of staves and small wooden shafts that shot their stun darts. When I looked at them I felt a small itch on my neck where the dart had hit me a week ago. I grabbed a couple of the stun shafts and my rifle, which sat alone on a table.

When we returned to the station two other Dawnians had joined the group. I handed them the shafts and they took them, looking at me then to Laraar. He nodded to them as if giving permission to use the weapons alongside me. Jortu made some kind of commotion drawing our attention.

"*Jortu has finished . . . test device . . .*"

Brilliant. I ran up to the display screen on the device and was lost immediately by all the icons and symbols. I asked how to speak to Al and Ponta reached across me, pressing a silver colored symbol that looked like a cross between Chinese letters and hieroglyphics.

"Al, can you hear me?"

Static sounded, but no words or voice spoke through it. Jortu knelt down and manipulated wires underneath the console. Static turned to buzzing. Buzzing turned to an uncomfortable high pitch squealing sound, then I heard his voice as though a distant echo. After a few more tweaks from Jortu I could finally hear Al.

"Captain. Do you hear me?"

"Yes Al, I'm here now. Are all systems functioning properly?"

"This technology is remarkable Captain. Though there is a complex amount of circuitry within this device, the entire station is charged without an external power source. I am unable to compare this type of power with anything else in the -"

"Al," I interrupted. "I'd love to hear all about it, but I need you to start analyzing right away. Meanwhile I am going to try and find Cessa and bring her back here. If all else fails she may be our only hope of stopping Erebos."

"Acknowledged sir. Good luck."

In any other situation, even though he was a machine he would have scolded me in some way for interrupting his breakthrough hypothesis and findings. I would tell him I don't have time for it. He would tell me to make time because something he says could be valuable information one day. The argument usually ended when I told him I would listen to him next time, though I can't claim that I always held my word.

I told the two trackers whose names were Grimal and Crotu to stand by as I closed my left eye and concentrated on the surrounding grass and dirt with my bionic eye. The task of finding Cessa's footprints wasn't easy. Even though she was only one of two humans on the planet, days had passed and winds shuffled the ground, not to mention the intense amount of activity while the Dawnians repaired their village. I remained persistent despite the odds. This area was the last place I saw her and it was my best chance of picking up her trail.

The first footprint displayed in my vision about two meters to my right. Idza passed her translator to Grimal so that they could understand what I was saying, but unfortunately they didn't have any training in human speech, one more thing I blamed on the empyreus. They must have figured that with their technology and resources, no more than a couple of Dawnians would need to learn it.

I requested that the two of them stay behind me so my scanners wouldn't be distracted by their presence in my line of sight. They kept their dart guns at the ready in case we found Cessa. The footsteps were far apart from one another, which indicated that she was taking giant leaps during her escape from the village. The path led us into the forest, which is where I counted on Grimal and Crotu to assist me. Each of them took a turn showing me something that could indicate her direction such as flattened plant life on the ground or broken branches hanging off of trees.

I heard a crunch and a snap from beside me and I quickly rotated toward the sound, raising my gun with my finger on the trigger. The animal I mistook for Cessa was large and covered in silver-white fur. Black markings covered its head and legs and its hooves were twice as large as a horse on Earth. Two bright golden eyes stared at me. I had clearly startled him as much as he startled me. I lowered my gun and my heart skipped a beat when a whooshing sound sent something past my ear. A dart landed in the animal's elongated neck and it dropped to the ground. I turned to give the shooter a sour look, but found both Dawnians rubbing at their stomachs.

Ah, dinner.

Now I knew where my mystery meat came from. Crotu ran over to the beast and checked it over, confirming it had been neutralized. After that we continued our trek through the forest for Cessa. After every few steps my eye would be unable to locate any footprints, but spending a few minutes looking around and focusing on various terrains would reveal another.

She must have kept to rocky surfaces as much as she could, but there weren't enough to mask her flight completely. I wondered if she had stopped anywhere for shelter or if she had been on the run since the night she attacked. I decided I would only search so far before turning back to the village. The top priority right now was to assess the arrival of her reinforcements.

We made our way through a heavily concentrated area of the forest where the tree trunks nearly touched each other. A couple of times I had to sidestep in between them, but there was a silver lining or at least I hoped there was. I could smell smoke and judging by the lack of wind, it had to have been close by. A number of possibilities could have explained the smell, but I hoped the source was a fire, one she would have to keep warm. In as few and most basic words as possible I asked my two colleagues to increase the distance between each of us. If Cessa was close by there was a chance that we could flank her position. The biggest problem was while Crotu and Grimal were traveling in complete silence, I was snapping twigs and brushing against plants every few steps. I slowed my advance as the two of them continued to my right and left.

I found my first clue of Cessa's whereabouts when I came to a narrow tree that had fallen. I traced it back to its trunk to see that a blade had cut straight through it. The surface of the cut was smooth to the touch and a cold tingling sensation traveled up my spine. Continuing forward I saw more trees that were used as targets. The surrounding air was becoming increasingly grey from the smoke. I readied my weapon and switched from plasma to stun rounds. I wasn't sure how the empyreus would affect the stun rounds, hopefully nothing as intense as the plasma or I might put Cessa in a coma at the very least.

Ahead of my position I thought I saw a figure of some kind, which blinked on my display. The creature was humanoid in shape, maybe Cessa, but maybe another Dawnian.

I stepped into a small, unnatural clearing. Every tree within twenty or thirty feet had been sliced at the bottom of the trunks. The wood that had been cut was burning, the flames rising tall. Sitting on the other side of the fire, Cessa's legs were crossed inward with her sword lying across her lap. Her eyes were closed and her mouth a straight line, until I snapped on yet another tree branch. My hunting skills were poor. Cessa smiled.

"Daniel. I thought you might come looking for me."

Hearing such a sweet and soft voice come from someone so cold and murderous made my skin crawl. I set my finger on the trigger and slowly advanced towards her position.

"Get up Cessa! Now!" I had to continuously take deep breaths to keep my hands from shaking. Without placing one hand on the ground she simply turned her feet down and pushed herself into a stance. She opened her eyes and looked at me and my weapon, then smiled at me.

"Look at you, the soldier. I feel like I'm experiencing deja vu, don't you? I stand a few feet from you with your gun pointing at me . . . Remind me again how that ended last time?"

My eyes narrowed and I made sure a target lock was kept on her using my bionic eye. She had the stealth and agility of a snake and a lioness mixed into one. She was standing still now, but give her a couple of second's hesitation and her sword would be smeared with my blood.

"This time it's different. You don't have an unarmed body to slaughter in cold blood."

Her mouth parted and her eyebrows strayed from each other. She acted as if I told her she lost her favorite puppy or something.

"I'm hurt Daniel. I was merely doing my duty. I can't help it if some righteous vile creature wants to be a hero. Heroes are an illusion Daniel. Take you, for example . . ." She walked toward me. I dug the gun into my shoulder and kept it aimed at her. "You think you're being a hero right now by finding me? Do you think you were a hero when you stopped my beasts from devouring the village? This all happened because of you."

The last of her words echoed through my mind.

No, I thought. *There's no time to question yourself.*

"You're wrong Cessa. We are responsible for our own actions. I may have been the one to bring you here, but you chose to betray me and murder the people of this planet. Now you're going to answer for it. Let's go!"

I waved the gun back in the general direction I walked from, hoping she would oblige and do as I said. Of course, she didn't.

She stood there and raised her sword to me. The blade reflected the little sunlight shining down into the clearing. The edge was so sharp it could easily cut me in half. My mind couldn't help but summon mental pictures of Ashley stabbed to death, but the images weren't as frequent or intense this time. Cessa must have expected me to flinch, because I saw her blink and her eyes darted to her sides, looking for an escape. That's when the dart from Grimal's blowgun hit Cessa in the neck. She had enough time to swipe her sword in the direction it came from, but a second later she fell to the ground.

Grimal and Crotu walked into the clearing and to my astonishment Grimal was flapping his hand open and closed, unbelievably reminiscent of when humans use a similar expression to show the other person is talking too much. I mentally imagined Grimal singing 'blah blah blah' and I couldn't help but laugh. The two of them looked at me and then laughed themselves in that quick high pitch progression.

Score one for the good guys. Crotu carried Cessa over his shoulder and Grimal held onto her sword. He offered it to me but I refused. Normally having the sword so close reminded me of the past, bringing up the unpleasant images of Ashley's death, but for some reason the memories weren't affecting me as intensely as they did before. Did talking to Idza help me face the pain or did her music help heal my soul? Either way I was confident that I could face my future without any further interruptions. At least I hoped that was the case. The three of us walked back to the village though our speed was a little slower with our fresh cargo, Cessa and the beast. At least we knew where we were going. Er, I mean they did.

SEVENTEEN

The sun lowered into the horizon and the village was fully active. From the outskirts I saw adults working and tending to their homes and children running and playing with each other. The music that emanated from the scene warmed my heart and helped me forget about the dreadful conversation I had with Cessa in the woods. The three of us marched straight back to the center of town where Idza, Laraar, and a few others were stationed watching the terminal do its work. I always knew Al would have no trouble drawing a crowd.

Everyone seemed very pleased to see us with a few loathsome looks focusing on Cessa, unconscious in the arms of Crotu. Laraar placed his hands onto my arms and smiled.

"*Relieved . . . You are well.*" He said.

"Yes, thank you."

Grimal dropped the beast on the ground and motioned for a couple people to come and handle it. Then he handed the translator back to Idza and spoke to her for a moment. When they finished he beckoned Crotu to follow him and they walked in the direction of the two cells we had previously occupied. Cessa wasn't going to be happy when she woke up and found herself back there. I might have to be present for that.

I walked up to Idza after she finished setting her translator.

"The trip back was quiet. How did it go for Grimal?"

She smiled, and held back a laugh.

"*He says . . . Daniel excellent distraction.*"

My shoulders slumped, but I guess I couldn't argue with his assessment. Everyone around me laughed. I let them do so at my expense as I approached the computer console to check in with Al.

"Talk to me Al. Tell me you have something."

"Something would be an understatement Captain. This empyreus is extraordinary. The raw energy it gives off allowing all surrounding devices to be wirelessly connected is unprecedented by our current technology. Not only do all devices integrate with each other, but they act on a network reminiscent of a beehive, doing one specific job and transmitting it to the next and so on. Simply remarkable."

I tapped my foot impatiently.

"Al, that's great and all, but I'm speaking of the transmission Cessa sent. What's the word on that?"

"Of course sir. I finished that over an hour ago, just after you left. Taking into account various equations and calculations such as signal strength, current star charts, and the average slingspace velocity for a star cruiser, I estimate that anyone who received the transmission would arrive at this planet roughly 16 to 43 hours from now."

Gulp...

"So what you're telling me is Raymond Erebos will be here in less than two days?" I asked him.

"Precisely, sir."

If what Al said was true then there was literally no time for preparation. I didn't so much walk as trudged towards a torn down home close by and sat on the steps in front of the entrance way. I rubbed my temples with my fingers. We needed soldiers, a defensive strategy or better yet a number of high powered weapons. Unfortunately less than a handful of Dawnians had any natural aggression. That meant that if it came down to a fight, I would have myself, Chorta, Horku, and Laraar. I had the Belle which still held enough plasma charge for a fight, but with Al disconnected she would have to be piloted manually. We were screwed. I didn't have to be a genius to know my rifle and a run-down armament of plasma bursts weren't going to stop Erebos and whoever or whatever he was bringing with him. The question is what exactly he would bring with him, what kind of force and firepower? I needed answers.

"How long do your sleeping effects take to wear off?" I asked out loud to anyone willing to answer.

"*Matters not . . . Can be woken,*" Laraar said to me. I looked up at him and smiled.

"Idza, please come with me." The two of us walked back towards the encampment where Cessa and I were kept. Technically the last time I slept in my cell was four nights ago, but since I was out cold for most of them it felt like just yesterday. On the way we stopped briefly at their hospital so

Idza could retrieve the supplies she would need to wake Cessa up. When we arrived at the cells I looked at the one I previously occupied. It was strange seeing it empty.

I moved in front of Cessa's cell and stood there with my arms crossed, waiting for her to wake up. Idza injected her with some type of serum and it took a minute for the grogginess to wear off. When it did Cessa sprang up like a cat, a vile hissing sound coming from her mouth. I half expected her to extend claws out of her fingernails or for her hair stand up on end. She screamed at the top of her lungs when she realized where she was and punched and kicked at the walls violently.

"Settle down," I said over the noise. I allowed myself a small grin to show her I wasn't afraid of her. "You'll only end up hurting yourself."

Cessa stopped and focused on me. Her hands were hanging at her sides clenched hard enough that I thought she might draw blood inadvertently. Her shoulders were tense and her breathing hard. As Idza walked around the cell to join me, Cessa took notice and smiled.

"Oh Daniel," she breathed, "You as well as anyone should know that mating with an alien creature is illegal by government law."

I shrugged at her. "You can stop toying around with me. It's not going to work, not to mention you're really not in the best position to be intimidating."

She didn't respond or flinch at my comment, but kept her eyes locked on mine, watching me and my every move, clearly both physically and mentally.

"I need to know what Raymond Erebos is planning. What are his intentions?"

At the sound of her master's name she drew a wide grin and furrowed her eyebrows. Her body shivered in what appeared delight. Even stars and planets away he still held total control over her like a loyal pet.

"Did you really think he was going to trust you with a task like this? You were merely the chauffer who had information he needed. He could have easily extracted it out of you, but instead he made you a player in his game. You lost by the way. When he gets here, he will claim this planet for himself and use the power it contains to fuel an unstoppable empire."

"That's . . . very ominous and evil sounding," I said to her with a touch of sarcasm.

Looking at her now I could see she really didn't have any other card to play but manipulation and intimidation. Free and with her sword she was lethal and dangerous, but without them she had to rely on her ability to wear down her opponent mentally, whether it was by lowering their self-esteem, seducing them or outright terrifying them with her frightening personality. She made it her job to toy with a person's emotions and in the short time I knew her I'd seen her be damn effective. Her problem was that she already used all her cards on me. The deck had been dealt and she was out of aces.

I continued my interrogation by asking if Erebos would kill everyone on the planet. She tilted her head back and laughed at that question.

"That's a good question. I imagine he will kill some and enslave others." She paused for a moment. "Anyone he doesn't kill will be forced to do his bidding . . . men . . . women . . . and children."

I think I got everything she would be willing to tell me at that point and for the most part, it seemed to be everything I needed. For Erebos to accomplish what she teased, he would need a small army. I turned away from her and walked away.

"You should just run Daniel," Cessa yelled out to me, "we all know that's what you're best at. You couldn't stop me from assaulting the village. You certainly won't stop him."

I stopped for an instant almost turning around to say something back to her, but thought better of it. That's what she wanted so I just kept on walking.

"I'll kill you Daniel! You threw me in this cage like your pet Dawnians! I will find you all and cut you down!" She screamed as we walked out of sight of the encampment. I'll admit that when I couldn't see her anymore I stopped and rested my hands on my knees. She knew how to make me feel helpless, I'll admit that. She was good. I would have to be better. She said I couldn't stop him, but it wouldn't stop me from trying.

Idza and I returned to the village center and I brainstormed ways to defend the town and its people. I also had to find a way to keep Erebos from getting his hands on any empyreus, which was going to be fluxing hard. None of the Dawnians had any ideas other than shooting as many of them as possible with blow darts, but I doubted they had that many blow darts. Still, just to help them feel useful I told them to put that plan into action and get blowguns into as many hands as they could.

I tried to think back to my training as a security officer without setting off any nightmarish images. During my lessons at the academy our instructor told us that when we are cornered into a tough situation, it was imperative that we use whatever assets we have available. Think as if you're defending yourself from a well-oiled machine, just by disconnecting the smallest cog you disable the machine entirely! What did I have? A numerous amount of people who lacked any battle training and spent their days talking in song. What was I going to do, arrange a chorus to welcome Erebos in song?

Stars above . . . That's it!

An idea presented itself to me and it was like opening a door to a room full of windows into additional ideas. I stood there in a daze, completely zoned out of reality as I calculated a plan inside my head. The music, the Belle, Al. For the first time, I felt somewhat hopeful.

"Idza! Laraar!" I practically scared them when I called out their names.

"I want a meeting with the townsfolk and authority right away. Go arrange it now!" They looked at each other then back at me, nodded, and left.

"Al, you said the empyreus allows you to connect wirelessly and work with any device in the village. Are you able to access the Belle's navigational system?"

"To a degree sir. I have the ability to code in some of the systems automated functions, such as star charts and course plotting."

"No, no! Can you fly her from here?"

"Negative sir. Even if you energized the Belle itself with empyreus the ship is still missing the key components to control her remotely."

Damn it. I took a deep breath and tried to tell myself there was always an option. If the Belle couldn't be used without a pilot I would have to find another way to keep the situation from exploding into chaos.

I literally stood in one place unmoving for what felt like an hour. I considered every option I could think of, every solution no matter what the cost would be. Then I nodded to myself and turned to the computer.

"Al, make sure you keep your countdown running. I know it's only an estimate, but right now it's the best we have. I want you to be able to alert anyone and everyone when Erebos is close."

"Acknowledged sir. May I ask where you are going?"

"I'll be back. I'm just going to take the Belle for a ride before all hell breaks loose."

EIGHTEEN

An entire alien race and one determined human stayed up through the night to plan and strategize for the impending invasion that Raymond Erebos would bring. I flew the Kestrel Belle to a secure location close by, but first I flew past the mountain of empyreus crystals. It towered above me and I mentally replayed my trip inside with Laraar, witnessing the unbelievably beautiful crystal structures and seeing how it was processed into the biomechanical fuel anyone would kill to have.

I snorted at that last thought. Anyone would kill for empyreus and here the Dawnians hardly ever harmed a fly, or whatever their version of a fly was. They used the fuel in their everyday lives, sharing it together, connecting their love of nature and technology to form the ultimate society. Now that doom was descending upon them, their perfect society was useless against the might and intentions of Erebos and his men. I wondered what would happen to everyone on the planet without the empyreus. This mountain and its capabilities were at the heart of the problem. If worst came to worst, would they be willing to destroy it? Would they stay the way they were for a while, relaxed and content with everything in their life or would they begin to feel and crave for more out of their lives as the effects of the energy wore off?

Once I safely secured the Belle and returned to the village Grimal led me to the Authority chamber room. I don't know if that's what they called it, but it sure looked like it. The walls curved in a wide circle with the familiar Dawnian dome ceiling. Rows of wooden benches were placed in four sections of the room, about ten benches down each row. In the front of the room sat the Authority who sang out a loud song, summoning their people to the chambers.

I told everyone my plan, how it was not guaranteed to work, and how it would be necessary to potentially be in the line of fire. There was a good chance many Dawnians would die, but I tried to emphasize that they would die protecting their village and people. A lot of them seemed to sit up at that. Chorta had stood a long time ago singing out a tone of approval when I spoke. It felt good to finally be somewhat accepted by him. When I finished and the entirety of the room rose up in support of my plan, we all broke off into groups. My group walked out towards the open field outside the village where Al was nearly certain the enemy would land. The other groups went off into the forest as the golden sun was rising.

Those of us in the field equipped ourselves with dart guns. I had my rifle, which was powered up on empyreus and ready to go. I paced back and forth down the defense line making sure everyone was motivated and ready at moment's notice. I put on a brave face and strode down the line like it was my job to command these people, when in fact I was terrified. I had no idea if these people were ready for this or if they could even comprehend what was about to happen. Hell, I didn't know if I was ready.

Laraar joined me handing me a small device that looked somewhat like his translator. He held it up, wanting to put it around my neck. I let him.

"Created . . . myself . . . Using our technologies."

Suddenly a voice was speaking to me. Al.

"Captain? Do you read me?"

My eyes glossed over.

"Al, you don't know how happy I am to hear your voice."

"I am incapable of discerning human emotion Captain so you are accurate, I do not know. If anything I would assume from your vocal pattern that you are in distress."

I laughed at his comment.

"Happy distress at the moment Al."

With the empyreus connecting all devices wirelessly it was a simple job for Laraar, working with Al, to create a portable communication device allowing me to speak with him on the fly. Laraar and Idza would also have the same ability with their translators. The idea and execution was brilliant. I rehearsed all the scenarios I could come up with for when the attack began and I could only hope Al could adapt to what happened around the village. Now I wouldn't have to wonder. Some of the nerves receded. Not nearly enough, though.

The stage was set and all the pieces were in place except for one. Laraar gave the people around us his version of a thumbs up and the two of us walked back to the village. It looked like a ghost town that would have fit in perfectly with one of the western stories my grandfather loved to tell me as a boy. I kept a lookout for tumbleweed but didn't see any.

Cessa was standing in the middle of her cell and watched us approach. I didn't let her get the first word in.

"Look!" I yelled, "It's your two favorite people!" I could have been imagining things I suppose, but I thought I heard her growl at us. Of course, I forgot that Laraar was the one currently holding onto her sword. That was like pouring salt into an open wound.

I raised my rifle to her. "Place your back to the door and hold your hands together"

She hesitated for a moment wondering if I was serious, but ultimately obeyed my command. Laraar, using a durable type of dark red rope secured her hands behind her back. When he was satisfied with the work he did he nodded to me and moved to the front of the cell, unlocking it. Cessa looked at both of us, dumbfounded that we would do something so idiotic.

"Don't try anything Cessa. You're going to walk slowly with us. I know you're fast, but you should know my gun is seriously doped up on some groovy energy. One pull of the trigger and half of your body might be vaporized."

I was slightly bothered by the words I used. That didn't sound like me, but then again I was trying my hardest to keep a stern and determined focus on defending these people. I guess when you do that you tend to get a little extra aggressive. Cessa seemed both shocked and amused by my words. She stepped out of the cage and made no attempt to escape. Laraar grabbed her arm and led her forward. I kept my distance on the other side of her in case she tried to use her legs to take us down. She was surprisingly obedient as we walked back to the main group.

A chorus of the musical equivalent of boos and hisses erupted from the crowd as we stepped to the forefront. Everyone here knew who Cessa was and the destruction she caused. She didn't seem to be affected by the noise as she maintained a bored expression and stared out into the open field. I could only imagine what was going on inside her head. It must be a scary place in there.

The group had been standing and waiting for over an hour and some decided to rest, sitting on the ground. Laraar maneuvered behind Cessa so he was standing right next to me. He was about to say something when my communicator buzzed. Al was calling. I knew what he was going to say.

"Captain. The enemy ship is approaching the planet. The device I'm connected to does not have an accurate scanner to determine the exact design model."

"That's okay Al, I think we know who's coming. Stand by for my command."

"Acknowledged."

My stomach spun in circles, turning my insides as if they were stuck in a turbine on one the Belle's wings. I yelled out to everyone to stand by and be ready. Laraar stood next to me staring up in the sky; everyone did including Cessa, though she held the same bored look on her face. The only thing we could do now was wait.

The wind picked up and blew past us as if it was fleeing the scene. I wish it could have taken me with it. Confrontations were never one of my strong suits, which is likely the reason I couldn't get hired for a mercenary job if my life depended on it. Mercs were paid to accomplish their mission by any means necessary, and I could only ever accept doing what I considered to be the right thing, whether ignoring an order to kill, kidnap, or steal from someone I didn't think deserved it. What was the right thing to do in this situation? I didn't like to kill people, but would I have to do just that in order to save the Dawnians from extinction or slavery? Was that even possible at this point?

My thought process was interrupted when I saw movement in the clouds. My eye counted off the numbers of ships flying in. One, two, three, six, ten, fourteen . . . fourteen ships flew on route to us. They weren't large cruisers, but instead shuttles. Except for one. One of them was larger than the others, but still not a full size cruiser. If anything it was a heavy trooper carrier. As they broke through the clouds into the blue sky my bionic sight zoomed in on them to get a more accurate reading and my heart dropped into my stomach when I realized they were familiar shuttles. I recognized their shape, their power output, and the name of their mother ship that was painted on the side.

ESA Echelon. Sarah King . . . she was here. For all I knew she was on one of the shuttles. I just wanted to collapse to the ground, curl into a ball, and scream at the top of my lungs. Cessa sent out a message that was picked up by the fluxing Echelon, the tainted ship of the ESA fleet, the home to all my nightmares.

"Flux . . . no . . . it can't be," I whispered to myself.

I could suddenly feel eyes on me, a lot of them. Every Dawnian within my sight was staring at me, and what were they seeing? They all looked at a man who promised to protect them, staring up at the ships terrified. I couldn't let them down. I couldn't let myself down. I forced my eyebrows together and tightened my jaw in a scowl. I checked my rifle and set it to EMP rounds. Then I mustered all the vocal power I could and turned to the people counting on me and shouted, "Stand tall and ready"! They didn't understand me, but Laraar translated for them and it made me feel a little better shouting it.

I felt a hand on my shoulder. Laraar smiled at me.

"Gratitude . . . you stand here . . . fight your own people . . ." He said to me.

"These aren't my people. Humans are flawed and imperfect, but most of us have the potential to grow and learn, show compassion, and stand up for what's right. But there are others who refuse to adapt and evolve and they start living only for themselves. Those types of humans are who descend on us now."

I turned to Laraar and extended my hand to him. He looked at it for a moment then mirrored my gesture. I pushed my hand into his and gave him a firm grip.

"These people were always my enemy, but I am honored to fight with you. No matter what happens know that it has been an absolute pleasure to know you."

I looked around at each and every Dawnian who stood beside me. I felt like I should say something to them, something to motivate them to help them get ready for the inevitable battle ahead. I took a few steps forward then turned around to face the crowd, asking Laraar to translate as best he could.

"The empyreus that flows in each and every one of you reacts to your emotions and amplifies them. As time passed and you felt safe and secure, it calmed your state of mind, your body, and your life force. The time for serenity is over! People like the one who attacked your village are about to land to take what belongs to you and possibly kill or enslave you. Focus on your anger. Remember that you are a race of honorable beings and your home needs to be defended."

Laraar sang out in a loud, but beautiful tenor voice translating everything I said. I thought of how the late Grent had made a fool out of me in our first meeting. The Dawnians truly had power. I told them that the enemy would arrive with weapons and that the key to defeating them was to get in close and fight hand to hand. I told them that I would stand beside them and fight for them and, like I told Laraar moments before, to meet them and make first contact with them was a true honor.

When Laraar stopped singing the people raised their hands up in the air and sang back to us. Baritone and tenor voices all joined together in melody, in harmony, shouting out an epic progression of sound. I could feel the music inside of me, giving me courage and strength. I felt taller, figuratively of course, and more than anything I felt hope. Laraar didn't wait for them to finish as he walked up to me, his eyes glazed over with tears. I gripped his hand and gave it a supportive squeeze then turned to the incoming ships with my rifle raised.

Although I felt righteous at the time, the ESA being here drastically escalated the situation. At the same time it didn't really change the game plan all that much. Knowing that helped me calm the storm raging inside me, but only slightly. Eleven of the ships landed on the ground, while three including the heavy transport ship hovered in the air. I made sure my eye had the chance to scan every one of them, locking on sight in case I had to attack quickly.

"Al," I said. "I count three airborne ships." I wanted to make sure I kept him appraised at all times.

The aft doors opened on the grounded ships and two types of troopers poured out. One group wore the standard military battle suit of the ESA and the other group was dressed more casually. They reminded me of common thugs, but thugs holding intimidating weapons. The mixture of thugs and troopers confused the hell out of me, but I stood tall and held my ground as they lined up opposite us. Two figures, a man and woman from the lead ship stepped off and walked toward me, both of them smiling, both responsible for why I was here. I wanted to throw up when I realized that the Echelon was *meant* to pick up the transmission.

Raymond Erebos and Sarah King stood in front of me, together.

"Well, well," Erebos said clapping his hands together. A cold feeling crawled up my spine listening to his voice once more. "This is quite the welcoming party. Thank you, Mr. Quinn."

What do I do? What do I say? At the moment my thoughts and voice betrayed me and I just stood there like an idiot. No, I couldn't allow that to happen, not again. The last time I let Erebos shut me up was during our first meeting. I had to stand up for myself for once in my life. I had to stand up to a man who terrified me and a woman I hated more than anything.

"I wouldn't exactly call this a *welcoming* party," I said to him. The first word out of my mouth was a little shaky but my vocal chords came through and supported the words I spoke. Erebos, being who he is, smiled at my comment.

"Despite whatever this is," he said, waving his hands in front of him. "You have accomplished the duty I requested of you. Depart back to your ship and you will be given a bank account with a large sum of money available to do with as you will."

"Like hell," Sarah interjected. While Erebos was amused by the scene, Sarah King was focused solely on me, her eyes sharing the same hatred I had, her mouth twisted in a snarl.

"I come to this planet and find two of the three things that belong to me, the energy source and Quinn. I'm willing to bet the third item is here as well. I want my artificial intelligence program."

I did my best not to flinch or blink when she said that. I usually had a terrible poker face. She walked up to me and I raised my gun in response, completely forgetting the EMP rounds were active. The most damage it would do is give her a nasty shock, maybe reboot her nervous system. It didn't matter. When I raised my gun at least fifty soldiers pointed theirs right at me. I had no choice but to let Sarah put her hand to my neck, grab the ring hanging from the chain, and rip it off of me. I had to force myself not to lunge at her as she held the ring meant for Ashley.

"You won't be using any tricks to escape this time, Quinn." As she placed the ring around her neck, I reminded myself that there was more to the situation than just King and me. This helped to keep the rage that was building at bay.

"Now, now, let's come to an agreement where, what's the expression . . . everyone wins?" Erebos said. He took a step forward.

With his words I connected certain dots in my head. The gears were turning smoothly and opening doors to things I originally thought were coincidence. At the same time, my heart was pounding like a hammer against my ribs and my stomach was attempting to hit the abandon ship button. I took a deep breath through my nose and reminded myself that hundreds of Dawnians behind me were taking their cues off of me. I took my own two steps toward Erebos and King.

"This entire time... " I turned to Erebos and shared my conclusions. "I wondered how you knew so much about, well, everything. You knew my past. You knew I had access to data on the empyreus. And you . . ." I turned to King. "It was no mystery now how your agents on the station found my exact location. I thought I was just being paranoid at the time, but you were simply waiting for Erebos to give up my location and send your own thugs in. The two of you were working together the entire fluxing time. The only question I have now is who works for whom?"

Both Erebos and King looked at each other and shared a soft laugh at my expense.

"The lovely Captain does not work under my employment, much to my disappointment. Let's just say that we have a mutual understanding of what needs to be done for the good of mankind," Erebos said. "I am a business man, Daniel. I never put all of my eggs in one basket. Contacting Sarah King was the logical choice. The two of you have a most interesting history."

At that, he smiled at me. I felt my anger rising.

"The good of mankind?" My teeth were grinding together and I swore I could feel my blood pressure rising. "Ashley's death, Captain Smithson's exile, the death and destruction of an entire race and their village . . . this was all for the good of the fluxing human race?"

Both of them actually sighed at the same time, as if disappointed in my questioning.

"Sacrifices are necessary," King said, her tone bland and uninterested.

"Daniel," Erebos said, for once using my first name. "It saddens me that you are like so many other idealists. Look at what humanity has accomplished over the years. We have accomplished miracles, proven our worth and power by the ships we fly, the stations we live on, and the worlds we explore. But do you really think as we travel through the stars that we will remain at the top of the food chain? You alone made first contact with an alien species that appear to be much more advanced than we are and that's just one race. As we expand further into the darkness think of the things we will find, not only astonishing, but terrible and powerful. We must make sure that humanity holds onto the high ground . . . and that starts here and now."

I was speechless. Until now I looked at these two like they were the ones with all the power. They terrified me. Erebos himself used fear to persuade me to take on this mission, threatening my life and my ship in the process. Sarah King was the cause of countless disturbing and horrible nightmares and images that had plagued my mind for the last five years. Never did it occur to me that these two powerful people were controlled by fear themselves, fear of the unknown. It all came down to being the dominant race in the galaxy. When you hold all the power, what else is there to fear but losing it? Then something Cessa had recently said about an empire popped into my head, and everything made sense.

"That's what this is all about," I muttered. My words grew stronger and more defined as I continued. "Going back five years to the mutiny . . . the Echelon, the artificial intelligence." I looked at King. "You are building your own fleet, using one of the flagships of the ESA to jumpstart your ascension and ordering additional sleeper agents to infiltrate other starships."

I turned my head to look at Erebos.

"And you are building your own empire. By joining together you are essentially creating a 'humans only' club. With the empyreus you would be unstoppable!"

Sarah King actually slow clapped for me.

"Give the kid some credit; he's not so dumb after all." Her words infuriated me.

Erebos put a hand up, motioning for her to quiet down. For the first time I saw his resolve crack. The corner of his mouth twitched into a scowl, but only for less than a second before his expression returned to neutral.

"Daniel," he said. I blinked as he again used my first name. "I think the time for negotiating is over. The last time we met I gave you a choice. I now give you another. Run to your ship, depart this planet, and I will still honor our original agreement. Your other option is to stay here. My men will capture you, torture you, then I will make you sit and watch as I slowly kill off every single alien on this planet. Then, I will tear out your heart myself."

"What about Cessa over here?" I asked him, nodding my head towards her and trying to pretend his words didn't scare the flux out of me. Laraar and Grimal were now both standing beside her. "Did you consider the fact that she's my prisoner? Are you willing to sacrifice her?"

The man didn't even flinch. In fact, he laughed out loud.

"Of course I am. She means absolutely nothing to me and she knows that. Do not think me a fool Mr. Quinn. Do you agree to my terms? This is your last chance. Think on it."

The time for talk was over. I clenched my teeth and thought about it for all of one second.

"You disgust me Erebos. You're everything that's wrong with humanity. I'm going to make sure someone here fights for the right kind, the kind that believe in justice and freedom."

He narrowed his eyes, pressed his mouth into a firm line, and spoke only three words.

"So be it."

NINETEEN

Honestly, I wasn't sure what to expect. Was I supposed to start shooting people? Were they going to attempt to shoot me first? I didn't exactly have any experience in starting wars. I raised my weapon toward Erebos and King and their soldiers all raised theirs. None of them would start shooting while their leaders were in the crossfire, which is why I grew nervous when Erebos and King simply turned and walked back towards their shuttle. Once they were out of harm's way, the slaughter would begin. I could only hope that the plan I concocted was ready to be put into action.

The first part of said plan didn't work out so well, as Cessa was still my captive, relatively ignored by Erebos. I suppose I shouldn't have been surprised at the lack of compassion from him. I looked at Laraar wishing he didn't have to do all my translating for me.

"Laraar, tell Grimal to get Cessa out of here! We don't need to be watching our backs as well as our fronts!" Laraar nodded and relayed the message. Grimal nodded without hesitation and pulled Cessa away. She fought, screamed, raged on about getting her sword back, but said nothing of Erebos's cruel words. Two additional Dawnians ended up assisting Grimal in dragging her away from the field.

I turned my attention back to the group of soldiers waiting to strike us down. My eye picked up increased power emissions from a number of shuttles, including the one Erebos and King were returning to. They were leaving, most likely headed for the mountain. I watched as he allowed King onboard first then looked to our group and waved his hand towards us, mouthing what I thought was, 'kill them all'. I didn't have time to yell at Laraar to tell everyone to evade and fire their blowguns so I just aimed my gun at the closest group of soldiers and fired.

With the EMP rounds activated and powered by empyreus, a blast of energy erupted from my weapon, firing out like a massive shotgun round. When it hit the soldiers they were electrocuted, their bodies shuddering and shaking, but otherwise the round caused them no serious harm. That was the point. As I turned my weapon and quickly fired a new round into another group, they raised their weapons and pulled their triggers. Nothing happened, which gave the Dawnians closest to them the perfect opportunity to move in at close range.

I wasn't quick enough to hit every weapon in sight with my EMP. That wasn't possible. Many of the soldiers opened fire at us. I immediately saw a couple of Dawnians go down and I had to force myself to keep my attention on the enemy. My battle suit would only take a few hits before their blasts would start penetrating.

My allies fired their darts as fast as they could. Many of the first line of soldiers dropped to the ground, unconscious. The unfortunate problem was the time it took to reload and aim the fluxing things. I watched three more Dawnians get shot while they tried to aim their guns at their second targets. So far five soldiers were put to sleep and another three were fighting close quarters with Dawnians. That still left a large number of soldiers firing their weapons at will and killing people. We wouldn't last very long like this.

That's when I heard it, the second part of my plan. Through the forest came a number of Dawnian women singing louder than I ever thought possible. Even though the edge of the forest was easily five hundred feet away from us, I heard them as if they were mixed together with our group. The song they sang was in a minor chord and the notes played out in an expression of sadness and regret. The somber song pierced my flesh and the loud resounding sound echoed in my heart.

Something was supposed to happen here. I knew it because it was my idea, but I couldn't bring myself to concentrate on anything but the sweet music. I lowered my weapon. I had no reason to use it right now. All around me, humans just like me were doing the same thing. The song was causing a ceasefire and that meant something to me, but damn it, what was it?

A hand violently grabbed my shoulder and spun me around. Laraar was shaking me, speaking to me, but what did it matter? As long as I could hear that amazing sound, nothing else mattered.

"Daniel . . . concentrate . . . stop listening!"

After a time the shaking and shouting overwrote the music and I felt the gears in my brain turning again. The music . . . right, I had set this as a kind of trap for the humans. The ritualistic music of the Dawnians was unbelievably powerful, even more so to the human ear. I had hoped that this would buy us enough time to even the odds. If it put those odds in our favor then I wouldn't complain.

"Right," I said, my voice shaking as I shook off the trance. "We have to engage them hand to hand. Try to take away their weapons. I'm guessing once they start to feel threatened it will break the spell. Tell everyone to get in close and try to stay alive."

Laraar turned to the group behind us and I had just enough time to look up at the sky to see the main shuttle carrying Erebos and King turn towards the group of women singing and open fire.

"No!" I screamed, raising my weapon and firing an EMP blast at their shuttle. I missed by inches. I tried to line up for another shot when multiple Dawnian figures leapt over me into the group of soldiers. I ran to an open spot, but I had to weave through multiple people. One of the soldiers who was already coming out of the trance saw me running and raised his weapon to shoot me. I fired a round at him which stunned him and momentarily rendered his gun useless. I thrust my feet into the ground hard and increased my speed, lowered my upper body and drove my left shoulder right into his gut. I heard a sharp grunt as he hit the ground. I pushed myself back up with my free hand and stepped on him as I continued to look for open ground.

When I finally got clear, I was on the opposite side of the battle from where the women stood so I couldn't see the damage that had been done. I had Erebos and King in my sights once again. I pulled up my weapon aiming at them, but instead caught sight of a missile launched directly at me from one of the other shuttles. I tried evading, but when it hit the ground there was a small explosion throwing me completely off my feet. My world turned over, under, sideways and I couldn't figure out which way was up until my back slammed hard against the grass.

All they had to do was shoot one more missile at me. There was no chance in hell I would get clear, but it never came. I heaved in a breath and tried to get up. The explosion had thrown me far, but the shuttles weren't focused on me, nor were they targeting the group in front of them. All four ships in the air turned on their axis and faced toward the southwest, the same direction where the mountain of empyreus resided.

I turned in a circle, looking for my rifle and getting my bearings. I retrieved it and then ran like hell for my ship. Erebos and King could not be allowed to collect the empyreus. Luckily for me they wouldn't be getting there without a small surprise in the form of our third Dawnian group, led by the ferocious Chorta and Horku. They would give them a fight for their lives. Still, it was my responsibility to stop them.

The ground in front of me blew up in small chunks and I hit the brakes. Two soldiers had broken off from the main battle and were advancing toward me, showering my position with countless plasma shots. I felt one impact my abdomen and another graze my thigh. I felt intense heat but my armor held.

"Damn it I don't have time for this shit!" I screamed at them, but they didn't seem to care. Both of them kept unloading their weapons toward me, but because they were running they lacked balance and the shots missed. I silently thanked the powers above that one didn't go clean through my skull as I watched them waste all their rounds rather than stop and take their time for a clean shot. When I was convinced their banks were low, I rushed them screaming a primal roar that would have made a lion quiver.

The two of them rushed me in response. There was no time for me to switch my rounds to stun or kill, so it was time to dance. Both of the soldiers dropped their weapons and sprinted full steam into me. I decided to keep my weapon. Why? Well the funny thing is, even when it's useless as a rifle, it still makes a fantastic melee weapon. Just before we crashed into each other I swung the weapon like a baseball bat. The first soldier ducked in time but not the second. The butt of my gun struck into his face and blood shot out of his mouth and nose. I quickly swung the weapon back the other way, but the first soldier was expecting that, catching my forearms in his hands and jamming his foot into my stomach. The air was forced out and my lungs attempted to retrieve it with no luck. I groaned for a moment until I saw the soldier swinging his right hand toward my face. I threw up my left elbow to block. The two of us traded blows back and forth until I realized that he outmatched me. The man was a skilled fighter. His initial attacks were soft and of no threat to me, except to wear me out as I blocked them at full force. I was tiring out and he wasn't.

The soldier attempted an uppercut to my jaw and I stepped to the side to avoid it, but the move was a fake out. His right leg had been sticking out and tripped me to the ground. I rolled to my back in time to see the bottom of his giant boot thrusting towards my face. If he connected he would smash my nose into my skull. Little did I know, the entire time I had been running clear of the fight Laraar was right behind me. Before the thug's boot could connect Laraar hit him, giving him a hard shove that sent him sideways of my position. I got up quickly and ran over to where he hit the ground and threw my own boot across his face. I saw teeth soar out of his mouth and he was still. I checked his pulse. Alive.

"Thank you," I said, my voice hoarse. Laraar nodded to me. "We don't have any time. Follow me."

Together we ran to the Belle. Once we were onboard I ran to the bridge and lifted her off the ground. Just before I engaged the thrusters to intercept the shuttles, I looked over the battlefield. Bodies of both races were down. I couldn't tell whether they were unconscious or dead. A lot were still standing, fighting each other. I thought that the Dawnians would easily outmatch the humans, but I suppose these humans were trained for ground combat and excelled at it.

I reluctantly hit the execute icon and the ship took off toward the mountain. Laraar and I sat on the bridge, listening to the sounds of our own breathing and the humming of the Belle's engines. It would take us three minutes to reach the mountain, which didn't sound long, but in that place and time it seemed like an eternity.

"I'm sorry for the loss of your people," I said to him, just in case I didn't get a chance later to apologize.

He looked sad, but shrugged his shoulders.

"You do . . . what you can . . . we understand . . . risks."

I nodded, still feeling incredibly guilty.

"I don't know what will be waiting for us when we get to the mountain, but I will do anything to keep Erebos and King from getting the empyreus. They will not take this planet as long as I'm alive."

At that, the corners of Laraar's mouth turned up slightly giving me a gentle smile.

"Let us hope . . . you stay alive."

I smiled. Yes, let us hope. The mountain was in view. I could only hope Chorta and his group was holding Erebos and King off, but what if they failed? What the hell could I do to stop them from getting the empyreus and retreating in their shuttles?

What if they didn't have shuttles? I thought.

Of course! The Belle was equipped with weapons, but nothing significant enough to make a dent in a large space craft. However, these weren't large crafts. They were shuttles, smaller than the Belle herself. Her plasma disrupters should easily be able to remove that problem.

"Laraar, have you ever flown a ship before?" I looked back towards him. He nodded, though hesitantly.

"Many of us . . . when life force was young . . . flew our ships," he said.

I asked him to stand behind me and gave him a quick crash course in piloting the Belle. I showed him the navsphere and how it worked, how to punch the throttle or hold it back, and also how to engage the weapon systems. There wasn't time to explain everything about the tactical console, but locking onto a target and firing the forward plasma guns was a simple process. The most important thing right now was to keep it simple. I handed over the reins.

"Why?" He asked me. I couldn't exactly distinguish anxiety or nerves with their song patterns, but I thought he looked a little nervous to handle my ship.

"You're going to drop me off about 70 meters from the side of the lake. Once I'm on the ground, you need to take the Belle to the mountain and blow up those shuttles. I think there were four of them. The only downside is my weapon systems can't lock onto that many targets. You have the ability to take out two ships at once, but then you'll need to swing back and take out the rest. If we destroy their shuttles, they'll have no way to fly back to the village or their ship."

"*What happens when shuttles at village contacted to come?*"

"Let's just deal with one thing at a time. Take these ones out and go from there. Okay?" Laraar nodded. "Great, let's do this."

Laraar set the ship close to the ground as we neared the forest that bordered the mountain opening. I educated him as he manipulated the controls. Overall he didn't do a bad job. For a second time I explained the weapon system, which buttons to completely ignore and which to focus on. After a couple minutes I was only delaying the inevitable. I touched his shoulder, giving it a squeeze, then exited heading back to the bay. I waited until the door was halfway open then reversed the lever and ran like hell. When I jumped from the closing door the ship was about twenty feet off the ground. I dropped the rifle and used the inertia to drop into a roll to minimize any damage done by the long fall.

As soon as I was safely on land I looked up to watch the Belle take off toward the mountain. I may have imagined it, but I could have sworn I saw her wavering a bit. I hoped that Laraar would be able to control her. There was so little time, but Erebos and King weren't exactly going to wait for me to give Laraar a flight exam.

I checked the status of my rifle then set the rounds for plasma burst. I winced as the gun's charge read 100%, knowing what firing plasma would do to a person, but I didn't see any alternative going forward. EMP rounds would be useless. They could be used to back up Laraar if he failed at taking down the shuttles, but an EMP would only disrupt the power for a time. I needed the ships to be destroyed. Stun rounds could potentially work, but I had to face the possibility that Erebos and King had used the empyreus to energize themselves and I wasn't sure stun rounds would bring them down.

Moving quietly through the trees, I heard the first and second explosion.

Yes! Laraar had done it. A lot of shouting and screaming followed, all human. With the thundering noise of the shuttles exploding I sped up my advance into a sprint. The lake was just ahead.

"Quinn!" I heard King shout. I raised my gun and spun around in a circle, looking for her.

Idiot, she thinks you're on the ship, I thought.

I moved forward reaching the end of the forest and planted myself behind a large tree. Looking around the side of the tree I saw a large fire and debris where the shuttles had been. A number of men were scrambling around the wreckage. I couldn't tell if they were looking for something or just freaking out. When three Dawnians pounced on them from between the wreckage, I confirmed it was the latter. Chorta, that wonderful son of a bitch was still alive and kicking. Literally.

My attention was quickly distracted by activity at the lake. A number of humans were at the shoreline. I saw King, but not Erebos. He could have been inside the mountain. What drew me to her and her cohorts were the large, seemingly heavy objects they were pushing into the lake from the larger transport ship. That and one other shuttle were all that remained. I was at a terrible vantage point to see what those shapes were, but knowing what Cessa kept with her on my ship it couldn't have been good.

Chorta and his men were beating down on the humans by the shuttle debris when reinforcements ran up from the two remaining shuttles. Chorta didn't see them. I made my move as they crossed my position. My bionic eye counted four men, all armed with weapons. I ran behind the first two and bashed their heads together, sending them quickly to the ground. The third soldier turned and aimed at me, but I swung out with my rifle and knocked his out of his hands. His eyes widened as I followed through with a kick to his chest. He fell into the soldier behind him who had aimed and pulled the trigger of his gun, but the impact caused his weapon to misfire into the sky. As his comrade fell on top of him, I leapt toward him and smacked him in the head with the butt of my rifle.

"Quinn! Well done, well done!" Sarah King bellowed from the lake. The two soldiers who were assisting her previously now had me at gun point and I had them in my sights as well. Sarah was unarmed, an easy target. I considered the thought of putting a plasma round in her. The soldiers would retaliate quickly and kill me, but at least she would be dead and people like Ashley would be avenged. No, that wasn't right. Erebos was still here and these people were still in danger.

"Get to the shuttle. Go back for more soldiers," she ordered her two lackeys. The two of them crossed in between us, their guns trained on me the whole time.

Come on, just shoot them. If you take them out then you won't need Laraar to destroy the shuttles. What if he isn't making the return trip? And if he does, he'll just be doing what you failed to by destroying the shuttles. Do it! Now!

I shook my head violently trying to get rid of the morbid thoughts. I had to trust Laraar would be back. My job was to contain the people on the ground and I couldn't risk being shot. I let them pass. King laughed at me.

"Oh Quinn, how can you be so impressive one moment and then ridiculously stupid the next? My men are about to go for reinforcements and you refuse to stop them? Where is the sense in that?"

"Sense has nothing to do with it King," I said to her, screaming over the thrusters of the shuttles. It's just that my reinforcements are here before yours."

Don't fail me now Laraar!

The timing couldn't have been better. King was processing what I said, wondering what the hell I was talking about when two green plasma blasts hit the shuttle and the transport ship, followed by an overhead flyby of the Belle. The shuttle spun out of control and crash landed out of sight. The transport ship was instantly engulfed in flames. I slowly advanced on King, a smile playing on my lips. Chorta and his men joined me. We finally had her. Erebos would be next.

"Give up Commander! You're alone now! Get on your communicator and order the men to stand down!"

"Or what?" she asked incredulously. "You don't exactly excel in killing people. Besides, I'm a Captain now and with that rank come the benefits befitting of that rank. I'm the one in charge and the one who calls the shots."

As she spoke the lake rippled and I noticed small forms rising from it. I saw heads, shoulders, bodies, and was rendered speechless as I realized King pushed humans into the lake to energize them. Stars above… my confidence level went down a couple of notches as they walked out of the empyreus.

Upon closer inspection as they drew near, I saw what they really were. They weren't humans. At one point they may have been, but these things behind King were vile monsters. Metallic plating and mechanical devices coated various parts of their body. It fused so flawlessly into their skin that it looked natural.

Sarah King had created her own fluxing cyborgs. She knew what the empyreus did and immediately took advantage of it. Merging machine with human wasn't anything new. Hell, my eye had been installed in my retinal socket years ago, but no one had ever found the trick to making the transition smooth and painless.

That wasn't the worst of it though. As disgusting as these things were, nothing prepared me for what came next. One of the cyborgs approached us stopping beside King and I studied the human aspects of him, the light brown wavy hair and green eye. His jaw was a hard line and his eyebrows were bushier than any average man's. Only three quarters of his human face remained. Half of his jaw and his right eye were replaced, but I could close my eyes and easily picture him. He had saved my life.

I was looking at a cyborg created out of my best friend, Jason Hobbes.

TWENTY

All I could feel in that moment was the tearing of my heart. Heavy tears formed in my eyes, quickly dropping to the ground. All these years I hoped beyond hope that Jason survived somehow, whether he got away or made up a convincing enough excuse so he wasn't labeled a traitor. Never in a million years would I have believed that Sarah King had kept him as a prisoner and experimented on him. Now having bathed in the empyreus, the machinery and cybernetics attached to him had bonded with his physical body making him a cyborg.

"Stars above," I whispered. "Jason, damn it. Oh damn, what did she do to you?"

Jason and the other cyborgs stood in front of the four of us as their bodies, clothes, and cybernetics absorbed the powerful energy. I was on my knees, my hand free of its weapon. I must have dropped it when I saw my friend's intense eyes burning anger and hatred into me. Chorta was breathing heavily, his hand pressed against his hip where a discharge had burned him. We were exhausted and the sight of Jason made me want to throw up and just give up altogether. Horku and a third Dawnian were both hunched over. Sarah King laughed.

"My scientists weren't sure the specimens would make it here alive," she said to me, walking up to her cyborgs and weaving through them. "These two here," she pointed to the two cyborgs behind her who I didn't recognize. "They are volunteers of the program. Jason however was very resistant . . . at first. I persuaded him."

"You bitch . . . you fluxing bitch!" I screamed at her. "How could you do this?"

How did she even know it could be done? I watched in horror as more cyborgs rose up out of the empyreus lake. Eight of them now stood in front of me. I started to dry heave and choked on my own saliva. I'm not sure why, but during my episode I thought of the energy and how it was known as a myth throughout humanity. Then I thought of Laraar telling me his people have been among the stars before. I couldn't be positive, but usually if I have a problem answering a question I just pick the simplest answer.

"You found one," I croaked. "You found one of the Dawnians in space didn't you? That's how you found out about this place, about what the empyreus can do . . ."

"Well done!" She said excited. "Quinn, I have to be honest, I never thought you were this bright yet here you are solving all these little mysteries. It's exciting isn't it? I thought the same thing when we stumbled upon our little alien friend. When we tore his ship apart and found out how it was powered we were astounded. Then when we tore *him* apart and found the same fuel. Well, we knew this was priceless, absolutely priceless."

I was told during my incarceration on the Echelon that the mind does strange things when it hits its breaking point. Sometimes it just shuts down, but sometimes it goes into a sort of overdrive mode, lashing out at the first thing it can. In all of a few seconds my mind sorted through various images from Ashley's dead body, to leaving Jason on the Echelon, to a dead Dawnian opened up on an examiner's table. Then it returned to the form of Jason, but mutated into a machine. At the center of it all was Sarah King who was standing right in front of me.

Something inside of me snapped, like someone flipped the light switch from on to off. Suddenly, like entering a dark room, I had no idea where I was going, only that I was stepping through the door. It just so happened to be the door to hell. I didn't care anymore about anything. I didn't care if I died or what the outcome of the battle was. Now that I think about it, I'm not even sure I was in complete control of my own actions. It felt more like my body went into autopilot. My rifle rose up before I realized it and in the blink of an eye I pointed my gun at Sarah King and opened fire. One of her cyborgs stepped in front of her and took countless plasma shots through the chest. When I saw him still standing there heavily injured and still functional, I couldn't believe it.

"Kill him!" Sarah shouted, and then eight cyborgs, one heavily wounded and leaking blood or oil, came rushing at me. Even Jason ran toward me. I opened fire again and unleashed a hell-storm of discharges at every cyborg in my sight. With empyreus fueling my weapon, the plasma banks never dropped.

I kept shooting until my arm was numb and my shoulder ached. Two of the cyborgs dropped to the ground, one whose head had been vaporized. The other one, the same one that protected King was motionless.

Stars above, I just killed them. The worst part was how I quickly resumed firing at every single body I saw in front of me. I relentlessly unloaded multiple discharges while the cyborgs charged, piercing their human skin, denting their metallic plating. A loud, angry screech of fury was carried on the wind. I realized it was me making the noise and it was nearly inhuman.

The cyborgs were almost on me. Then a large, muscular shape jumped in front of me wrapping its arms around three of the cyborgs and tackling them to the ground. Chorta's team screeched out a sound of fury much like my own, probably just mirroring me, and ran to engage the cyborgs. I joined them, screaming out as much frustration and anger as I could.

Our two groups reached each other and all hell broke loose. Jason threw a punch to my chest. I intended to block it, but he was too quick. The hit connected and I flew backwards, my chest erupting in pain. My armor was designed to take physical attacks, but not one that felt like a spaceship had just hit me. I couldn't breathe for several seconds and Jason leapt toward me, his knee bent, intent on smashing into my face. I rolled out of the way as the ground beside me shook from the impact. I quickly swiped my leg under him trying to knock him over, but when my leg connected with his, it felt like hitting a metal bulkhead. I howled out in pain, wondering if I just cracked the bone.

Jason took that moment to grab me by the throat and lift me off the ground. I grabbed his arms and tried to push against them to ease the pressure, but he kept squeezing. With his immense strength, it would be a matter of seconds before he broke my neck.

"Jason, it's Daniel," I said hoarsely, calmness breaking through my mental breakdown. "Jason, please…"

There was no recognition in his eyes. They didn't waiver or hesitate. Whatever she did to him, he truly saw me as his enemy. He had been left behind and paid for it with his life. I wondered if somewhere inside that body the real Jason was somehow trapped within his subconscious.

I told myself whatever I needed to for motivation. I had to keep living, stop Erebos and King and find a way to reverse this monstrosity that was once my friend. I allowed more of the anger and hatred that was flowing through me to come to the surface. I grabbed hard at his wrists, planted my feet against his chest, and kicked hard. If I couldn't release his hands at all the move would break my neck, but luckily I parted them just enough that I kicked him away and fell to the ground. I had seconds to see that the Dawnians were not doing well. The cyborgs had the clear advantage and were landing punches and kicks, completely overwhelming them. I admired their dedication and honor, especially Chorta. Every time he was knocked down he kept getting back up no matter how hard he was hit.

There wasn't really anything I could do. The cyborgs were pumped up on empyreus and we were tiring out. We wouldn't have the time to throw ourselves in the lake and absorb the energy. There was no way I could think of to power these bastards down.

Wait . . . yes there was!

Jason rushed me again, and I pushed myself out of his path and ran for my rifle. I dove on top of it as if I was sacrificing myself by jumping on a live grenade. I rolled to my back and entered a code onto the side panel. Before I could complete the sequence Jason was on me again. His knee thrust into my groin, causing me to cry out. His hands grabbed at the rifle and pushed it down to my neck, trying once again to choke me to death. With my peripheral vision, I caught sight of the other five cyborgs fighting around us. We were all in close proximity to one another. I turned my head to the side to get a better view of the weapon's panel. With my vision starting to turn red and my lungs unable to pull in any air, I used my last moment of life to finish the sequence with my pinky finger.

This is going to suck, was my last coherent thought.

The rifle had been a gift to me from my former Captain, Greg Smithson, the same man who was betrayed and went into exile to keep himself and ESA secrets safe. He had entrusted me with Al and helped me modify the weapon to access the various ammunitions. I hadn't used it all that much, but when I did it got the job done. The problem with the rifle was due to its multiple rounds, charges, and technology; the weapon could overheat if used too much and go into overload. I could only imagine what would happen if the empyreus-powered device was manually set to overload, and therefore self-destruct. After I managed to finish the sequence, a red warning message blinked, and I was about to find out.

I used every last ounce of energy and adrenaline I had and kicked against the ground to roll over on top of Jason. I let go of the gun as a high pitch noise began to reverberate through my ears and it came smashing into my face, which hurt like hell, but it also knocked me off of Jason. I braced for the explosion and when it came, a wave of energy passed over me and jolted my entire system. My body shook violently and an electric current traveled along my nervous system. I couldn't move or breathe. All I could do was lay there, my mind registering that my entire body was in agony.

When I had the ability to think coherently again, I was on my back and could only see through one eye. The EMP overload had knocked out my bionic one. Everything else about me seemed to be functioning for the most part. I could feel all my limbs and I was breathing. Every part of my body was in some type of pain, but nothing I couldn't handle for the moment.

I didn't so much turn my head as I just let it fall to one side then to the other so I could assess my situation. Everyone was on the ground. Chorta seemed to be breathing, but I looked at Horku for a moment and detected no movement whatsoever. Damn.

Something grabbed at my leg. I tried lifting my head to see what it was but couldn't. It slowly inched its way up towards my chest and each time it climbed higher, I felt five distinct joints. Fingers. Someone was pulling their way up to me.

Jason. He lived, though I didn't know how he could move.

His face was slashed in multiple places, assumingly from the debris of rifle parts that flew at him when it blew up. The cybernetic implants on the side of his face and leading down to his shoulder were sparking, and I guessed offline. He couldn't move his left hand which was mostly machine. Our eyes met, mine full of sorrow and his full of hatred.

"Danny," he spoke, but his tone of voice didn't match with the look in his eyes. He sounded like he was reaching out to me, the *real* Jason.

"Jason? Flux, can you hear me?"

He didn't answer me at first. His mouth looked like it was forcing itself shut, but he was still trying to talk. His face turned red as if he was putting intense pressure on his own head. When his mouth parted, it let out a gust of air as well as two words which weren't articulated, but easily understood.

"Kill me," he begged.

"What? You were trying to kill . . . Wait no. No! I won't! Not a chance in hell!"

"Danny" he groaned, his voice sounding more distance with every word. "I can't control it. I'll kill you. Please stop me. Kill me."

Flux. The EMP blast knocked him back to his old self, at least a part of him. His eyes kept that same look of hatred and his hand was close to wrapping around my throat for a third time. He was literally unable to control his own body. I couldn't even imagine, couldn't begin to process what a nightmare that would be. If I killed him, I would be ending his suffering and by his word saving my own life.

But I couldn't. I would die before murdering my best friend. I told him that or tried to through the tears and sobs.

"I'm so sorry Danny," he whispered to me. He tried to speak again but his mouth closed and his face simply . . . relaxed. The cyborg persona was taking back control. His hand rose, closed, and hammered down into my chest. The pain was intense. I coughed out violently, tasting blood in my mouth. He raised his hand again to throw down the final blow. I knew there was no way I'd survive another hit like that. A small part of me was okay with this being the end. All that my friend had been through on my account, I felt like I deserved it, but how would he feel? There was definitely a part of Jason still alive inside the monstrosity in front of me. I guess he would feel somewhat similar to how I felt now for what was done to him.

A staff, Chorta's staff, swiftly flew over top us, striking Jason in the head and knocking him off me. I breathed deep, my heart hammering against my chest. I really thought that was the end, but someone else changed my fate. A lavender colored hand reached out above me and I grasped it. I thought it was Chorta because of his weapon, but I looked up at the Dawnian that saved me and despite the immense pain I felt, I smiled and let out a small chuckle.

"Laraar. That's at least three times you saved my life. Thank you."

"*No need*," he said returning the smile.

"Is the ship okay? Where are Erebos and King? I saw her moments ago."

"*Relax . . . a moment. Ship safe*," he said as he pointed into the forest behind me. "*Humans in mountain . . . your status?*"

I was happy to be alive for the most part, but had a hard time bringing myself to look down at the mutated man I called my closest friend. Everything hurt and my two worst enemies were still alive. I shut my eyes hard, trying to push past the pain and despair.

With my eyes shut I never saw her. I didn't even hear her. Before I realized what was happening, Cessa had leapt behind Laraar, grabbed her sword from his back, and plunged it straight through his chest.

"NO!" I heard myself screeching.

I caught Laraar as he fell to the ground. There was no time for us to have a heart to heart. There was no time for me to thank him for everything he did for me. Laraar saved me from the mechanicals dogs, stood up for me during the blood price match, and saved me twice during the battle for Dawn. I owed him my life, but now I would never be able to repay him for all he did. Laraar looked frightened, but at the last moment his face relaxed and he breathed out one word.

"*Honored.*"

The whole world was a blur. The only thing in focus was Cessa, who wore a grin. A *fluxing* grin.

"I promised him Daniel," she said to me. "I promised that I would kill him for locking me up and taking my sword. I think I made you a similar promise."

She raised her sword to me, but I didn't even give her a second to consider throwing it down. The fire inside of me turned into the deepest, richest flames, from the levels of hell itself. My teeth were gritting together so hard I was shocked they didn't break. Every single muscle in my body tensed itself and the rage intensified with the power of hatred and vengeance.

I pushed up off the ground, my pain irrelevant as I rammed my shoulder into her abdomen, knocking her off her feet. She landed gracefully enough and thrust the sword toward my stomach. I threw my right arm under hers and heaved up, redirecting the aim from my stomach to my shoulder. The blade cut right into my armor and I felt an extreme burning sensation. I didn't care about the wound and besides the burn there was no additional pain. My anger and hatred smothered it. Cessa quickly spun her blade so the sharp edge was level with my neck. She made an attempt to make me a headless corpse, but I managed to throw up my left forearm blocking her. My armor held that time and I saw a moment's hesitation in her eyes. She didn't expect me to block that one so I used the millisecond to throw a right hook across her jaw.

Cessa recovered from the hit quicker than I expected and tried to kick me right between the legs. I managed to get my hand low enough to catch her foot, but she used the opening I inadvertently created to throw her own punch. It landed and my cheekbone flared with pulsating pain. I stumbled backwards and she grasped the hilt of her sword with both hands, winding it up like a baseball bat ready to swing. I could almost hear her blade cutting through the air. I simply allowed myself to fall to the ground, the sword missing me by less than an inch. I'm fairly certain some of my hairs were sheared off.

I landed on my ass but thrust my legs forward. The bottom of my boots connected with Cessa's knees. She hunched over, screaming out, and I took the opportunity to grab the wrist of her sword hand. She fell on me trying to stab me in the face, but I tilted my head and the blade pierced the ground. I folded my legs in and Cessa landed on my knees, but she wasn't there for long. I grunted and threw my legs back, sending Cessa tumbling over me. When I stood up both of our hands were touching the sword, but I had the leverage I needed and wrestled it away from her.

I stood over her using her own sword to pin her to the ground. The point of the blade rested against her throat, and I wanted nothing more than to simply push it into her.

"Do . . . it . . ." she rasped, her breaths labored like mine.

I raised the sword up to strike, to kill her. I wanted to do it so badly. She deserved it. How ironic would it be if she were killed by her own sword, the same one she used to kill others? I looked into her eyes and a moment before striking I saw how wide and afraid they were. That wasn't why I stopped myself though. It was the blood that stained her sword, the blood of my friend. I mentally pushed with all my strength to lock the aggressive emotions behind a door. I felt the fatigue and injuries the more I closed it.

"I'm not . . . like you . . ." I replied. Blood ran down from my shoulder and dripped from my chin. I spit blood toward the ground.

From behind the two of us that damn slow clapping sound had returned. I moved my body slightly around Cessa so I still had her in my sight and could see Sarah King and Raymond Erebos returning from the cave in the mountain. My legs went numb. I managed to back away from the three of them and dropped beside Laraar's body. I rested one hand on his chest and the sword across my lap. My lungs hated me right now, trying their best to keep oxygen flowing through my blood. My eyes were stinging from the tears and sweat. Now that I had calmed my emotions down my heart just wasn't in this fight anymore. Too many people had died.

"I have to say, when you get angry you are quite impressive," King said to me. "I wish I knew this back when I framed you. Maybe I would have just experimented on you instead of your friend."

I looked at Jason, who was still unconscious. Other cyborgs and Dawnians were too.

Erebos looked at me with a mixture of disdain and disappointment. His hands were folded together in front of his stomach. I almost laughed. Everyone else surrounding us was dirty, beaten, and bloodied, but these two fluxers looked like they just got here. Neither of them had a scratch or even a hair out of place.

"Mr. Quinn, I can admire your valiant attempt to stop us, but ultimately it was futile. Now that you've run out of options I think it best you surrender. I will rescind my statement of killing you and you can serve in my employ. How does that sound?"

In response I spit blood at his feet. He dropped his hands.

"We have the empyreus, Quinn, and now we have you," King said. "Now all I need is the A.I. program. Make no mistake, my soldiers are searching for your precious ship. They'll find it and take it apart piece by piece."

Al. Stars above, I still had one more fluxing card to play.

I reached down to my communicator, and my heart sank when I realized that I had been wearing it when I set off the EMP explosion. The device was useless now and I was out of options. *Unless . . .*

I turned to Laraar, who still wore his translator. Technically since all devices were powered by empyreus, they should all be connected. That's what Laraar told me anyway. I wouldn't have time to test it without the two of them suspecting something. Even Cessa was beginning to catch her breath. She would be up in moments and assumingly would want her sword back. Over my dead body. I would only have one chance to do this.

"Erebos, go to hell . . . and commander . . . you still have a problem looking right under your nose." I quickly turned my head and all but threw myself on top of Laraar, screaming into his translator.

"AL! BOOM!"

It's unbelievable the number of thoughts that can pass through your mind in no time at all. I couldn't help but feel that if I put this plan into action a lot sooner, then maybe so many people wouldn't have died. As they say, nobody is perfect, me least of all. I tried to do everything I could to save the Dawnians and protect their way of life, but in the end if they couldn't keep control of the empyreus then no one would have it. I could only hope I would be forgiven and didn't condemn their race when I placed the explosive cargo boxes Cessa packed on my ship within the mountain. I literally added fuel to the fire when I enhanced every one of them with empyreus. Now whatever job they had been meant for, whether it was exterminating the Dawnian race or just blowing up my ship didn't matter.

Because I just blew up the entire fluxing mountain.

TWENTY ONE

My entire state of being felt disconnected from my physical body. When I opened my good eye the entire area was shifting and moving. When I tried lifting my arm I saw the blurry outline of it in my vision, but I didn't really register that I had moved it at all. If anything it seemed like my brain had a two or three second delay before any messages reached my limbs. Was it just my imagination or did the explosion totally screw me up?

As the time differential between my brain and limbs balanced itself out I got to my feet, though it took a couple of attempts. Most of the world was still a total blur. The only thing I could hear was a high pitch noise passing from ear to ear, hammering the inside of my head in the process. I smelled nothing but smoke and fire.

Though my eye was still trying to piece together everything it was seeing, one thing stood out right away and that was the lack of a giant mountain in front of me. Instead I saw large piles of rubble, rock, and crystal. Smoke rose into the sky, reminiscent of a mushroom cloud. Other people, both human and alien, were on the ground, some face down, some up. I knew in the back of my mind that Erebos, King, and Cessa were all there somewhere, but the first thing I did when I saw the mountain or lack thereof, was turn the other way and run. Well, I tried to run, but couldn't so I stumbled forward step by step.

Something in my path caught my foot and I fell face forward to the ground. I didn't even realize I still held Cessa's sword in my hand until I let it go when I fell. I quickly rolled over thinking whatever had tripped me was alive and waiting for me. My paranoia was on full alert, but as I looked at the body on the ground I saw Sarah King, unconscious. I kicked away from her and reached to grab the sword. That's when I noticed something just under her shoulder. My ring. I slowly reached out moving my eyes from the ring to her face every couple of seconds. I imagined grabbing the ring only for her to awaken and lunge at me. I moved as fast as I could and managed to grab it. The rope I used to tie it around my neck was gone, but I didn't care. I kissed the ring and closed it in my fist. I stood back up with the ring and sword, moving away from the area before anyone conscious found me.

My sight and hearing slowly returned back to normal as I stumbled through the forest, though normal was sort of an exaggeration. My head pounded and my shoulder burned with pain. The cut still bled, though not as bad as before. My chest hurt, probably from the literal pounding that Jason gave me.

I stopped for a moment, cursing myself that I didn't look for him in the aftermath of the explosion. I almost turned to go back, but stopped myself. He wasn't really Jason anymore, at least on the surface. If I went back and he regained consciousness, he could kill me and the enemy would still win despite the loss of the empyreus processing machine. I had to find my way back to the village. I hoped someone there was still alive to help me.

Numerous times I tried to activate my bionic eye, but it was still offline. I wondered if it would ever come back online or if the power of the EMP was great enough that it damaged the circuitry beyond repair. I passed by a number of trees and large shrub-like plants, and took sight of something beautiful, something mesmerizing.

The Kestrel Belle stood right in front of me.

The bay door was open, and while I remembered that Laraar didn't have full knowledge of the ship's systems, I also remembered Sarah King had people out looking for it. For all I knew soldiers were onboard now. I proceeded slowly and as quietly as I could, though I grunted with each step I took.

The bay itself was empty. I stopped and found myself looking at the area where Cessa's damn boxes were previously placed. That's when I heard a noise come from the corridor up the ladder. There was definitely someone here and they didn't care to be quiet about it. I gripped the sword hard and moved forward, climbed the ladder, and peaked over the scaffold. I could hear voices, but I was too far away to discern what they were saying. Judging by the direction of the sound and the number of differentiating tones I guessed two of them were on my bridge.

I walked through the corridor and saw nothing out of place. It seemed like they went straight for the bridge, presumably to look for Al's mainframe. The door was closed but not latched, a small sliver of light showing through the gap. I proceeded with caution trying to be as quiet as I could. I peeked through the small opening and saw one guard on his knee, bending over to look at the circuitry and computer components under my navigational console. The panel had been broken and wires were dangling from the inside. The other guard sat in my chair, looking over my configuration for any signs of Al. The bastards were gutting my ship at its brain.

Without thinking I smashed the door in, leapt forward, and grabbed the kneeling soldier from behind. Before he could say a word, I placed the sword against his throat. The second soldier turned to find us locked together. His eyes widened. He opened his mouth to say something, but stopped as his eyes met mine.

I could only imagine what I looked like right now. I assumed the sight the guard got was one of a beaten man, bruised and cut with blood on his suit. There was still blood on Cessa's sword as well.

"Do you have weapons?" I heard myself ask. Neither of them replied, so I applied a little more pressure to the soldier's neck.

"Do . . . you . . . have . . . weapons?" This time my voice sounded like an enraged animal. The soldier in my seat shuddered and he slowly drew his gun, a small plasma gun, standard weapon of the ESA infantry.

"Drop it to the floor . . . now!" I screamed, and watched as he followed my order. The soldier acting as my hostage drew his weapon as well and quickly threw it on the floor. I tightened my hold on him and he cried out.

"No! Please! I don't want to die!"

"Right then," I said, not recognizing my voice, the force and anger mixed with fatigue. "This is how it's going to work. The two of you will leave this ship without your weapons. You will not disobey me or put up a fight. If I sense deception in either of you, I will kill you both."

I'm pretty sure I meant it at the time, which is why I was slightly relieved when they ran out of the ship. I shut the door to the bridge and took a moment to breathe. I was alone. There was no Al. With my communicator deactivated I couldn't contact him . . . unless I did so through the Belle itself!

I jumped over to the communication console, cursing myself for moving too fast, which only made my body hurt worse and flood my mind with dizziness. I turned a couple of knobs and searched for Al's signal. It took me less than a minute to find it.

"Al! Al come in! Do you read me?"

Please let him be safe, please tell me the village is still standing . . .

"Captain? Yes, I can read you."

"Flux, thank the stars above. Listen, I'm on the Belle and I have no idea what to do now. What's the status at the village?"

"The battle seems to be over Captain. Being installed in this computer does not give me a wide range of sensor ability, but I can scan the immediate area. The Dawnians are all being herded together one hundred yards south of my position. I also scanned multiple humanoid signatures moving in range. They appear to be joining the larger group. Captain, there are a number of humanoids that register . . . rather oddly."

I sagged in my chair. The cyborgs. That meant King probably survived, maybe even Erebos and Cessa.

"Captain, I must also inform you that the starship Echelon has made landfall."

"What?"

"Just moments ago the ESA Echelon lowered into the atmosphere and landed outside the village."

I really had no fluxing clue what to do now. I thought maybe with the destruction of the shuttles that King would request more, but I didn't think in a million years that she would bring the flagship onto the planet. Unless . . . with the destruction of the mountain, did she intend on flying the entire ship into what was left of the empyreus lake to absorb it? That had to be the plan. I had to stop it from happening, but how?

"Al," I said softly as I returned to my command chair, leaving the comm signal open. "I'm going to manually pilot the ship to collide with the Echelon."

"Sir, is this a wise course of action? I will confirm that if you maintain full thrusters the impact will destroy both ships, but are you sure this is your only choice?"

Al actually sounded concerned for me. It felt good and helped me stand firm in my decision.

"I'm sure Al."

When I punched in the sequence to lift the ship into its hovering mode, nothing happened. I activated the thrusters while still on the ground. Nothing happened. I looked down at the hanging wires. The soldiers must have disconnected the navigational system while they were looking for Al. Stars above! I was actually ready to sacrifice myself and still something went wrong!

"Damn it to hell! Can't a guy catch a break when he's trying to save a civilization?"

"I regret that you are unable to pilot the ship to defend these people," Al said after I explained the problem to him. "If only the autopilot was still installed on the ship, I could pilot it remotely from here."

In that moment, the moment I gave up hope and wanted to quit and just wish for it all to end, I had one more thought. Suddenly another option presented itself, an insane one that would only work if the damn stars were aligned perfectly, but this was our last option.

"Al," I said with a renewed enthusiasm. "I need to get to you quickly, but . . . damn it. I'm in bad shape and the ship's navigation is out. How the hell am I supposed to get to you? If only I had your portable module . . ."

"You should have it Captain," Al said.

I blinked.

"What? How? Isn't it with you?"

"Negative sir," Al said. "The module was disconnected from my mainframe during the uninstallation process, though you should know your chances of a successful teleport are no greater than they were before."

I dropped to the floor searching for the module. I couldn't remember the exact success rate that Al mentioned over a week ago, something under 60% I think. I searched and searched, looked under every station on the bridge. I finally found it pushed into the corner of the floor. I grabbed it and attached it back onto Ashley's ring. It looked the same as the day I purchased it, though at the time the diamond on top was actually a diamond. With the ring in one hand and Cessa's sword in the other, I stood up and kept still.

"Al. Found it. Execute teleportation now," I said with a renewed determination.

Within a minute I felt the familiar pull of each and every part of my body. It took Al longer to calculate and activate the module than it took me to teleport to him. When I rematerialized my body was in the air a few feet above the ground. I dropped and my legs couldn't support the fall. I did my best to ignore the pain and stood up, looking around. There wasn't anyone in sight, though I heard a large commotion somewhere across the village. In that same direction I looked up in the sky to see the outline of the giant Echelon. Seeing her on the ground made her all the more magnificent and at the same time, terrifying.

I had to move quickly. Someone could spot me here at any moment. Not only would they arrest or kill me, but they would more than likely study this station and learn of Al's existence.

"Okay Al, you said you can't control the Belle because the autopilot wasn't functional, not to mention the bastards tore apart navigation . . . anyway, what if it *was* functional, but on another ship?"

The Belle couldn't be remote controlled, but maybe the Echelon could be! Al had been installed in that computer core as well, and should have prior knowledge of how to manipulate the systems. I knew that King and her minions would've had to reinstall certain components after Captain Smithson removed Al, but most of the computer systems should still be compatible. I waited for Al's response, hoping it was a good one.

"Captain, I am tied into the Echelon's navigational control."

"Al, see if you can . . . wait, what? I didn't tell you to do that," I said, a puzzled look formed on my face.

"Captain, I believe it is something you call . . . improvising and you did request I work on it, did you not?"

I laughed out loud.

"Al, you're the most amazing non-sentient being I've ever known." I stepped up to the control panel of the station and the two of us input commands into the Echelon mainframe. Al wasn't the only one who had knowledge of how their computer systems worked. I was going to make sure we gave them quite a shock and I explained my plan to accomplish that to him.

"Captain, if my sensors are correct, the Dawnians being held south of our position are about to be executed. I detect weapon systems charging from multiple devices."

Flux! I had to stall them. I could only think of one thing and I cringed at the thought of doing it, but I had little choice.

"Al, is Idza still alive? Can you sense her life signs through her translator?"

"Yes Captain. She is among the people who are about to be terminated."

I asked Al to patch into her translator so I could talk to her. I thought carefully about what I wanted to say and how I would say it.

"Idza, it's Daniel. I'm alive, surprisingly. I'm so sorry that all of this happened to you and your people. I never meant for it to be this way . . ." I paused taking a deep breath before continuing. "I think I can save us Idza, but I need your help. I need your music, your song, to persuade the soldiers to disengage one more time. It doesn't have to affect them for very long."

I stopped and waited. She responded with a question, one I expected.

"*Laraar?*"

I didn't know what to say or how to break the news. It didn't matter though. My hesitation told her what she needed to know. She didn't say another word into the translator and there was nothing but silence. Suddenly I heard a soft, low humming that was carried on the wind. More voices joined in and from my position in the village I could hear a ballad that was lovely and at the same time sad. The emotions poured into me and I felt even worse.

I knew that the soldiers would be feeling the same way I was.

"Al, put our plan into action now. I'll see you later if I'm not dead."

I left Al to do his work and ran toward the singing, hoping I wouldn't be shot or killed in the process. When I turned at a junction in the village's path, I saw the crowd of humans and Dawnians. Forty or fifty humans stood in front of them with their guns lowered. A lot of the Dawnians still lived, too many to count, but I knew many had already died. They were on their knees, hands placed on the ground and they were swaying, singing their beautiful ballad. I stopped for a moment to listen, feeling tired of battle and death.

Snap out of it! Snap out of it, I told myself over and over. I tuned out the song as best I could and ran up to the group. I saw Raymond Erebos, Sarah King, and Cessa along with a number of cyborgs. One of them was Jason. Their entire group was covered in dust and dirt, the aftermath of the mountain's explosion.

The cyborgs were moving to attack the Dawnians. The musical spell didn't work on them. Before they could do anything, I screamed out over the music.

"Stop! Stop!"

When Erebos looked at me he smiled, King frowned, and Cessa looked directly at her sword. Erebos raised his hands and told everyone to stand down, though most of the soldiers and thugs were still reeling from the effects of the music. King ordered the cyborgs to return to her position and they waited as I caught up to the group and stood between the humans and Dawnians.

"Mr. Quinn, never in my life has a day gone by where someone has impressed me as many times as you. You have defended this planet and its people with honor, but ultimately you have to realize the folly of your attempts. There was never any way you could win."

"Mr. Erebos," I replied to him, mocking his tone. "Never in the time I've known you have you looked so filthy! It's nice to see that you're finally getting your hands dirty!"

I quickly switched gears, changing my tone to something more serious and sincere.

"Do you even give a damn about the people who lost their lives today?" I asked

"I think we previously established that sacrifices are necessary to obtain one's goal," Erebos said. He smiled and raised his hand up toward me. "You yourself know this. You blew up their mountain, separating them from their ability to harness the empyreus. How do you know that you didn't condemn their race to death by doing so?"

He had a point, but this conversation wasn't meant to guilt trip me. I'd feel plenty of guilt later if I wasn't dead. All I needed to do now was distract him.

"I don't know what the consequences will be, but I stopped you from getting your hands on it. Speak all you want about what's good for the human race, but I've seen the monstrosities you intend on creating with it. The universe itself could only know what other demonic plans you have."

"Demonic?" Erebos asked, tilting his head back and laughing. "I won't try to persuade you anymore Mr. Quinn. You've chosen your side. Unfortunately it was the wrong one because you've only delayed the inevitable. I can wait here patiently while the creatures you call friends rebuild their facility for me or die by refusing."

A communication device attached to King's hip flashed blue and red and then beeped in furious successions. A young man's voice spoke through static.

"Captain King! Captain King! Urgent!" I stretched my lips as wide as they could go in a successful smile. *Al, you amazing son of a bitch you did it!* I couldn't help but use the moment to taunt Erebos one more time.

"Well Erebos, I think you will be waiting longer than you expected." I looked at King, who was trying to ignore her officer calling in. "You may want to get that . . . Commander."

She tore the device from her belt, shouting into the speaker. "What the hell do you want?"

"Captain, the Echelon is prepping for departure!"

Every human, from the soldiers and thugs to the assholes who controlled them turned to the Echelon and stared in shock. King turned back toward me, her mouth parted and eyes wide. I winked at her.

"What are you talking about?" Her head trembled, which made me wonder if it could explode.

"Something is overriding the controls, Captain. The system is set to take us out of the system in two minutes!"

She stared at the comm device and then looked back at me, rage boiling over in her eyes. She knew what I had done and how I did it, by utilizing the very artificial intelligence program she sought.

"Do you think yourself clever? You think you can scare us away like this? How do you know I won't just leave my soldiers here to take control of the planet?"

Wait for it . . .

"Captain!" The same voice shouted, though noticeably more scared. He didn't even wait for her response this time. "Our self-destruct program has been activated! It will destroy the ship in less than ten minutes!"

Her rage slowly turned to confusion, then panic.

"You wouldn't," she said, trying to convince herself I wasn't a murderer. She told me this very fact, reminding me that more than just soldiers lived on the starship, commoners and families. She knew I would never kill an innocent. That's why I gave her one more piece of information with the best game face I could muster.

"You're right. I would never kill innocents, but the thing is I don't have control of the self-destruct sequence. The only one who can deactivate it is the artificial intelligence program. Personally, I don't think he cares about commoners or families."

Just saying those words left a bitter taste in my mouth, but I had to do it to prove my point. "Take all of your humans with you King, including Erebos and Cessa. Once you're onboard and the ship takes off, the self-destruct will be deactivated."

"Why the hell should I trust you?" She snarled. I shrugged.

"Don't then. See what happens."

Wow, if looks could kill.

She stared at me with a hatred so intense, so maniacal that I swear her hair was standing on end. Her fingers dug so hard into her palms I was surprised blood wasn't dripping from her hands.

"You son of a bitch," she growled. "I won't forget this. I'll be back for you."

"Sorry but I won't be here. If you want your precious A.I., or me, I suggest you come looking for me elsewhere. Oh, and one more thing," I said as I tapped my finger against my bionic eye, which replaced the one she took from me. "I don't forget either."

She turned from me and stomped back to her ship along with her soldiers and cyborgs. I watched Jason as he turned to leave, wishing there was something I could do for him. I wanted to call out his name, convince him to stay behind. Unfortunately the persona that held control over his original personality couldn't be trusted. He could easily snap my neck if I was caught off guard. This wasn't the end though, I promised myself I would find him and do whatever it took to help him.

That left me with Erebos and Cessa, who both looked at me incredulously. Cessa's eyes kept darting between mine and her sword which rested over my shoulder. Then Erebos did something I didn't expect. He shrugged his shoulders and smiled, but the smile didn't show through his eyes at all. They burned their way to my soul. I shuddered.

"Well done Mr. Quinn," he said. "It is foolish to not respect those who stand up for what they believe in. You have won this battle and I lost." He gave me the slightest bow with his head. "However, our business is not yet finished. As I said, I can wait patiently. As I do, I'll be watching you."

"That's . . . kind of creepy," was the only thing that came out of my mouth. Erebos finally turned and walked back to the ship. Now it was just Cessa and me.

"I want my sword," she said to me. I held it in front of me and examined it. The craftsmanship was superb, the blade itself sharper than any I ever saw. I kept my eyes on it, waiting for some nightmarish image to pop in my head, but nothing came of it. The weapon itself represented a symbol of everything I feared and tried to run from. Whether it was Ashley's death or Laraar's, maybe it was time to face that fear and use it as a reminder—not of what I lost, but what I had.

Plus, I was a mercenary and I was fairly certain the payment Erebos promised me wouldn't be coming.

"The sword belongs to me now," I said. The words were like an ocean of fuel poured onto a wildfire. She bent her knees, seemingly about to strike until a loud booming voice called out to her.

"Cessa! Come!"

The loud angered voice of Erebos was terrifying. In the time I knew and interacted with him I hadn't heard him sound so . . . evil. In that instant I thought I saw something pass over Cessa's face. Her eyes widened, her mouth cringed. She looked terrified. I wasn't wrong when I said Erebos controlled her and did so by using fear. I couldn't help but feel pity for her in that small moment. Then, as quickly as I had seen it, her face returned to the cold, hated expression I was used to.

"Keep that close Daniel," she said to me, turning away. Finally the last of my kind boarded the ship. I felt a body stand next to me. Idza.

"Destroy their ship . . . would you have?"

"No," I said, watching the massive starship lift into the sky. "I would never sacrifice so many innocent people. Thankfully my bluffs are getting harder to read."

"Bluffs?" she asked me. I told her I would explain later, but she wasn't done asking questions.

"Why do they not fire on us . . . destroy us?"

I smiled and took my eyes off of the ship.

"Al and I did a little reprogramming of their computer. Thanks to the empyreus in his system we managed to hack the navigation and weapon control. They're probably trying to figure out why their weapons won't fire right about now."

We stood there awhile longer before she spoke again.

"They will be back," she said softly.

"Yes," I replied. "But it will take them a lot longer than you think."

TWENTY TWO

A brand new day was about to begin on the planet Dawn. The human threat had been contained and sent on its way. Unfortunately it came at a great cost, namely the destruction of the Dawnian's ability to process the empyreus. My actions in triggering the explosion left me responsible. Sure, at the time it was an easy decision. If I didn't do it who knows how the battle would have ended, how many more monstrosities King would have created. I kept telling myself it was for the good of the Dawnians *and* the universe.

Idza agreed with me for the most part. After the Echelon had cleared orbit we continued our discussion. She was interested in why I didn't think King and Erebos would be back anytime soon.

"Al and I just make a great team. He activated their autopilot and their self-destruct while I deactivated their weapon systems. Then I decided to take a detour into their star charts and did a little scrambling. When they get back to human space they're in for a shock when they realize Dawn isn't listed where it's supposed to be."

I gave her a thumbs up and a smile.

Idza looked pleased by that and then ordered me to the hospital for treatment. She didn't like the way I looked with my body bruised and beaten. I didn't feel all that well either. There was a good chance I had some internal damage from Jason hammering his cybernetic fist into me. After washing up with empyreus, using as little as I could manage, I slept for a few hours. When I awoke I felt amazing and my bionic eye finally started to work again. Idza was waiting for me and together we walked outside of the village to help in the cleanup, collecting the dead and unconscious.

"Can you find another source for the empyreus crystals and build a new processor?" I asked her during our walk.

"*The . . . crystals grown in the mountain . . . only grow there.*"

She told me based on the amount of empyreus left in the lake, if used sparingly it would last them another seven to ten

Earth years. If they planned to excavate the rocks and boulders from the cave's floor, as well as build a new processing facility, it would take them roughly half a century. No one really knew what would happen when the empyreus ran out. It made the Dawnians strong, focused, and peaceful. Their way of life was as melodious as the music they sang. Empyreus helped them realize their true potential, but I couldn't help but wonder if they had already reached that potential, and because of it they didn't know where else to go or how else to evolve. They forgot what it was like to live for something, to fight for something. There wasn't a care in the world until humanity entered their lives. When Erebos and King invaded, the Dawnians were ill prepared for it.

How would all of this change in the next few years? Would it be like an addict detoxing off drugs? Or would they start to realize the wonders and terrors that still eluded them in space?

Flux, I was exhausted. I couldn't help but replay the last few days over in my head, the fight between Chorta and me, the battle between human and Dawnian . . . and Jason.

Stars above, Jason.

He protected me, saved my life years ago, and he paid the ultimate price. Now he was trapped in a grotesque form of himself, bonded with various metals and bionics. Although a part of me was convinced the cyborg wasn't Jason anymore, I knew somewhere deep inside he fought to survive. At least in his own way, his soul still lived.

I made sure to collect the bodies of all the humans who were either knocked unconscious or dead. For the deceased, I dug out their graves myself, wanting to give them a proper human burial. This was never meant to be a battle between Earthling and Dawnian. I didn't think of myself as some kind of defector. I liked to think that I acted in the best interest of everyone involved. I wanted to believe that I did what was right, not only for the Dawnians, but for the better side of humanity.

When it came to the humans that were still alive, Idza brought me to the Authority who had their own plans. They sang their song to me, letting Idza translate.

"Humans will remain with us . . . they wanted our planet . . . wanted us. We wish to understand . . . we want them to understand."

They put their foot down and I wasn't getting much of a choice in the matter. In a way it made sense. These humans, assuming they cooperated, could learn a lot from these creatures. Maybe they could even grow to befriend them, to see the lives they almost destroyed. I couldn't help but wonder at times whether they even realized what they were doing from the beginning. Did they know the endgame or were they following orders blindly?

"If they remain here, will you give me your word, your vow that no harm will come to them? Will they be treated well?"

I waited for the translation to go through. They nodded and sang back to us.

"Yes . . . our intention is to learn from each other . . . over time . . . if they do not prove violent, they will be free to walk among us."

Well, that was that I suppose. I bowed to them, but they weren't finished. More singing rang out among the tent. I looked to Idza for the translation, but she hesitated to say it. Her face grew somber.

"They . . . request you honor your promise . . . you will leave the planet."

Ouch. That felt like a figurative sucker punch to my stomach. They must have seen the wince I made when they said that. They sang again, this time it was a little softer.

"We are very grateful . . . you saved us . . . we do not deny it. You must also realize you have some fault in what happened. Many of us will honor you . . . some of us will not forgive you for deaths of loved ones . . . the destruction of sorania machine. You said you would leave if you saved us . . . all we ask is you honor your words."

There was no argument against what was said. I did tell them I would leave. After all that happened it shouldn't have been surprising to me that I was a reminder of what they had, how peacefully they lived until I arrived. In a few years when the empyreus runs out, they'll remember what and who caused it, but I wasn't ready to leave just yet.

"I will honor my promise and leave you, but only after I am allowed to stand with you during the burning of the fallen. I wish to see Laraar one last time before his life force is released from his body."

The three of them looked at each other, deciding whether they would allow it. I watched a small tear form in Idza's eyes. The Authority accepted my request provided that I would leave shortly after. I agreed.

The Belle's repairs finished within a couple of days. Al, of course, was reinstalled into it. His mainframe had fused with the Dawnian technology, but they were willing to sacrifice some of their components. At first they wanted to keep him as well as the human soldiers, but I refused it. I made a promise to Greg Smithson that I would keep Al safe, and since my father was one of the engineers that designed Al, I would never let him out of my sight as long as I could help it. With Al integrated into my ship, I felt like I had a little piece of my family with me every day.

I gathered together with the Dawnians one last time as they set fire to their fallen. So many of them died, some of whom I never had the pleasure to meet. Horku and Grimal were among the fallen, now burning in the fire. Their life force would soon be reunited with Grent's. I held Idza's hand during the ceremony. My eyes burned with tears as we watched Laraar's body burn to ash. The Dawnians sent their people off with a soft, yet powerful dirge, which didn't make it any easier for me to contain my emotions. I would never forget the bond that Laraar and I created and I would miss him terribly. Idza told me that he would stand among the honored fallen of his people. If it wasn't for him, I would have never had the chance to blow the mountain or send away Erebos and King. He not only fought for this world, but I felt like he fought for me.

Afterwards it was time for me to depart and Idza accompanied me to the Belle. I didn't even get a chance to talk to the human soldiers. I hoped that everything would work out for them, and maybe one day in the future I could come back here and see the progress that was made. Even though I would miss this place, the thought of being back in space gave me goose bumps. It's where I belonged. I looked at my ship, assessing the damage to the hull and took notice of my starboard wing, more specifically a section of paint that was scraped off. That wasn't there before. It made me smile.

Laraar and his piloting skills, I thought. At least I knew with the paint missing, I would always be reminded of him. I would never fix it.

"*Will you be able to make it home?*" Idza asked me.

I tried to calculate the amount of fuel I had left. With over half of my cells sacrificed there was a good chance I wouldn't make it. For whatever reason that didn't scare me. I had my ship, I had Al, and the people of this planet were safe for now. I told this to Idza and she produced a small canister from a pouch hanging on her waste.

"Empyreus? No I can't. You should save what you have left."

"*Daniel, you still try and hold blame . . . Had you not destroyed the mountain, the humans may have taken all our lives. You say you did us wrong, but I say you did us right. Forget the others . . . believe me. Take this and go home. I insist.*"

She held it out to me, her eyes pleading. I felt like I would be insulting her if I didn't take it, so I did and thanked her. The two of us stood across from each other and time seemed to stand still. I could only hope that everything I did here wasn't in vain. The honor and sacrifice of Laraar and countless other Dawnians depended on humanity staying away, at least for now. I hoped that at some point I could share everything I learned and experienced here. I worried about what would happen if this planet fell into the wrong hands, but for every wrong there is a right. I firmly believed that one day there could be peace between our two races. I told this to the Authority and Idza before leaving.

"I keep a mission log on my ship and I'll make sure the time I spend traveling back to my sector of space will recount everything I experienced here. My people have similar authorities like yours and I hope to one day present them with the log and bring good people here, people who will work and learn from you, just like I have."

I walked toward Idza, opened my arms, and put them

around her, pulling her into a tight embrace. At first she kept still, but then I felt her hug me back. We stayed that way for a while. When we let go my eyes were misty and I felt tears building up.

"I'll miss you Idza."

"*Your presence has been an added piece to my life force. It will not be the same.*"

Every minute that passed was just putting off the inevitable and if I didn't step onboard the Belle right then, I might have just stayed despite the order of the Authority. But believe it or not, with all the trouble waiting for me I was ready to face it. My feet touched onto the metal floor of the cargo bay and I turned to wave to Idza as I pulled up the latch. The first tear didn't fall until the door shut, separating us, but after the first came more and I broke down as I walked to the bridge. When I finally sat down, I couldn't help but smile at the second rate controls and cracked display screens. The ship was a hunk of junk, but she was my hunk of junk and she had carried me safely from one end of the galaxy to another.

"Captain," Al said. I was happy to hear his voice again. For a time I was worried they wouldn't be able to reintegrate his system with the ship. He may not be sentient, but after the years I worked with him, I honestly considered him a friend and confidant. I wouldn't tell him that though. It would drive up his ego too much. "Based on your apparent emotional state I feel obligated to ask if you are okay."

I laughed at him. The statement was so serious yet I knew that was his way of showing concern for me.

"I'm okay Al, thanks. Let's activate the reactors and get out of here."

The Belle buzzed with energy and lifted off the ground. I stared out of my window at the wonder that was Dawn; beautiful trees, blue colored grass, golden sun, and, most of all, the village in the distance where the people were busy repairing their buildings, their homes, and their way of life. I turned the axis of my ship slightly to see Idza standing below watching the ship take off into the sky. I knew she couldn't see me, but I saw her and I kept the ship hovering there for a moment before finally punching the execute button. The ship turned and took off quickly through the clouds and up into the atmosphere. I leaned back in my chair and took a deep breath. I tried to focus on the hum and rhythm of the ship's engines, which normally acted as an agent to calm me down, but for once they had little effect on me.

"Captain," Al said, startling me awake. "I must inform you that we do not have sufficient fuel to return home."

Without responding I stood up and left the bridge, walked down two floors to the engine room, and used a small amount of the empyreus on my engine cores. The two large engines hummed appreciatively and power levels spiked to maximum. Even after I witnessed the power of empyreus multiple times, it still bewildered me. When I returned to the bridge, Al actually sounded excited.

"Captain, correction of previous statement: at maximum slingspace velocity the ship will reach human space in 5 days, 2 hours and 17 minutes!"

My eyebrows shot up at Al's time estimate, which was half as long as it took to get here.

"Well, let's not be in too much of a hurry," I said. "Although it would be fun if we beat the Echelon back."

I laughed, though it felt strangely hollow. I looked out into the vast, endless reaches of space hoping to feel relieved, but I couldn't help wondering about the Dawnians I left behind and how they would adapt to a new lifestyle. Surely Raymond Erebos, Sarah King, and Cessa would be keeping an eye out for me for all the wrong I did them. So much happened in the last few weeks and I wasn't sure who I was anymore. I killed. I destroyed the energy source the Dawnians relied on and you can't just move on from things like that. I had a feeling the trip home was going to bring a new set of nightmares.

Still, there was one thing I was absolutely sure of. I was Captain Daniel Quinn of the Kestrel Belle. Nothing and no one would ever change that.

"Orders, Captain?"

"Take us back to humanity's little corner of the galaxy Al," I said. "Let's take it slow and steady. I think we've caused enough trouble . . . at least for now."

Coming soon!

Keep reading for a special preview of:

ANTAGONIZE
FROM THE LOGS OF DANIEL QUINN

There's something to consider when you're traveling between alien planets —they have no idea how to cook a human meal. I sat in a bistro created by the Karthans to facilitate comfort for smugglers and travelers who delivered to their planet, and all the while I stared down at the plate of 'food' using my fork to poke at the grey looking pasta.

A distraction in the form of a young alien joined me at my table, his small mouth turned in a wide grin. His skin was pale blue and there were no ears on the sides of his head. Instead a pair of antennae protruded from his thick, blue hair. I knew he wasn't a Karthan because they never showed themselves to you above the surface of their planet. They used service bots and droids to play host to visitors. Rumors suggested that Karthans were short beings, half my size, and large around the midsection. I also heard the under city of planet Karth was a thriving utopia, but since they never allowed any aliens access, none of the rumors ever changed to facts.

"Rotu nah-oh," he said to me in a high pitch voice. "Nah-oh ja Daniel Quinn!"

I recognized the language . . . He was a Restra from the planet Tristain. I never traveled there personally, but I spent the past year familiarizing myself with all aliens and languages in my ship's database. Twice in my mind I played his words over so I could translate them.

I know you, you are Daniel Quinn!

Confusion would be an understatement. I figured Karth to be the perfect planet to visit. From outer space it appeared desolate and floated within toxic nebulae, making you wonder how the damn thing was habitable. I arrived less than a day ago, transporting chemicals and weapons to their dock, and now I sat waiting for payment. Smuggling jobs were the only kind I accepted. When you use the Starcade to apply for jobs, you risk taking something more extreme, such as sending a message to the buyer's enemy or outright killing someone.

Somehow in my short time here, this Restra found me. Alarms in my head rang out, warning me that potential danger could lie ahead. The Restra just stood there with the goofy grin on his face, and tapped two of his four fingers on a computer tablet of some kind.

I did my best to appear hospitable to the young being, but under the table I cocked back the hammer of my revolver.

"Ih na, buu Ihn rinya ri tis karta-oh," I said. *I am, but I'm confused why that excites you.*

"Oh ja rikrik?" *Are you kidding?* The more he spoke my mind translated his Restran words almost in real time, becoming less and less difficult to understand him. "You're a hero! Is it true that you went to an uncharted planet and saved the lives of the natives?"

I nearly fell out of my chair when he described my time on the planet Dawn. How the hell could he possibly know this, unless he was working with one of the enemies I made on the planet? I slowly gripped the handle of my gun, wrapping my finger against the trigger.

"Who the hell are you and how do you know about this?" My voice broke slightly.

Tress's excitement faltered as he registered my confused, frustrated expression.

Don't dwell on the past. Just worry about the present, I thought to myself. I breathed deep and exhaled slowly in an attempt to relax.

"You know about me and you've met me, but you still haven't told me what you're doing here or how you found me in the first place."

"I can answer that for you, Captain," a voice said from the entrance. Turning, I found a stocky man gripping the door frame. His forehead glistened and his chest heaved.

Although there were accommodations for humans, the chances of two of us being on Karth at the same time were slim. The man stepped over to my table, favoring his left foot as he did so. My stomach churned like a raging tornado and I felt cornered. I blinked hard, disguising it by rubbing my eyes. When I opened them again my right eye—a bionic one that replaced my biological eye after a skirmish against Sarah

King—displayed a series of scans and readings of my surroundings, including the human and Restra. From the outside, the eye appeared real unless I shifted my vision to night or thermal imaging, so they didn't know I was scanning them. The human's pulse was racing; his heartbeat dangerously high, but he didn't carry any luggage or even identification. All he had was his clothes. His clean shave and combed hair made his appearance this far out in the galaxy odd. And when I looked at the Restra, a faint energy signature emanated from behind him. A weapon?

"His name is Tress," the man said, his hand gesturing toward the alien beside him. "And my name is Damon Derringer. Tress's planet is within the same solar system as mine, Captain Quinn. I enlisted his services to help locate you. It would seem that I made the right call." He gave the young alien's back a large pat. His hands, however, trembled. The alarms in my head, my uncomfortable stomach, they all indicated something was wrong here, and I'd be damned if someone tried to make a fool out of me.

I eased my revolver from its holster, lifted it above the table, and pointed it at Derringer.

"Captain! What are you doing? I'm not here for trouble!" He practically spit out the words as he raised his hands.

"I don't really care who you are," I said with agitated roughness. "The fact that the two of you know who I am makes me nervous and I don't like being nervous."

"Please, sir "

"Shut up." I kept my composure calm. If things escalated, I wanted to maintain control. "The last time a strange man joined me at a table it resulted in a few near-death experiences and he almost enslaved an entire alien race. So here's what we're going to do. Get up and get out of my sight before I count to three and pull the trigger."

"Captain!" he yelled as I counted to one. "I know about what happened on Dawn! That's partially why I'm here!"

"Two," I growled. Damon backed away to the door.

"Please, sir! Just let me explain! I am here for your help!"

A high intensity plasma beam burned straight through Damon's midsection and passed within inches of Tress. A smoking black hole was scorched into the wall of the bistro. Damon didn't get a chance to react. One second he lived and pleaded for his life and the next he fell onto the table, dead.

I never counted to three. I didn't fire my weapon. The target reticle in my eye scanned behind Damon's last position where a hole had been burned through the door.

Tress dropped to the floor squealing as I jumped behind a table for cover. My hands gripped the revolver hard as I kept myself low to avoid the additional shots, but none came. I risked a glance to the side, but no one attempted to fire on me.

Seconds later, energy shields activated and dropped from the window and door frames. We were locked in and, even better, the killer was locked out.

The Karthans don't take well to killing, especially when an off-worlder does it. The planet's surveillance system was advanced by my standards. An electronic security web runs down from the dock to the town and everything is under the scope of a camera. Whoever shot Damon Derringer, it's likely the Karthans are pursuing him now.

With the blast shields activated, I felt safe enough to stand and take stock of the situation. The weight of Damon's body on the table caused it to topple during the lockdown and he was now on his back, facing the ceiling. The wound in his chest smoked and smelled like charred meat. It had been cauterized from the plasma. Tress stood beside me and stared at the recently deceased.

"Is he gone?" he asked.

In reply, I shoved him against a wall with my forearm and pushed my gun under his jaw. His hands flailed and smacked my arm and the wall, but I was stronger. His mouth trembled and his eyes shifted color to a shade of indigo, which announced his fear.

"Enough! What do you want with me?" I asked. The revolver's chamber spun and charged its plasma round. The weapon was lighter and more compact than my multi-chamber rifle, which I destroyed some time ago. I'd spent months building the new one. Well, no, that's a lie. Technically, I built it but my advanced artificial intelligence on my ship, the Kestrel Belle, instructed me.

"Please," he muttered. "Please, please... don't kill me! We came here to talk to you!"

"Right." I growled. "Talk. Except your buddy down there has a hole blown through him so the time for talking is over."

"I don't know anything about that! I don't know why he was shot! Please! I don't want to die!" The alien, no older than a teenager, cried out hysterically. The indigo in his eyes glowed brighter and radiated a neon kind of intensity. My conscience overpowered my survival instinct at that point and I eased off Tress.

There was a time when I couldn't hurt a bug, let alone another humanoid, but after the events on the planet I named Dawn, I wasn't sure what kind of person I was anymore. I killed men on that planet and now I was nearly ready to kill Tress.

Get a grip Daniel, I thought.

A loud humming emanated from behind the bar across the room. A small, square-shaped droid hovered toward our position. At the top of the cube a bright read beam scanned Damon Derringer.

"Human. Dead," it said in perfect English. Behind the robotic voice and static, I heard another voice with intonations native to the Karthan language. These carrier droids were controlled by operators and worked as translators for other alien races, which was impressive. It turned and scanned us.

"Human. Restra. Elevated heart rates and minor scratches, but no critical injuries detected. Do you require assistance?"

"Just finish my payment so I can get off this rock," I said while moving to a table with a little less Damon on it. The droid lingered, but when Tress didn't say anything it returned to its point of origin behind the bar.

Tress reluctantly joined me at my table, his hands entangled in one another and shoulders hunched. He never took his eyes off of Damon.

"So, you're not going to do anything?" His voice was soft.

I shrugged. "If you don't have any idea what Damon wanted me for, then it's none of my concern."

The words felt foreign as they left my mouth. I was jarred by the murder of another human being who seemed harmless. I wanted to stay off the radar as best I could, but the knowledge he had of me and my past left me wondering what he wanted. Of course, that answer died with him.

"He wanted your help" Tress said. "He said you could save lives . . . that you are a hero."

I laughed. I never thought of myself as a hero. A hero saves lives, sacrifices his needs over others. Was I a hero when I saved Captain Gregory Smithson's life on the Echelon? If I didn't act, Sarah King wouldn't only have taken the ship, but also his life and the artificial intelligence program. But in the end, the captain and I fled. King still got the ship, killed people, and even used my best friend Jason Hobbes as a cyborg experiment.

Was I a hero when I saved the Dawnians? It was my fault they were discovered in the first place. Sarah King and Raymond Erebos had the information on its location, but they would have needed months, maybe years to translate it all. I found it and tried to sell it and that led them to the most powerful energy source in the galaxy. How did I save the Dawnians? I blew up their processing facility and destroyed their technology, which was their only method for harvesting the powerful energy that powered their technology and their lives. King and Erebos didn't get it, but now no one could.

Hero was the last title I'd give to myself. If anything, I'm just a guy who gets in over his head and has to make up for it later.

The droid's buzzing sound returned. It hovered toward me.

"Is my payment complete?" I asked.

"We would like to negotiate the terms of your contract, Captain," the voice said.

"No, absolutely not," I replied. "We agreed the price on the contents I delivered—$575,000. I am not lowering it."

"Nor are we. In fact, we would like to double the amount."

It felt as if my jaw dropped to the floor. With more than a million dollars I could refit the Kestrel Belle, get her engine replaced, strengthen the hull, and more. But the Karthans weren't just offering that money freely. No one ever did, especially not after an establishment was damaged with me in it.

"What are your new terms?"

"The murderer of your fellow human has proven difficult to apprehend. We would like to hire your services."

"Why me?" I asked, interested in the offer, but curious about why they weren't looking elsewhere. Smuggling items was the best use of my mercenary talents. I sorely lacked skill in the bounty hunter department.

"You are the only other human on this planet, which makes you somewhat responsible for this situation. Our security droids have been unsuccessful up to this point and we feel a sentient life form above the ground may benefit our efforts."

"Wait a second, how the hell am I responsible for this? This man came to me. I was here first. It's not my fault he got himself shot."

"Those are our rules Captain," it replied. "Visiting species on our planet are responsible for their own kind."

"Well, all you had to say was *please*," I said with a sarcastic tone. I guess I should be glad Damon died in front of me and not on the other side of the planet. In truth, I could really use the money, but did I really want to go up against Damon's murderer? Was he killed for talking to me? And if so, why? What information did he intend to give me before his death?

If Damon was murdered for talking to me, that meant I was already involved somehow. All I could do at this point was speculate, but it nagged at me—Did the killer have the same information on me that Damon did? He might have shot me after all, but missed his opportunity when the barriers dropped over the bistro. Right now I was safe in the sanctuary of a protected building, but what about after?

"What can you tell me about the murderer?" I asked.

"Leondren male," the droid said. "We estimate his height at seven feet tall. Weight unknown. He is currently advancing to the docking gate and carrying a briefcase that likely holds the weapon responsible for the murder of the human."

Leondren. I heard that name before, likely from researching the alien database with Al on the Belle. I couldn't picture them or recall their capabilities, but he was obviously a skilled marksmen. He managed to accomplish a precise kill shot from outside the bistro without collateral damage.

"Is it just one Leondren?" I asked.

"Affirmative."

There was considerable danger going after the killer, but it could be worth it for the payout. Money wasn't everything to me, but at the same time it made the starships go around the galaxy.

"Alright, I'll agree to your terms," I said, pushing my thumb to a print scan on the droid. "I'll make an attempt to apprehend this Leondren, but if I find my life at risk I have the option to pull out and receive my original payment."

"Agreed, Captain," the droid said. The entrance's barrier deactivated. I stood and moved forward with my revolver still in hand, the plasma charged and ready to fire. I turned back to Tress, who sat there silently the whole time; his eyes still the same fearful color.

"You stay here. If you're associated with Derringer, then you may be target as well."

His eyes glowed, but he nodded at me.

"Be aware, human Quinn, you are advancing into danger," the droid warned.

"Yeah, don't I always," I muttered.

I ran for the dock. The town looked to be deserted. The buildings were covered in light brown sand and metal barriers covered all the windows and doors. I ran past domed buildings, ones that ended in sharp points, some square, and others circular. Each building was designed with the idea of familiarity and comfort to any visiting species. The bistro I dined in before things got tense, was constructed when the first human scheduled a visit to Karth. The actual surface of planet was a desert—all sand and rock. There may have been plant life, maybe something reminiscent of cacti on Earth, but none within view. The biggest problem for me was the humid weather and bright sunlight, which left me sweating and panting after about a hundred steps. I'm in pretty good shape, but the heavy atmosphere from the gases surrounding the planet caused my lungs to argue with me. I imagined them saying, 'this is why you should carry an oxygen mask with you'. My body begged me to stop and rest, but I pushed harder.

I saw bodies when I was about halfway to the docks. They weren't humanoid or alien—they were the security droids, all of them scattered on the ground. Claw marks covered their metallic bodies and wires hung from limbs. I couldn't guess how many of them were there. Plasma burns striped the ground, but not the droids. Using my bionic eye I scanned over the area. The plasma fire was consistent with the type of rifle the droids were equipped with. Could the killer seriously tear these machines apart that easily, alone, through those blasts? I continued with caution.

By the time I reached the large, grey walls separating the town from the starships, my clothes were damp with sweat, which also burned my eyes. A crowd of aliens were pounding and screaming on the sealed doors. I couldn't recognize most of the aliens by their appearances. A few of them were half my size with silver spiky hair and long arms hanging down to the ground. A handful of others wore thick white robes that covered their entire bodies, but their bare feet looked soft and round, almost like a suction cup. Their fingers ended in the same shape. I also caught glimpses of a family—two adults and child, their skin light brown and textured with lines crossing over each other. A Karthan announcement repeated over the loud speaker. The aliens must have been outside the buildings before the security measures had activated. I couldn't translate the entire announcement through all the noise, but it basically said the doors were sealed due to criminal action on the planet.

This was a lost cause. Even using my bionic eye I could detect dozens of different weapon signatures. I dropped to the ground, exhausted from the thick air and frustrated at the sight in front of me. I didn't know what I was supposed to do next.

"They all swarm the gates like insects, don't they?" A deep, raspy voice startled me.

I jumped to my feet and spun to find a . . . well . . . a lion. He looked enough like one, except he stood on two feet like a human would. A radiant brown mane surrounded his head and his flat, wide nose ended in triangular nostrils. We stared at each other and goose bumps crawled up my arms and legs when his humanoid round eyes contracted into slits, the irises colored gold. He produced a sly smile that showed white teeth formed into sharp points. He wore form fitting armor the color of dull silver. Held at his side was the long, metallic case the Karthan droid mentioned.

"For a Leondren, you speak English well enough," I said. I felt my heart beat against my chest a little faster, but I remained outwardly calm. He bowed to me.

"I am humbled by your knowledge of my race."

We both assessed each other. Every second that passed, the crowd at the doors grew louder. My fingers twitched and the hand around my gun tightened its hold. My legs argued for movement, but I forced myself to stay still.

"So . . . are you looking to get off this rock like the rest of the . . . what did you call them . . . insects?"

"I am. My job here has been completed," he replied. His composure was calm, his smile warm and welcome. It made my stomach churn.

"And that job was? Do you mind me asking?"

"I do not," he said. "I am proficient in silencing individuals who step over their bounds." He talked as if he were boasting about his job. The hairs on the back of my neck stood erect. Despite the Karthans hiring me to apprehend him, the Leondren seemed conversational. Why not push the discussion further?

"You're an assassin," I suggested.

"I suppose your kind would give it that title, yes."

His composure, his mane hovering in the soft wind, he looked like he could crush a stone in the palm of his hand. Would I even have time to raise my revolver? I could only assume that the Karthans were sending more security forces this way so maybe I just needed to keep him busy until then.

"You silence people, even when they're defenseless? Can you justify murder when a man's back is turned?"

"When the price is right, I can justify anything," he said, a soft purr emanating from his throat. His voice was cold as if he didn't care for anyone. I swallowed hard but tried to look calm.

"What's your name?" I asked him.

"Granak," he replied. "And I already know your name, Daniel Quinn."

That didn't surprise me.

"Well, Granak, what happens next? Your contract here is done. I know you killed Damon Derringer, but what about me? How do I fit into all this?"

To my surprise, Granak laughed.

"I will not be killing you, Daniel Quinn. At least, not yet."
He turned toward the crowd and walked away from me.

That was it? Not yet?

I pointed my revolver at his back.

"Granak! You aren't going anywhere. Stop right there or I'll open fire."

He stopped and looked over his shoulder at me, the smile on his face never faltering. He regarded me, then the crowd of aliens at the dock.

"If you miss your mark, Captain, you'll kill one of these helpless insects."

I hesitated. That was all the time he needed. Granak reached into his pocket and pulled out some kind of mechanical sphere. My bionic eye acted instinctively and scanned it. A sonic detonator.

I fired a direct plasma blast, thinking I could hit him before he threw it, but he let go as the shot hit him in the upper back. I watched as the sphere traveled toward the crowd. My breath stuck in my throat. They were all about to die. Maybe there was no hope, but that didn't stop me from screaming at them.

"Everybody down! Detonator!"

The device exploded just before making impact. A violent shockwave erupted from the source of the explosion, hitting me like a shuttlecraft. My eye flashed static, my eardrums blew out, and it felt like all oxygen was forced out of me, my lungs and body burning with the need for air. The ground came up and hit me. I couldn't hear a damn thing except a high pitch ringing and when I touched my ears I felt blood. I opened my human eye, though blurry, and watched as Granak walked through the aftermath. He stepped on bodies or what was left of them as he strode toward his escape, his hulking mass taking his time and surveying his work.

All I could think about was the number of aliens he killed and his careless attitude toward life. I pushed myself up to pursue him, but fell in a dizzy haze before I could take a single step. All I could do was watch as his ship, nothing but a giant blurry spot to me, took off into space.

Meanwhile, a voice in my head kept asking, *What the flux am I supposed to do now?*

TWO

"You have sustained hearing loss, Captain. There will be bruising on various parts of your body from being flung by the explosion and your ankle has been sprained, but otherwise all injuries are minimal."

We were back inside the bistro. I couldn't hear the medical droid speak, obviously, but a screen on its chest flashed the diagnosis to me. I nodded to him as I jammed my fingers in my ears, attempting to clear out a blockage that wasn't there. The ringing in my head was a raging battle between a high pitch noise and a constant ringing.

Shortly after the explosion and Granak's escape, Tress came to investigate and found me lying on the ground with blood oozing from my ears. He helped me walk back into town, which I had to admit was impressive, especially considering I threatened his life less than an hour ago. I later learned that only two other aliens survived, though both were missing appendages, while I got away with a twisted ankle, a few cuts and bruises, and the hearing loss.

Tress didn't understand the concept of hearing loss and as such he felt it necessary to blabber on about how sorry he was for the position he put me in. The medical droid was kind enough to type out Tress's apology to me, though I wasn't terribly interested. All I could think about was how fluxing stupid I was for landing on this forsaken rock of a planet.

Two disposal droids were bagging Damon's body. The image of him being shot replayed in my head, and as it did I noticed things. Both Tress and Damon came looking for me, but Granak only killed Damon. At first I thought the barriers stopped him from killing Tress, but if that's the case Granak wouldn't have told me his job was completed. Didn't Damon say something about their planets being in the same solar system? If that's true, Damon was marked before he even left his home planet.

If I knew I was going to die, but I had to find someone, how would I pass on my information? Find a partner to deliver the message I couldn't. But Tress didn't know anything unless he was lying to me. Then I remembered the faint energy signature coming from behind him.

"Tress," I tried to say, but not hearing my own voice was jarring. I must have screamed at him, because he jumped as I spoke. I grabbed his hips and spun him around in a circle, then reached into his waistband and pulled out a metal, rectangular object.

An electronic memory drive. Damon Derringer you smart son of a bitch, I thought.

Tress screamed out something, but I couldn't even read human lips let alone alien ones. I pointed toward the medical droid and typed on the keyboard.

"This drive can record and contain memories and files. I use something similar to record logs on my ship. Damon must have known someone was following him," I said. Tress's eyes turned pale blue, but I didn't know what that meant. I reminded myself to ask Al what the color combinations within a Restra's eyes meant.

The droids finished the containment process for Damon's corpse. They loaded him onto a large hover bed and the droid closest to me turned and spoke to the medical one.

"Where would you like the body?" The words on the screen said to me.

"Um, come again?" I typed.

"You are the only other human on the planet, Captain. You are granted all rights to the corpse and are required to transport it off Karth."

"Flux." What the hell was I supposed to do with a corpse on my ship? I didn't know this man or where he came from. What were the Karthans going to do about the various remains of aliens around the docking gate? Call their native planets and request a pick up?

"We do not understand your use of language, Captain. If you are unable or unwilling to remove the corpse, we do have the option of vaporizing it."

I nearly said yes just to have it finished, but my conscience took over. This man traveled far to find me, and to leave him on this barren rock would be a disgrace to whatever legacy he may have held back home. But maybe his memory drive would tell me where he came from. Would it be such a bad thing to return his body to his family?

"No," I typed. "I'll take him. Deliver him to the Kestrel Belle, docking platform thirty."

"Yes, Captain. In regards to the Leondren, we are still willing to hold our terms of the contract."

"Forget it," I said. "That lunatic spent no effort killing a dozen aliens at the dock. Just pay me the original fee."

"His attack on our dock escalated our need to capture him," the droid typed. "If you will pursue and apprehend the Leondren, we will not only pay you $3 million Earth dollars, but we will submit favorable Starcade ratings to your account."

"Ratings . . . as in plural?" The Starcade is an intergalactic bulletin board for mercenaries, rogues, and anyone trying to work outside the law. It's a simple system where you apply for a job and, depending on your rating and reputation, you're either hired or you're not. Often times I was looked over because of my low rating. Give me a smuggling or courier job and I had no problems getting it done, but a lot of Starcade jobs required assassinations, forms of violence, and outright murder. I wasn't comfortable with that and I lost a lot of job opportunities because of it.

If the Karthans were willing to make this new deal, I wouldn't just have a ton of money to spend on the Belle and myself, but my Starcade rating could rise high enough to earn me better jobs with better pay. How could I turn that down?

But I would have to face Granak again. If another face off situation arose, did I have any chance of winning? For all I knew he was halfway across the solar system by now on his way to a new job and target.

"I agree," I typed. "But I want an advance of my original payment."

The Karthans agreed. Now I had the money I was originally promised, with more on the way provided I take down Granak. If I never saw him again, it would be no different to me. Something in the back of my mind told me we would meet again, though.

An hour passed as my cargo was loaded. The medical droid was able to manufacture a serum compatible with human biology and the ringing in my ears slowly faded, but was replaced by bleeps and bloops of the computer in front of me. I could hear Tress muttering something, too. But my hearing wasn't completely restored and everything sounded as if it came from across the room.

The Karthans cleaned up the mess Granak left behind while I checked over my weapon and armor and signed the new contract for them.

"Captain Quinn," the bistro's service droid announced. "Your cargo has been successfully loaded and your ship has been cleared for departure."

"It's about time," I muttered as I stood. Tress followed suit. Stars above. I didn't even think about him, but obviously I couldn't leave him stranded. I still felt guilt over threatening his life, but maybe I could make it up to him. Damon mentioned Tress lived in the same solar system, so I could drop him off on his home planet on the way.

"Doratu no ja!" I said sternly to him. *Listen to me!* Finding the right words to say in his language took me a while, but I managed to roughly say, "You follow my rules on ship. You lock door to your room if there is trouble. You leave ship if we need to abandon. Understand?"

He nodded his head violently.

"Ta!" *Yes.*

Get a grip Daniel, I thought. *He's a frightened teenage Tristain. It's not like he's a cold, ruthless, assassin who seems to befriend you only to betray you later.*

Oh wait, that was my last passenger.

The docking gate was ruined when we approached it. Entire sections of the surrounding wall were missing, cut out in the shape of Granak's sonic shockwave. I walked past it and wondered whether the ground I stepped on was actually dirt or dusted remains of the fallen aliens. Somewhere in dock, a number of ships were now up for grabs without a pilot to captain them. The thought nearly brought me to tears. Being a captain myself, I was affectionate of my ship.

I found her right where I left her; the Kestrel Belle. The model was an antique design—only a handful of Kestrel class cruisers remained afloat in space—but she was nimble and quick. She resembled her namesake, the falcon. The bow ended in a sharp point which faced downward like a beak, the midsection was elongated and smooth, and the wings curved outward with the slingspace turbines attached at their backs. Her color was supposed to be dull silver, but various sections on the belly and starboard wing were bronze-colored plates that had been fused to the original hull to repair damage.

Two carrier droids that prepared Damon's body hovered down the ramp to my cargo bay.

"Cargo is secure, Captain," the one on the right said with a faint sound of Karthan language still audible behind the droid's voice. "Don't forget our agreement. Deliver the Leondren criminal to us, dead or alive."

"I haven't forgotten," I told them.

When I stepped onto my ship all the stress and worry of the day slowly evaporated. I was home. The Belle was a three-deck ship. The cargo bay was the size of a miniature warehouse and was the only way to get on or off the ship. Technically there was an escape hatch outside the bridge, but I could never get the fluxing thing open. The ladder at the end of the cargo bay led to the second deck of the ship, which held a very empty and cobwebbed armory. From there you could gain access to the third deck, engineering, and the first deck with the bridge and crew quarters.

I made checking the cargo my first order of business. The Karthans surprised me with the research they conducted on our species. Damon's remains were placed in a crude coffin built with some type of sandstone. Belts and braces latched it firmly in place. The Karthans were a damn mysterious people, but they knew what they were doing and they treated their visitors with respect.

Everything was set. With Tress and me onboard, I pushed up the lever to the bay doors. The mechanisms creaked and moaned as the door closed. The natural lighting and humidity of Karth disappeared, replaced with the Belle's artificial life support systems.

Tress followed me as I climbed the ladder's cold metal rungs. Deck plates clanked as we walked across them onto the second deck. From there we climbed the stairs and walked down the corridor towards the bridge. I stopped at the first door on my left and tapped it with my knuckles.

"This here will be where you stay," I said to Tress. As my hearing improved, my Restran language flowed smoother than before. "There are a handful of beds. Choose whichever one you want."

The familiar sounds and smells of the Belle made me smile as I left Tress to inspect his new quarters. I walked through the small arch onto the bridge and closed the door. It was the size of a large closet with three chairs and stations. The left station was used for tactical and security purposes like weapons and shields. The right was main operations, where maps were reviewed, courses were evaluated, and engineering and other ship statistics were calculated. The center station was for navigation—my station—though the two consoles that surrounded it also connected functionality with tactical and operations. In front of the chair was a silver globe; a navigational sphere, or navsphere as I came to call it, which controlled the ship.

I sat. The familiar texture and shape of my chair melded with my body. I cleared my throat.

"Al, you there buddy? Time to wake up," I called out. A number of indicator lights on the right console flashed blue and red, and I heard a deep computerized voice come from the speakers around me.

"Captain, may I remind you that because I am a machine, I do not sleep. The correct term would be 'hibernate' or 'standby'."

Stars above, Al, I thought.

"I am relieved to see that you are not harmed, sir," he continued. "I detected the explosion at the space dock. Before we continue our discussion, I feel I must warn you—"

"Yes, Al," I interrupted. "I know we have a passenger on our ship. Activate passenger protocol immediately."

The protocol was designed to keep Al a secret from any and every passenger I took onboard. He was the most advanced computer intelligence humanity had ever created and he had been installed on my ship so I could keep him safe. There were people out there like Sarah King who would, and did in fact, kill to acquire this technology. As long as we had passengers, Al and

I would only communicate by text unless, like now, I isolated myself on the bridge.

"CAPTAIN," Al typed out on my front console screen. "THAT IS NOT WHAT I MEANT—"

There was a loud knock at the door. I stretched to open it for Tress, who poked his head in with his antennae shifting from side to side.

"Captain Quinn," he said. "Who are you talking to? I heard two voices coming from this room."

Oh flux.

"SIR, THE RESTRA PASSENGER CAN DETECT ME SPEAKING, EVEN BEYOND THE BRIDGE."

I sighed. I guess passenger protocol wouldn't be needed then. I deactivated it. I considered that Tress's antennae were used as his primary sense, but I never thought they'd be so strong as to hear past a thick metal bulkhead. I introduced him to Al.

"Ra chintu comp?" Tress said. *A living computer?* Al was the one who had been teaching me alien languages for the last year, so I wasn't concerned with him translating the question.

"In a manner of speaking, yes," Al answered back in Restran. "I am an advanced mechanism with the potential to learn and grow as I absorb new information."

Depending on the level of interest Tress showed, this conversation could keep them busy for hours. I took hold of his shoulders and eased him into the communications chair. I buckled him in and returned to my seat to fire up the thrusters.

"What is your primary function?" Tress asked Al as I flipped a couple of switches to ignite the main engine core. The Belle began to tremble as if it were anxious to get back into space. The navsphere, a silver ball with directional angles and numbers, hovered in front of me, its magnetic charge at maximum. I placed one hand on it as I used the other to grab the thruster lever.

"I serve mankind, more specifically Captain Daniel Quinn on his various missions throughout the galaxy," Al explained. "I process data, control the Kestrel Belle during autopilot mode, and I am programmed with a subroutine that allows me to provide council to humans in times of strife."

I snorted at that comment, never pegging Al as a psychiatrist. He was a good listener, though, I had to give him that much.

"I must admit I rarely get the chance to converse with other species," Al continued. "If I am correct, your home planet Tristain has similar atmospheric conditions to human worlds, does it not?"

"I, uh, suppose so . . ." Tress said hesitantly. "Are you capable of operating a ship without a human to command you?"

He changed the subject about his home planet. Interesting, I thought.

"I am more than capable of handling ship operations. In fact, I would find it more accurate to say the Captain cannot operate the ship without me."

"Har har," I muttered, though he was telling the truth. Cruisers like this operated best with a handful of crewmates, namely an engineer, a communications officer, tactical officer, and the captain. Al covered three of the four.

I activated the dorsal thrusters. They fired and slowly lifted the Belle into the air. Outside my shield window the town of Karth shrank away. I spun the navsphere to the left, turning the Belle towards the sky, and then transferred power to the aft thrusters. We launched upward and the dull blue color grew darker and darker until finally we cleared the planet and saw nothing but the vast reaches of space.

The reason I joined the Earth Star Alliance years ago was to explore space and meet new alien cultures. After I was betrayed by commanding officer Sarah King and was locked up, I thought space would be my prison. Now I did everything I could to make it my freedom, but those days seemed few and far between when I was given missions like this one.

I set an automated course out of the solar system and engaged. Once we achieved a safe distance from inhabited planets, I could launch the ship into slingspace, a speed faster than light. I pulled out Damon's memory drive from my pocket.

"Al," I said as soon as there was a break in his conversation with Tress. "I want you to download this and replay all information"

I plugged the drive into an open access port on the console to my right.

"Yes sir," Al said. "Processing . . . There appears to be audio and video files, twenty-four of them to be exact."

"Can you determine which file might have the most pertinent data, anything about a request, or orders, maybe something about danger?"

The room was silent except for Tress and my breathing. I didn't get a chance to learn what planet Damon came from, but I searched for Tristain on my star maps. Sector by sector the computer searched. I set my feet on the console and rested my hands behind my head.

A holographic image of Damon Derringer appeared in front of me and I nearly fell out of my chair. He wore the same suit as when I saw him—he must have recorded this message right before he found me.

"Captain Daniel Quinn, my name is Damon Derringer. I regret to admit that if you're watching this recording then I am most likely dead. I come to you now under grave circumstances. The planet Terra, my home, has been at war with its sister planet, Gaia, for 55 years. Millions of people are dying and I am asking you to help save our worlds."

Apparently my plans were going to involve one minor alteration.

The war between Damon's home planet of Terra and its sister planet Gaia has been waging since before he was born.

"Captain," Damon continued. "In the last two years, our planets decided that too much blood has been spilled, and thus a peace council was formed. Twelve of the highest ranking government officials signed a declaration in pursuit of a cease fire, one that would benefit both worlds and usher in an era of prosperity. But now the council is in danger. As I speak, members are being targeted for assassination, proof of which I obtained at great risk. This memory drive contains all the information you will need, as well as encoded passwords for my database on Terra. You must travel with haste and make contact with Harold Scott, commander of the Sentinels, the Terran security force."

As I watched Damon's hologram speak, I grew increasingly confused. What the hell was I supposed to do about this so called war? My skills in diplomatic relations were nonexistent. Besides, I never visited either planet and, to my knowledge, I didn't know anyone who lived there.

Just turn off the hologram and think nothing more of it, I thought.

Nerves crept into my stomach and up my spine. Memories surfaced, some old, some recent, but they all had one thing in common: Every time helped someone, shit always blew up in my face. My best friend was captured and mutated into a cybernetic freak when I helped my old Captain, Gregory Smithson, escape from the hands of the mutinous Sarah King. And an alien I bonded with, Laraar, was killed by a woman whom I had tried to befriend and show mercy.

Why the hell would I want to be placed between two warring planets? How could that end in any good way? What difference could I make? I considered asking Al to stop processing the information. If I did that, all I had to do was deliver Damon's body home. But how many people could die from this war?

There were never minor casualties in war. The lives lost throughout history can't be summed up by using numbers. I agreed to take Damon's body home. I would already be there anyway, so why not look around? Would it be so bad to take a look around?

Yes, probably, but despite my trepidation I stayed silent and let Al continue the download.

You want to involve yourself because you care, I admitted to myself.

But why do I care? Was I seriously having an internal discussion with my conscience right now?

You care because of all the wrong that's been done to you—Ashley's murder, your failed jobs, the destruction and deaths on Dawn, Jason Hobbes. You can't change the past, so you look for things you can change in the present and future.

I wanted to think of an argument against what I thought, but I couldn't. The holographic video ended and Damon's digital body dematerialized. I breathed in deep and let it out slow. I didn't have to do this. All I needed to do was chart a new course, somewhere far away, and hide.

Hide, like a coward.

"Al," I said, resolved. "While you're processing the memory drive, I also need access to any records we have on the alien race known as Leondren. One of them was responsible for bombing the docking gate on Karth. We're going to try to hunt him down."

"Acknowledged, sir," Al said. "Although, that will not be difficult. There is a Leondren starship precisely 1875 meters off our starboard bow."

"What?"

"That will not be difficult. There is a Leondren—"

"Al, shut up! I heard what you said the first time!"

I cut the power to the thrusters and scanned the area Al mentioned. There was definitely something out there. I rotated the navsphere gently to bring the Belle into position facing the object and then turned toward my operations console and zoomed in to the location I had submitted. I never got a chance to see the Leondren vessel up close, but the ship in front of me was the shape of a diamond with three separate wing structures on each side of her. The hull was a dark grey color, but my databanks couldn't register the metal. Sensors indicated the ship was stationed at a higher altitude than the Belle, and she was leaning down facing us, like a predator looking to strike.

Granak.

He denied every attempt I made at communication and scans of his ship revealed weapons fully activated and charged. The time for talk was apparently over. He said his business, successfully intimidated me, and pissed me off at the same time.

"What's happening?" Tress asked as he leaned over my shoulder.

"He's waiting to see what I'm going to do," I replied.

I wanted to attack, to fly in and unload a barrage of plasma, but his ship was superior to mine in weaponry alone, over a dozen launchers equipped, and I didn't even compare other systems yet. The Belle was agile, but could I really outmaneuver him if I made the decision to attack? I didn't want to take that chance. My mission was to apprehend him, but I needed to face him on even ground, wherever that may be. I hated to admit it, but the best option was to turn and run.

Live to fight another day, a voice echoed inside my head. It wasn't my voice, but that of Captain Gregory Smithson. He had said that to me after our successful escape from the Echelon.

"Al, do we have the coordinates for Terra?" I almost whispered as if Granak could hear me. I doubt he was going to let me escape so we needed to be quick and precise.

"Affirmative, Captain. The course is entered into navigation."

I reached to the slingspace primer, pushed it forward, and waited. The only way I could engage the ship faster than light was to reduce my thrusters to half power, but if I did that Granak would have no problem catching up and taking us out. As long as he didn't detect the buildup of my slingspace core, we should be able to launch without any reaction from him. At least, that's what I hoped.

"All right then," I breathed. I wiped my sweaty hands on my pants and placed them back on the navsphere. They trembled against the cool metallic device. "Tress, make sure you're buckled up."

I took my own advice and strapped myself securely into my seat. I breathed deep to attempt to calm my nerves. Power levels rose and the soft hum of the Belle grew louder. Granak's ship kept stationary. I imagined his feline eyes staring right at me, his mouth formed in an open smile with those sharp pointed teeth.

The slingspace engine core blinked green.

"Hard starboard," I whispered.

I thrust my hand to the right. The sphere effortlessly spun, turning the ship. That's when Tress started mumbling something.

"Look out! Look out!" I translated too late.

The display screen in front of me flashed red. Granak had fired his weapons.

"Flux! Al, engage slingspace!"

I reduced my thrusters to compensate for the energy output needed to launch, and expected to see the stars around me shift and fade away, but instead the Belle flew off course. The bridge violently shook and the straps around my shoulders dug into me as I jerked forward.

"Captain, impact on the dorsal midsection. Slingspace has been deactivated."

Granak knew exactly where to hit me. I grabbed the navsphere and activated the main thrusters. The Belle groaned but responded and we shot forward.

"Al, keep an eye on Granak and prepare to drop the aft weapons."

"Acknowledged. Leondren ship closing in at 300 meters. Mines are set and ready to deploy."

Granak's ship easily matched our speed as it fired another round. The disruptor fire missed but was close enough to make me hold my breath in anticipation of a hit. I took evasive maneuvers, turning left and right, diving down and shooting up. Every time I turned the Belle, I released one of the mines in the hopes that Granak wouldn't see it coming. I couldn't hear the explosions, but I felt the Belle shudder, the floor clanging. His weapons locked on to the mines and destroyed them shortly after I ejected them.

"We are dead!" Tress shouted from behind me.

"No we're not," I replied, though I wasn't completely sure of that answer.

That's when I remembered the marksmanship Granak displayed on Karth. He hit Damon in one shot, but after multiple attempts he either missed the Belle entirely or grazed her hull. He was toying with me. Just like back on the planet surface, he had no intention of killing me, but to what end? Was he going to give chase and fire at me until my power reserves drained out? Our two ships danced in the darkness of space. I lost track of how much time passed. Tress whimpered behind me, terrified.

"Al, divert power to the port thrusters and prepare to fire forward plasma guns," I said, tired of the battle being one-sided.

"Sir, that is not—"

"Just do it, Al!"

When the adjustments were completed, I cut power to the main thrusters and activated the port side. In the blink of an eye, the Belle spun 180 degrees and we faced Granak's ship.

"Fire!" I screamed. Two beams of pure green plasma erupted from my ship. A barrier of energy stopped the plasma from directly hitting his ship.

"Impact to vessel's forward shields, Captain," Al reported.

Flux. I returned all power to main thrusters and shot past Granak. He had more weapons and more defensive systems, but I turned toward him again and fired my plasma at his stern. Each hit met the same barrier as my first. I gritted my teeth. Anger fueled me, the same anger I used when I nearly shot Damon Derringer.

"Captain. This is futile. We will exhaust our plasma banks long before the Leondren's shields fail. I recommend a full course correction back to Karth."

Al wanted me to tuck my tail between my legs and run. That's what I tried to do in the first place, but Granak had other ideas. He wanted me to attack him.

He wanted me to attack him, I realized in a moment of clarity. *He's trying to cripple my ship... and I'm helping him.*

My slingspace drive was out of commission and the main thruster control felt sluggish the more I pushed the ship. If I continued my attack, I would be a sitting duck, completely defenseless.

"Stars above, Al," I said out loud. "You're right. I'm sorry. Set course back to Karth. Maybe we can get the bastard to follow us back."

If I didn't know any better, I thought I heard Tress sigh.

That's when Granak resumed his attack. His ship turned toward us, the exact same tactic I used against him earlier, and unloaded multiple disruptor blasts. Every one hit my ship. The lights on the bridge flashed red, a sign that hull integrity was dropping. In any other circumstance that would have scared the shit out of me; a hull breech on a ship this old could tear her apart. But before I could react, the computer station in front of me exploded and showered me with sparks and smoke.

Tress screamed; the sound came out of him like the combination of a loud whistle and the screech of an earth elephant. I threw up my hands and turned my head to guard myself from the damaged console and I saw his eyes shimmer deep, neon indigo. He was more terrified than when I threatened his life and I didn't blame him. I told him we weren't going to die, but the onslaught of weapons fire convinced me of that inevitability. In those last few seconds, I regretted bringing him onboard.

"Tress," I said. "I'm so sorry."

I closed my eyes and waited for the Belle to shudder, to split apart and suck me into the void of space, but the attacks stopped. The Belle didn't break apart like I thought she might. When I opened my eyes, Granak's ship was right in front of me, on the other side of the shield window. He won and I lost and this felt like his way of gloating. After a minute or so, the ship turned and thrust out of sight. A ripple effect from his ship traveling faster than light caused the Belle to drift backward. I unbuckled my harness and stood carefully. The left side of the blackened main console still smoked. The right side seemed intact as well as the navsphere, but when I attempted to turn the ship nothing happened. The thrusters were offline.

"Al," I said, hoping to hear an answer from him, but it didn't come. I called his name a handful more times, but heard nothing.

For the last five years, the only companion I truly had was Al. He was an artificial intelligence, sure, but he was the only voice I consistently heard. When he was first installed on the Belle, he spoke like nothing more than a standard computer, assisting me with operations on the ship. But he was designed to evolve and after years of traveling together, he began to show signs of emotion and sentience. He joked with me, insulted me, and I him. Man and machine became the closest of friends. He used his vast database to teach me about the worlds and races we met in space and I taught him how to behave more like a human.

Now Al's mainframe had been damaged in the attack. I wanted to scream, to throw or punch something. Al was literally a one-of-a-kind A.I. I didn't have access to replacement parts, nor did I have the technological prowess to repair him. And what if he couldn't be repaired? What if I had lost him forever?

Thomas R. Manning is the author of
Energize: From the Logs of Daniel Quinn. Born just outside the
city of Pittsburgh, Pennsylvania, Thomas spent his life in the
worlds of creativity and imagination, whether through drawing
comic books, performing in school musicals, or writing stories.

His love of science fiction inspired the Daniel Quinn series, but
Thomas is excited to share many other stories in various genres
in the near future. For more information, visit
www.thomasrmanning.com

"Like" Thomas R. Manning on Facebook:
www.facebook.com/authorthomasraymann

"Follow" Thomas R. Manning on Twitter:
www.twitter.com/thomasraymann

www.ingramcontent.com/pod-product-compliance
Lightning Source LLC
Chambersburg PA
CBHW060135130626
46556CB00006B/2353